TELL ME A LIE

DANA KILLION

Obscura Press

1

"Another corrupt alderman? Really, Andrea? Why are you even bothering with that story? Our city motto should be 'Pay to play. That's the Chicago way.'"

Brynn Campbell stood on the opposite side of my desk scowling in disgust the way only a not-yet-jaded twenty-something could. She'd been my assistant at Link-Media for almost a year and a half, after graduating from Northwestern University with degrees in journalism and computer science. Initially, I'd brought her on as an intern but quickly found her research skills indispensable and made her a permanent part of the team. As far as I was concerned, she was my secret-weapon fact-finding reporter assistant ninja, even if I was occasionally reminded of her fresh-out-of-college idealism.

Idealism. That was a trait I'd lost back in sixth grade.

"I get a kick out of watching these mini-mayors implode," I shot back. "Who knows, maybe this time we'll all be shocked and I'll find out that the latest no-bid city contract *didn't* involve massive pocket-lining. But that wouldn't be a lead story, would it?"

"No, but someone doing the right thing for a change would

be a nice surprise. Isn't there a genetic test or something for tendencies toward lying that would keep these self-involved, greedy pricks out of office?"

"I think it's called an election."

Brynn let out a roar of laughter before we reviewed the task list I'd compiled for her. Total campaign donations from Impact Soundproofing to Alderman Dominic Flores, estimates on the average cost of home soundproofing from other companies excluded from the bidding process, the number of homes near Midway Airport that had been identified as part of the target group—in other words, the background fact-based data that Brynn loved to gather and that would corroborate the extent of the corruption. My job was the people and the color.

We wrapped up our touch base, and Brynn returned to her desk while I turned back to my computer screen to flesh out the story as I knew it this early in my investigation. It had started with an anonymous tip, a phone message in the middle of the night left on my work voicemail. A cowardly competitor no doubt hoping for revenge mixed with an opportunity to knock Impact off its pedestal and to worm their way into sloppy seconds with the alderman.

Anonymous sources were the bane of a journalist's existence, but who was I to argue with information if it panned out, even if the caller had a personal motive. Eventually it all came out in the wash. First step was to make sure I wasn't being played.

I'd inherited the digital media company more than year ago, after my estranged husband died in a scandal of his own that had also nearly taken my life. I hadn't been ready for the role of owner, let alone the role of widow or divorcée or whatever I was supposed to be calling myself. Hell, calling myself a journalist had barely been a comfortable handle when he died. Needing time and space to process the events that had turned my life upside down, I'd promoted a coworker, Art Borkowski, to managing director and settled into my primary role as journalist.

It was a delicate and at times uneasy dance that Borkowski and I played—owner, boss, employee, reporter. We were figuring it out as we went along, testing boundaries and loyalty, as well as our own egos, in the process. It didn't help that certain members of my board of directors didn't think I had the balls or the background to pull off dual roles. At times I wasn't sure myself, but I wasn't going to admit it to any of them. After a near coup a few months back, we were now on steadier ground, but the relationship was one screw-up away from mutiny or massive legal bills.

I logged in to LexisNexis and started poking around for any threads that might show a connection between Impact Soundproofing and Flores. There had to be a cousin or a sibling or a drinking buddy between them. My phone rang as I jotted down names to check out.

Lane? Why was my sister calling?

"Hey, Andrea. Can you hear me? The cell service at my hotel sucks, so call me back if we get cut off. I've been walking around the resort with my phone in the air looking for a spot with more than one bar for fifteen minutes."

"Yeah, I can hear you fine, but I'm confused as to why you'd interrupt your Cabo jaunt to check in with me." I felt my stomach clench as I listened to the faint beat of Calypso music and waited for the ask. Lane never called just to chat. And if she was reaching out from Mexico during her annual Realtors convention, my gut was warning me I wouldn't like what was coming next.

"Oh, thanks, my flight was fine and the weather is a balmy eighty-five degrees. Thanks for asking. Jeez, Andrea, maybe you should be the one taking a vacation?"

"Come on, Lane. I'm at work, remember? Did you call to discuss our sisterly relationship, or did you need something?"

Lane always needed something. Money, a favor, a new guy who wasn't a jerk this time...

"Well, excuse me, I'll stop wasting your precious time and cut to the chase. Clearly you're in one of your moods. I need you to go pick up a deed for me."

"You need me to get you a deed? Don't you have an assistant who can do that?"

"Everybody's down here. All you have to do is run over and pick it up. It's no big deal. I bought this investment property at auction, and the contractor needs to get in. He can't do that until I have the deed in hand. I was going to let it wait until I got back next week, but the contractor called. He has an early opening and wants to start demo right away. If I lose this slot, he'll go on to another job. It'll be three weeks at least before he can get the crew back over."

"Fine," I said, regretting that I'd picked up the phone. "Where do I have to go?"

Even as I said the words, heard myself agree to another in a long list of favors, my stomach knotted. Boundaries were a problem in this relationship, and I'd just contributed to the problem. Again. Lane had nearly died last year from a contaminated sports drink, and despite my determination not to let her run all over me, guilt had been winning out.

"Great! I'll text you the address. They're in the Loop. But they close at 4:30. And can you go over to the house and see how much stuff was left? This was one of those take-it-or-leave-it foreclosure auctions, so I might need to get the junk hauler guys in first. Thanks. I owe you one."

The *beep-beep* of the dropped call bounced in my ear. I closed my mouth and tossed my phone back on my desk. Played again.

2

I pushed open the door to Higgenbotham & Hudson ten minutes before closing. Already I was irritated with the whole thing, myself most of all. There were fifteen other items on my to-do list, and serving as Lane's errand girl wasn't one of them. Why did I let her guilt me into these stupid favors? The auction house wasn't terribly out of the way, but I resented the intrusion in my schedule. Knowing Lane's history, I suspected there was bound to be something about this favor that wouldn't be as simple as she said it would be. It never was. I looked at my watch again, calculating whether I would have time to make it over to the property and then run back to my apartment to change before meeting my friend Cai for drinks and dinner.

Lane had emailed me a copy of the purchase receipt, so with any luck, this would simply be a matter of exchanging the receipt for keys and the deed. Then all I'd have to worry about was battling the rush hour traffic.

A young woman lifted her head up from her computer and smiled at me as I approached the desk.

"I'm here to pick up a deed," I said, handing her a copy of the receipt. "The property was purchased by Lane Kellner."

She took the sheet, glanced it over, then turned back to her screen and typed. "Just give me a moment to look this up."

After a few clicks of the keyboard, she smiled, got up from her chair, and walked around the corner. I opened my phone and typed the property address into my map app, trying to estimate how much time it would take me to get there. Forty-five minutes at least, this time of day. I was tempted to wait until the morning to check on the property, but a quick look at my calendar showed me that was an even worse idea. "Damn," I mumbled under my breath.

The receptionist returned, a large manila envelope in hand.

"Here is a copy of your deed, and we include some literature on various city resources, such as the contact for the zoning department and utility hookups."

I took the envelope from her and quickly flipped through the documents. Everything looked to be in order as far as I could tell. So I slid the envelope in my tote bag.

"Great, looks like the only other thing I need is the keys."

"Oh, these properties are sold as is. That means it's the buyer's responsibility to gain access. We don't ever have keys."

"No keys? So how do I get in?" I asked, feeling my blood pressure shoot up a few degrees.

"Well, it's possible that there is no lock on the door. That happens sometimes with these abandoned properties. If not, you'll need to call a locksmith. Just show them the paperwork, and there should be no problem."

She gave me a slight smile, and her tone was only slightly patronizing. Clearly I wasn't the first dumb schmuck unaware of the proper protocol.

No problem? Right. Had Lane known this when she'd asked me for the favor? Damn, damn, damn! I thanked the receptionist and headed toward the door knowing I was sporting an expression this woman had seen many times in the past.

I arrived at the property on Pierce fifty minutes later and scanned the stoop for signs of the locksmith I had phoned from the car to hedge my bet. Another hundred bucks that would go on Lane's tab. No sign of the guy. What a surprise. I shook my head and sighed. Going home to change was clearly off the table.

Humboldt Park was a transitional West Side neighborhood still mired in the inconsistencies of gentrification. Chicago's ethnic divisions still favored its Puerto Rican history, but rising property taxes were having their impact. This made the real estate vultures happy, and Lane aspired to be one. Having some inside knowledge, she flirted with property flipping, but her pockets were never deep enough, nor her contractor ties strong enough to rack up any serious profits. By the looks of it, this one would be break even, at best.

I parked across the street from the ramshackle brick home, then walked up to the chain-link fence and lifted the latch. Remodeling was one of my side passions, and I was always up for a challenge, but I wasn't sure what Lane saw in the place. It looked more like a teardown. Lane was likely in over her head and grossly underestimating the size of the budget she would need to make this habitable. The brick seemed to be in decent shape, at least nothing a little tuck pointing couldn't cure, but the roof was a tear-off, the porch needed to be completely rebuilt, and the windows were barely holding in their frames. One good storm would send glass shattering, if it hadn't already. I could only imagine what condition the mechanicals were in. Had Lane even looked at this property? Or had she gotten sucked in to another sight-unseen fantasy moneymaker from an online auction? Oh well. Her problem, not mine.

Where in the hell was that locksmith? I looked up and down

the street, hoping to see the van. Nothing. May as well check the door while I waited. I grabbed the handrail and put some weight on the first step, testing for strength and expecting wood rot to cause the whole thing to collapse. So far so good. Gingerly, I made my way up to the front door and turned the knob. Locked. I stepped to the right and put a hand up to the front window, trying to peer in through the dark and dirty glass. Inside I saw nothing but dark shapes.

"You Andrea?"

Startled, I gave a small jump, my purse slipping from my hand. I turned to see a red-faced middle-aged man whose waist circumference likely matched his height.

"Yes," I said, glancing at my watch in a deliberate attempt to make him feel bad for not getting here faster, a message he ignored as he huffed up the fragile stairs with barely a creak. Apparently they were sturdier than they looked.

"This should just take a couple minutes. These old locks are pretty easy to hack unless it's all rusted out. Then we just bust open the door." He grinned, apparently amused by the look on my face.

He pulled out a selection of files and tools I didn't recognize from his bag and got to work while I silently cursed my sister. There was no way I'd get back downtown on time. I sent Cai a text asking to push dinner back to seven o'clock, then pressed my nose back up against the dirty glass of the front bay window. If Lane expected me to arrange her junk hauler too, she was about to be disappointed.

The sound of a hammer hitting metal jolted me back. The locksmith looked up at me with an accomplished smile.

"See, I told you it was easy." He tossed his tools into his bag, then hauled himself up off his knees with a grunt.

I stepped over to take a look at his handiwork, seeing an

empty hole where the doorknob once was. "And do you put something new in there?"

"Did you bring one?"

I shook my head.

"Then nope, not today. That'll be a hundred and twenty-five bucks." He scratched out a handwritten receipt while I fished out my wallet and handed over the cash.

"Just give me a call when you're ready with that new lock set." He hoisted his toolkit to the other hand and wobbled down the stairs.

I placed a hand on the door and gave it a shove. It stuck briefly, then creaked as I pushed harder, swinging open with the additional force. A cloud of dust flew up, and the rank scent of mold and rotting wood assaulted my nose. I stepped inside, waiting a moment to stifle a sneeze and for my eyes to adjust to the dim light. A staircase rose straight in front of me, with a living room to my right. Beyond enough dust to cause an asthma attack, the room was empty.

Good. Maybe they were all empty and I'd be out of here in ten minutes. The thump of my feet sent hollow echoes as I walked through the living room toward the back. With this much dust, it was impossible to tell the condition of the floors, but the fireplace was boarded up with plywood, a sure sign it wasn't functional or had become a squirrel hotel. I wasn't going to be the one to find out.

I walked through a small, equally empty dining room into a kitchen that hadn't been updated since the '40s—chipped linoleum tile, a handful of painted wood cabinets, and two windows partially boarded up from the outside. The air was thick and stale and rancid. The build-up of dust I had inhaled was settling into my nose threatening a sneezing fit. Pausing, I fished around in my bag for a packet of tissues. My nose tended, I pulled open several of the upper cabinets to find only a smattering of old dishware before realizing footprints dotted the dirty floor. Not fresh, but they didn't seem like they'd been there for years, either.

I ran my eyes around the space. It was hard to make out whether more than one individual had left the tracks, but someone had used of the kitchen. Smudged prints ran from the back door, took turns through the kitchen, and continued on to a closed door on the left side of the room. I hadn't noticed prints when I'd walked through the living room. Had I missed them? I turned back toward the front of the house and saw only the clear prints of my narrow wedges in the dust.

My phone pinged a message. Michael.

You free tonight? his text read.

Dinner with Cai. Tomorrow? Call me later?

He sent back a thumbs-up emoji, and I put the phone back in my bag. We'd been dating for about nine months, and our relationship was both comforting and fear inducing, at least to me. *Skittish* was a more succinct way of describing how I felt. Despite Michael's best attempts at moving the relationship into more permanent territory, noncommittal was the best I could do after one failed marriage. It didn't sit well with him, but for the most part, he was giving me the space to work it through for myself.

I stood for a moment, contemplating the closed door and wondering if a squatter had taken up residence. No, the tracks weren't fresh enough. I stepped over to the back door and found it unlocked, the latch no longer functional. That was one explanation for the footprints. It was also a hundred and twenty-five dollars down the drain, but I was going to hit Lane up for the reimbursement anyway. I quickly scoped out the backyard from the doorway. Seeing nothing concerning, I decided I could leave the yard to Lane and instead moved my attention to the closed door in the kitchen.

Alert for intruders and even more irritated with my sister, I shook my head, turned the knob, opened the door a few inches, and listened for sounds. Hearing nothing alarming, I pulled the door the rest of the way open and found myself at the top of a dark staircase to the basement. Instinctively I reached for a light switch before remembering the utilities had probably been shut off ages ago. Pulling my phone out of my purse, I hit the flashlight app. Its weak stream shone about twelve feet into the dark stairwell. I cursed and gingerly moved forward.

Halfway down, a cluster of cobwebs grazed my cheek. I recoiled, brushing at my face. In the process, my heel caught on the wooden stairs and I wobbled. Reaching out to the stone wall, I steadied myself, then quickly pulled back as another web brushed my hand, sending a new shiver down my body. Why the hell was I doing this? Lane should be the one cozying up to arachnids. Enough of this. I'd go as far as the bottom of the stairs, shine my light around what would be an empty, filthy space, and then get the hell out of here. This wasn't my problem. And a spider factory wasn't what I had signed up for.

I let out a breath, shaking off the eight-legged creepy-crawlies as much as I could, and swung my light up and down, trying to read the obstacle course the spiders had created. Another four steps and I would probably be able to duck my head low enough to see if the basement was empty. Then I'd be gone.

As I reached my target, I leaned forward, swinging my phone into the darkness. Damn! Boxes were stacked as far as I could see, and the stench that I had first noticed upstairs was stronger now. Trash? A dead rat? I couldn't tell. It was earthy and rotted and repulsive. I panned the flashlight slowly over the assemblage. I had no interest in learning their contents, but it seemed odd that someone would go to the trouble of packing their belongings and then leave them with the house.

As the light inched over the containers, it illuminated a section of the basement clear of boxes. Beyond the last stack I could just make out a rug on the concrete floor and the edge of what appeared to be a vintage dresser with a mirror.

Why would someone lay out a rug in the middle of this mess? Curious, I continued down the stairs hoping to get a better view. As I got closer, I could see that a partially covered window well was washing light onto the rug. Hesitantly I stepped forward, drawn to the clearing. The stacks of boxes obscured much of my view, so I continued cautiously, listening for something other than the sound of my own breath, my thoughts on the footprints in the kitchen.

Once I'd reached the last tower of cardboard, I paused and debated my next move; caution was firing grenades in my brain. I could now see that the rug was an Oriental pattern and probably not a cheap one. My eyes went to the dresser, where an array of small items rested. From this distance, I couldn't tell what they were, but my sense was that they had been arranged. Sweat began tickling the back of my neck as I lifted my flashlight to the bureau. A reflection in the mirror stole my breath, and my phone clattered to the ground. Shaking, I scrambled to retrieve it, holding it tightly to my chest as I stepped around the cardboard wall. There, spotlighted by the light of the window well, sat a large wingback chair. In it, the decaying body of a woman.

3

"You sure you didn't touch anything down here?"

One of the police officers stood next to me giving me the can-I-trust-you look. I shook my head assuring him I had not, as I had the two previous officers who had inquired.

I remained glued to the spot where the first cop to arrive, an officer named Bernstein, had instructed me to stay. I could feel the cold, hard concrete floor sending spasms into my feet, but it was the body in front of me that was sending waves of panic and nausea through my body. Who was she? How had she died? And why? She was impossible to look at, and yet it was impossible to turn away.

Her age was difficult to pinpoint, as was her size, but judging by her ripped jeans and a sweatshirt, printed with a local band's logo, I guessed that she was under fifty. Caucasian. No polish on her nails. In life, her hair had been long and stringy and was a dull shade of brown that suggested it hadn't been washed frequently, or perhaps a poor diet, or maybe dried-out hair was just one of the effects of death I hadn't seen up close and personal.

Her body slumped against the wings of the chair, arms limp at her sides, feet bare, as if she had simply sat down and died. Given the tilt of her head and the length of her hair, I couldn't see her face and was thankful for that.

The maze-like space was now teeming with Chicago's finest. The officers kept clear of the chair, making room for the forensic photographer who had begun the painstaking process of recording the body in situ.

As I watched the team record the details of death and listened to the casual banter that masked the crush of trauma, my mind roared back to the footprints on the kitchen floor. Was she a squatter who'd been accessing the basement through the unlocked back door? It seemed a likely conclusion.

I ran my eyes around the clearing, trying to notice the details that had escaped me in the shock of finding the body. In the far corner behind the chair, boxes were stacked low, side-by-side on the floor, butting up against each other. A filthy blanket and pile of towels completed what appeared to be a makeshift bed. A small pile of shirts and underwear was stacked on the floor next to a backpack. Simple though it was, this had been, at the very least, a crash pad for some period of time.

The dresser was an old bird's-eye maple piece from the '30s, the kind with a bowed front, carved legs, and a mirror attached to the top. It seemed in reasonable shape for its age but was out of fashion and likely not worth much. Paired with the wingback chair and the Oriental rug, the furniture seemed straight out of almost any Midwestern grandma's house.

A collection of small items sat on the vanity in front of the mirror. The light was dim, so I could only make out rough shapes from my location out of the fray. My sense was that they had been arranged, merchandised even. The incongruence flashed warning lights at me. With the officers distracted by the body, I stepped over for a closer look.

A large, flat shell held a bundle of dried plant material. Its grayed leaves were wrapped and tied, contrasting with the pearly interior surface of the shell. The edges of the bundle were burned and remnants had collected below, the shell serving as a tray for the ash. Two small sticks of brown wood were also in the shell, their ends also burned. A faintly sweet smell emanated from the area, punctuating the smell of decay. Incense, perhaps?

A grouping of stones sat to the right. Or were they crystals? Some were black and opaque, their edges rough, others a deep murky green, and one larger, roughly six inches in length, and translucent white but shaped and polished, carved more like an obelisk than a stone.

"Are you okay?"

I turned to find Michael standing by my side. Once again his radar for when I was in trouble seemed to be working.

"Was the text I sent you cryptic enough?" I looked at him with a weak smile. I recalled sending him a text moments after calling 911 but had no idea at this point what gibberish I'd composed.

"More like get your ass over here, now!" He smiled and started to say something more when Officer Bernstein interjected.

"Hewitt, who the hell hauled your ass over here? We don't even know if our Jane Doe needs your services." The officer looked at Michael, then at me. "Ah, I see you got a private invite." He smirked, giving us a look that reminded us both of the complications of dating a detective. As if I needed reminding.

"So, what *do* you know?" Michael asked. "I suspect Jane here is doing a lot more talking than you realize."

Michael shot me a look that was half eye roll, half don't-worry-I've-got-this. Taking me by the arm, he led me back to area of the room that kept me out of trouble, then stepped closer to the body.

"By the looks of it, we got a squatter using the place to get her fix," Bernstein said. "Wouldn't surprise me if the tox screen comes back singing. Happens all the time. These dumbasses shoot up when there ain't anyone around to call 911 when the trip ain't so rosy."

"Well, thanks for the analysis, but let's not declare the case solved until we've been here at least half an hour," Michael responded. I knew it annoyed the hell out of him when the beat cops came at their cases with preconceived ideas. I watched Michael as he took in the scene, staring intently at the body. Then he turned his gaze to the room, not moving from where he was planted and noting, as I had, the makeshift bed and the small comforts that had been arranged in this dark, depressing place. He stood still, observing, forming questions in his mind, processing, before moving slowly around the chair. He stopped as something caught his attention, then stepped close, kneeling next to the body. He seemed to be looking at a tattoo on the inside of her right wrist. For a second his eyes widened, and I saw him take in a sharp breath of air, as if something familiar about the small mark slapped him with reality. The look stayed on his face for a only second before being replaced by the mask of professionalism.

"The front door was locked?" he said, directing the question to me, his voice holding a hint of fear.

"Yes, I had the locksmith break in before I realized that the back door in the kitchen was unlocked."

Did he know her? My eyes went back to the spot on her inner wrist that had caught Michael's attention. Between the darkness and the pooled blood in her limbs that tinged her flesh, it was difficult for me to make out any of the details of the marking. But Michael had reacted to something.

"Well, she's definitely been here awhile," the officer said. "What do you think? A couple months?"

"Probably," Michael said, not looking up. "Cold basement would have slowed down decomp. She's been here awhile all right. The ME will have to nail that down." After a moment Michael stood. "Any idea how long the property has been vacant?" he asked, again directing the question to me.

I couldn't make out the expression in his eyes, but emptiness had replaced the warmth I normally saw there. It pained me to hold back the questions brewing in my mind, to stop myself from being at his side while he ached, but keeping our relationship under the radar was the agreement we'd made.

"I'm afraid not. My sister bought it at auction, which, as you know, isn't a fast course of action. Mortgages, bankers. Back taxes. Foreclosure process. The property could've been in limbo for years. We'll have to ask the auction house what they know about the original owner."

"We?" Michael shot me a look that said don't-you-even-think-about-it. As if his tone could prevent me from asking questions. *Was* this a story?

"Did you notice the dresser?" I tilted my head.

Michael walked over, Officer Bernstein following behind him like a puppy looking for approval.

"What? Burned weeds and a couple rocks? What about it?" Bernstein asked.

"It's odd, don't you think?" I said, my body releasing a shiver. I didn't know if it was the chill of the basement or my adrenaline normalizing but my body was recording the shock. "If she was here just to shoot up, why aren't we seeing drug paraphernalia and Doritos instead of pretty rocks?"

"You haven't spent much time around druggies, have you? That's like trying to explain why the moon sets every night. When these guys are hopped up on a little horse, logic and common sense are foreign concepts that just don't apply. Not worth the energy trying to explain anything these people do when they're all fucked up," Bernstein said, while Michael remained quiet.

For the first time since I'd found the body, Lane came back into my mind. She was going to freak out when I called to tell her that her new purchase came with a dead body.

"Those weeds are dried sage," Michael said. "You burn the bundle and let the smoke travel around a room. They call it smudging. It's used as part of a cleansing ritual."

4

I looked at the clock for what seemed like the fifth time, calculating the zone change with Mexico and the likelihood of catching Lane during that slim window before she got pulled into her moving meetings or skipped them altogether to indulge in mai tais at the pool. No sense speaking to her before she was coherent. There were too many late nights and too much booze between us.

I'd been at Lane's investment property well past ten last night answering CPD's questions, primarily with the phrase "I don't know," and I wasn't sure Lane would have any more answers to their questions than I had. I'd canceled my dinner plans with Cai without going into detail, left Michael at the property with the rest of the crew prowling for answers, and made my way home to an apartment that suddenly felt desolate.

Normally the emptiness of my co-op felt like a refuge, a private space where I answered to no one. I could work all night, stay in my jammies all weekend, and eat nothing but raw veggies for dinner if I wanted, all without the disapproving eye of another human being. Last night, however, I longed for another voice, even if that had just been the presence of another person at the end of the sofa as I ate the late-night tuna salad I'd forced myself to ingest. Walter, my Ragdoll cat, had done his best to make me feel loved, but I couldn't help but credit the tuna for his show of affection.

The discovery of the body had led to a night of fidgety, on-again, off-again sleep as I obsessed about the victim and how she might have died. Although I had people who would look for me should I ever disappear, thoughts of dying alone were impossible to shake.

With sleep elusive, I'd gotten an early start on the day at my office and was poring over my notes on the Alderman Flores story, but the dead woman reinserted herself into my thoughts at every opportunity. Michael had yet to respond to my text for an update.

Was she a story? So far, it seemed straightforward: one more sad, heartbreaking life lost to overdose. A story that meant everything to her family but, sadly, little to the population at large. Overdoses came too fast and too frequently to warrant much attention by the media. For now, it was up to the cops to figure out. In the meantime, I had an existing story to work on, and that meant a call to Dominic Flores's office.

"Good morning. This is Andrea Keller with Link-Media. May I speak with Elena Sanchez?"

"I'm sorry, Ms. Sanchez is in a meeting," said a squeaky female voice on the other end.

Hmm, someone new.

"May I take a message?" she asked.

Meeting, my ass. I'd already put in six calls directly to Flores, and this was call number eight to his office manager. Not a single message had been returned, and I would bet money that this call would be no different.

"I'm sorry, I didn't catch your name," I said, hoping the newcomer would be chatty. At this point, the normal receptionist, Elena, had been well trained in the art of telling me to drop dead. "Perhaps you could answer a question? I have a deadline for this story I'm working on and only need a minute or two. Even a brief quote would be helpful."

"Um, my name is Juanita. But I'm just the part-time receptionist. I really don't think I can help you with this."

"Well, I've left a number of messages for both Mr. Flores and Ms. Sanchez. They seem to be having a hard time getting to the phone. Is there a better time of the day for me to reach them?"

When it came to working a lead, stonewalling was my least favorite response tactic. It seemed weak or cowardly even when the reasons were legitimate. At least I could respect the creativity in a good boldfaced lie. Yet avoidance seemed to be the default methodology for people with shady business dealings. However, I could always find someone willing to talk if I was persistent enough or stubborn enough or creative enough. I never knew how one little thread would lead to another and another after that, until eventually a structure came into view. As a prosecutor, I had always enjoyed solving the puzzle, and a story was just that, another puzzle with pieces that hadn't yet found their places.

"I'm not sure about today's schedule, but Ms. Sanchez gets into the office quite early in the morning. I think it's normally around 6:30. If you call her before 7:30, she might be easier to reach. I can give you her direct number."

Bingo. "Thank you so much. I really appreciate your help."

I jotted down the number as she read it off. If I couldn't get Elena Sanchez to answer the phone, I could always resort to staking out the parking lot early one morning.

I thanked her again, ended the call, looked at my watch, then dialed Lane.

"Hey, sis," she said, answering on the second ring. Her voice was bubbly, as if she were actually happy to hear from me. In reality, I recognized it as her sales voice. The classic Realtor intonation that implied she was so enthused, so confident about a prospective deal, that her voice was as smooth as maple syrup. "How did things go at the property? Please tell me they didn't leave a whole bunch of shit."

"Well, just one surprise, and it's a big one."

There was no easy way to break this to Lane, but I was struggling with how to couch the message.

"Okay, that doesn't sound too bad," she responded. "I'll just get the junk haulers over there rather than leaving it to the contractor. I've got them on standby just in case. How big of a truck do they need?"

"No, you're not understanding. You won't be needing the junk hauler. This particular…treasure…has already been removed." I was hedging, trying to delay the hysteria that I imagined was moments away and a little confused that CPD hadn't already beaten me to the punchline. "Has anyone from the police department been in touch with you?"

"The police? Why would they call? I did get a couple calls from a number I didn't recognize, but I didn't pick up. Unless it's a client ready to sign an offer letter, the world will have to wait until I have time to listen to my voicemail. And why would CPD need to talk to me, anyway?"

"Because there was a body in your basement," I blurted out.

"Excuse me? A body? You mean like a dead body?"

Her voice had risen an octave or two, and she was speaking in a clipped staccato. I could imagine her carefully manicured nails digging into her palms until they left a mark. It had been her stress response ever since she was a teenager.

"Yes, there was a dead body in the basement of this property, and I found her." I kept my voice low and controlled, anticipating a reaction that would be neither of those things. "Please tell me that you had no idea. Didn't you inspect this property before you purchased? I mean, not even a peek in the windows or anything?"

I could feel my body tense with the memory and cold sweat re-form at the back of my neck. Like it or not, I was reliving the shock of finding this poor woman who had died alone and not been found for what was likely months. Who was spending sleepless nights wondering where she was and if she was all right? What family members jumped with every phone call, prepared for either the best or worst of news?

"Oh my God, you can't be serious. You mean like a skeleton or something?"

I could hear the panic in her voice as reality hit.

"No, I mean a real woman who still had a face. The cops think she's been there for months. They don't know yet when or how she died."

"How in the hell am I ever going to be able to sell the place now? Does it stink? I'm going to have to have the place fumigated. Wait, they took the body away, right?"

She rattled on, processing her shock, her questions nothing more than stream of consciousness, not expecting answers from me. Which was good, because I didn't have any.

"Yes, Lane, they removed the dead woman's body," I said, as if speaking to an elderly aunt who was hard of hearing. Leave it to Lane, a human life was lost and her first instinct was to rush ahead to how it would affect her. "What do you know about the property?" Yesterday's conversation, if I could call it that, was floating back into my mind.

"I told you, it was an auction. Standard foreclosure as far as I could tell, but there isn't much background provided in these types of purchases. Ownership transferred to the bank after a mortgage default. It's called an REO, or real estate owned. Banks aren't in the business of managing properties, so they hire an auction company and pay them a cut just to get it off their books. I bought it for little more than the price of the back taxes. There's never an inspection option for these types of purchases. This was an as-is purchase."

"Did you go to the property before you bid?"

"No, I just punched the address in to Google Earth and then ran the comps. Worst case scenario, it's really about land value. If you get lucky, you can flip the house with minor capital investment, and if not, raze it and sell the lot."

Discussing the details of the purchase seemed to bring her back to solid footing.

"Well, now a number of Chicago's finest *really* want to talk to you," I said. "Your contractor isn't doing anything in that house until the cops release it. You should probably book a flight back this afternoon."

"Don't be melodramatic. The body's gone, right? What do the cops need from me? I don't know anything more than you do about what happened."

"Just answer the phone, okay? It's up to them to decide what they need or don't need from you. I'm not interested in moderating the discussion."

"Fine," she huffed. "Well, I need to go. There's a breakfast meeting by the pool that I'm late for, and I still haven't put on my sunscreen. I'll call you when I'm back next week."

Typical Lane, downplaying anything that she wasn't the center of. At least she might answer the phone now when CPD called, leaving me out of this mess. Feeling I'd turned over the responsibility, I could get back to my own work. I pulled my notepad closer, searching back through the pages. The anonymous contact who had been dribbling information to me about the shenanigans at the soundproofing company seemed to be clamming up. And management was being just as evasive as the crew in the alderman's office. What I needed was someone in the front office. Someone who had an admin or bookkeeping role and might be worried about keeping their own ass out of trouble.

"You got a minute?"

I looked up from my notes to see Brynn eyeing me over the top of her extra-grande coffee mug. I motioned her in, and she settled her athletic frame into the chair opposite mine.

"I've got calls into the city on those building permits, but they are about as talkative as cabbage. Feels like someone has told them to stay quiet. Doesn't make sense. Permits are not some big dark secret. This might sound crazy, but I'm wondering if Flores has an inside guy? If all of the soundproofing permits were signed by the same person, that might mean there was a little cash flowing under the table."

"Could be. And that would be an interesting twist," I said, running through potential scenarios. "I wonder what the going rate is for low-level graft? Good hypothesis. Keep working it. Sometimes you have to get in their faces a little bit, so a trip down to city hall might get better results."

"Yeah, that's what I was thinking. Just wanted you to know there might be another route to take on this story." She got to her feet.

"Can I add one more thing to your to-do list before you go?"

"That's not a serious question, is it, boss?" Brynn laughed and rolled up the cuffs on her Oxford shirt one more time.

"No, I guess not. I need you to research ownership of a house. It's a foreclosed property in Humboldt Park. A single-family that was just sold at auction. I want to know the backstory. Who owned it, dates, how long they'd been in arrears, etc." I scribbled the address on a piece of paper and handed it to her.

"You thinking of investing? That's a hot area for development right now."

"It's hot all right. My sister just bought this property. The previous owner included a gift with purchase. A dead body."

5

"What do you mean, a body?"

Brynn stared at me as if I'd just announced that Martians had taken over the state house. I couldn't blame her. I was still stunned by last night's events myself, and I'd been there. It was surreal. If I hadn't had to scrub the smell of death out of my hair and nostrils last night before going to bed, I might have thought the whole thing had been some awful nightmare.

"There was a corpse in a chair in the basement," I said, matter-of-factly. I hadn't processed any of the competing emotions that had kept me awake last night, and I recognized in my tone that my analytic tendencies were popping to the surface. Everyone had go-to behaviors that kept us grounded, and searching for facts was one of mine. "Female. Youngish. But hard to identify her age given the state of decay."

"Gross. That's disgusting!" Brynn said, shuddering. Her monster mug of coffee sloshed its contents over the edge and nearly slipped from her hand. "And you were the one who found it—I mean, her? Who is she?" Brynn slumped back down into the chair as if not trusting her legs to hold her.

I handed her a tissue. "I have no idea who she is, was." I shook my head, the image of the decaying body fresh and unyielding. "I'm afraid the medical examiner may have his work cut out for him. I hope they can find dental records."

"Maybe she's the prior owner? It's hard to pay your mortgage when you're dead," she said, stating the obvious and dabbing at the mocha droplets on her fingers.

While that theory was the most logical first conclusion, it didn't immediately ring true for me. Why hang out in a cold basement if you had the whole house to play in? And why would the homeowner have dumped all their furniture and instead slept on a box? Surely she could have salvaged a mattress even if she had some legitimate reason to stay downstairs.

"CPD seemed to be speculating that she was a druggie using the abandoned house as a crash pad, at least that's what the responding officer seemed to think. No official word yet."

Given the limited creature comforts in the basement, that made more sense to me, yet I hadn't made it above the first floor. Perhaps the second level showed clearer signs of habitation, which would shift the inquiry back to the homeowner.

"You don't look convinced."

My legal training had drilled into me a solid respect for the gut-check. Facts mattered, of course, but a well-developed gut instinct told you when to question whether all of the facts had been revealed. Brynn didn't have my legal background, but she had developed a sense for knowing when my mind was still uneasy.

"I'm not sure about anything I saw last night," I said, releasing an exasperated sigh. "But that's just my gut talking, or maybe the shock or the lack of sleep. I don't know. There were a couple of odd things in the space, and I can't wrap my head around it yet. Have you ever heard of smudging?"

"Only if you're talking about smeared ink."

Movement outside of the glass walls of my office stopped me from explaining further. Michael was pushing his way past my fellow coworkers toward my office. In tow were the responding officer, Bernstein, and Michael's partner, Karl Janek.

Janek? What was he doing here? Was this about the body?

"Looks like we're about to be interrupted, Brynn."

She turned and looked over her shoulder as Michael hit the door. "Got it. I'll catch up with you later on this stuff. Hello, Detective Hewitt," she said, giving me a small wink.

Although Brynn certainly knew we were dating, I hadn't been overly vocal about my relationship with Michael, at least not at work. It was too complicated, too fraught with innuendo, for eyebrows not to be raised. So I tried to convince myself it was nobody's damn business. I wasn't hiding the relationship, exactly; I just didn't want it to get in the way of my job. I knew Michael shared the same concerns about complicating his work life, but his solution was to jump past the dating phase into something more committed, apparently believing that no one would find our relationship inappropriate if we lived together instead of just occasionally sharing a bed. Maybe in a man's world that might be true, but I knew my reality would be an unspoken bias that I'd slept my way into every story that involved CPD.

I also had one other little problem: ice-cold feet. Once burned, twice shy and all that. In the meantime, we played annoying little games with our public lives and private lives that made us feel better but probably fooled no one.

"Gentlemen, what can I help you with today?" I said, trying to keep the smile off my face as I looked at Michael. I always enjoyed seeing him in work mode. There was something a little decadent about it, as if it were a secret just between us. In reality, it just made me want to see him naked.

"Come on in, have a seat." I motioned to the chairs and pulled another over, but no one took me up on the offer, so I stayed on my feet.

"We have a couple questions for you about the property," Michael said. "Can you tell us again why you were there?"

His voice was all business, but I recognized the way his gorgeous brown eyes lit up when he looked at me, and I smiled anyway. Although I'd answered a million questions last night, I knew that repetition and checking my consistency were just part of the investigative process. This wouldn't be the only question that I would be answering more than once.

"As I said last night, my sister, Lane Kellner, purchased the property at an auction just before she left town on a business trip. Her contractor had an early opening, so she asked me to pick up the deed and do a quick check on the condition of the home while she was away. So, I met a locksmith at the property. He did his thing, left, and that's when I went inside and found the body."

"And what did you do when you got inside? Can you retrace your steps for us?" Michael continued while Janek and Bernstein stood silently.

The blush of seeing Michael was starting to wear off, and I was now acutely aware of the serious expressions the men were sporting. Whatever had happened, this was not an average overdose. I could feel it in their eyes, hear it in Michael's voice.

"I walked through the living room and dining room. Both rooms were empty, so I continued to the kitchen."

"You didn't go upstairs at that point, correct?" Bernstein asked.

"That's right. When I got into the kitchen, I noticed footprints on the floor, as if someone had been using the room. I was curious, opened a few cupboards. There were a few basic kitchen items but nothing more interesting. I did find the back door unlocked. Looked like the latch was damaged. I should have checked before I called the locksmith, but I was in a hurry. Anyway, I looked outside briefly but didn't see anything concerning at that point, but that's not why I was at the house, so I didn't give it much attention."

Michael and Janek exchanged a glance. "Is that when you went to the basement?" Janek asked. His voice was tight in a way I couldn't read, but I immediately knew something was wrong.

"Yes, there were clear footprints leading to the door, so I went downstairs, found the body, and called it in. I think you know the rest."

"And your sister, where is she?" Michael asked.

"She's down in Mexico, at a resort in Cabo, for a real estate junket. I spoke to her this morning and updated her."

The men looked at each other.

"You spoke to her?" Michael said.

"I did. I assume you've been trying to reach her. She indicated that she'd received several calls and had chosen not to answer."

"Does she have a habit of ignoring cops?" Bernstein asked.

I tamped down a smile. "Obviously, you don't know my sister. Let's just say she's flighty. Right now she's sitting by the pool talking deals and drinking things with fruit and lots of rum. She simply couldn't be bothered to answer your calls. As far as I can tell, she's as in the dark as I am about who the dead woman is or why she's there. Right now her primary focus is how inconvenient all this is for her remodeling schedule."

I couldn't keep the sarcasm out of my voice. Michael and Janek knew all about Lane's character flaws, and it was clearly inconvenient for them to be on the receiving end of her drama.

"And when will she be back?" Bernstein continued, clueless to the underlying history.

"Next week, I think. She just got down there," I said, trying to recall if she'd specified a day. "But she doesn't share her schedule with me. Given last night's development, I encouraged her to come home and deal with this herself, but she didn't seem inclined to cut her trip short."

Michael raised his eyebrows and shook his head. He knew exactly how infuriating Lane could be.

"And when you saw the victim, what did you do?" Janek asked. "Did you step close to her? Did you touch anything?"

There was the slightest bit of a waver in his voice, as if he were struggling for words. The Karl Janek I knew didn't waver when he had something to say. He could be the strong, silent type, but this was something else, something emotional.

"Quite frankly, I was so shocked, I couldn't do much of anything," I said, keeping my eyes on Janek. "I first saw her in the reflection in the mirror, and it startled me. I dropped my phone. When I had it back in my hands, I got to within maybe eight feet of her and couldn't move any closer. Obviously she was dead and had been for quite some time. That's when I phoned you guys. I didn't touch anything other than retrieving my phone."

Small pricks of confusion were pinging in my head and beginning to pique my interest as I watched the men, and confusion meant I had questions.

"I got the impression last night that you guys were viewing this as an overdose," I said. "A typical overdose doesn't get personal attention from guys in your pay grade. Is there more to this?"

"Just covering all the bases until the ME can determine cause," Michael said quickly. He avoided my eyes. He wasn't being truthful.

My reporter instincts were knocking. "Do you think the items on the dresser mean anything? If this was just a place for her to squat and get high, I can think of a whole lot of other things that would make more sense to have around than a bundle of sage and some rocks. The way everything was arranged, it feels more like it was an altar."

Although I hadn't consciously considered the idea that the dresser had been an altar before this moment, the intensity of Janek's response had my mind running hot and fast. I had nothing other than sparks of confusion and intrigue, and I couldn't ignore them.

"It's not worth making sense of. Logic goes out the window when these guys need a fix," Bernstein said, dismissing my concerns. Whatever Michael and Janek were considering, they hadn't clued him in.

Janek's jaw clenched. The beat cop had been quick to judge and even quicker with his self-professed knowledge of addiction. Hard to fault a guy who only saw the aftereffects on bodies and lives lost, but the quick answer was never a complete picture. I looked again at Janek, then back to Michael. There was a tension present that I didn't normally see. Michael was watching his partner, as if reading him. Or waiting for a reaction.

Something was playing out between the men, and I didn't know what. It was as if this case was hitting close to home. Did Janek have some personal experience with addiction, or was this about the identity of the body?

6

My thoughts were as snarled as the afternoon traffic on the Stevenson Expressway. I was driving west out of the city to make a personal appearance at Impact Soundproofing. I should have been formulating questions about the absence of a bidding process and the company's history with Flores, but the image of the dead woman in the chair kept drawing me back. The loneliness and isolation of her body haunted me. Who was she? And why had she died alone?

Although the drug overdose theory had merit, it felt like there was something more to her story. I couldn't attribute my suspicions to anything other than instinct, but after all, if it was a simple overdose, why would two detectives be on the case? Forensics would do the heavy lifting on cause and identification.

Michael and Janek had not shown their hand while in my office, so I'd been left with a suspicious mind and my overly active imagination. Just the scenario to occupy my thoughts as I drove.

Thinking rules of the road didn't apply to him, a huge Suburban zoomed up on my left and tried to Pac-Man his way into the spot in front of me. I jammed on my brakes and laid on the horn. He could have flattened my dinky Audi with one wrong move, all to get off the expressway five seconds faster. Keeping idiotic maneuvers like this at bay was the only benefit I could imagine to self-driving cars. I swung off at Central Avenue, my heart in my throat, and then turned south toward Midway Airport.

Siri directed me to a bland brick building without windows where a faded hand-painted sign identified the business and a second directed me to parking in the back. I maneuvered into the narrow alley between the building and the chain-link fence that separated it from its neighbor. The rear of the building was no more illuminating than the front. I pulled into a slot, nestling my small city car between the oversized pickup trucks that filled the rutted blacktop.

Exiting, I saw three bays of large, rolling overhead doors dotting the exterior. And to the right, a small stoop had been constructed out of two-by-fours, providing access to a haphazardly painted green door labeled "Office."

Although my repeated phone calls had done nothing to convince the owner of the business to speak to me, in-person appearances were harder to avoid and carried the added benefit of surprise. I marched up to the door and went inside, finding a paneled room with three chairs, a plastic philodendron, and a pass-through counter. A security camera was trained on my face. A Hispanic woman about my age sat on the other side of the glass, scooping up some rice dish, which smelled amazing, out of a takeout container. A small name plate identifying her as Vanessa sat on the counter. She looked me up and down as I approached, appearing none too happy to have her lunch interrupted.

"I'm here to see Mateo Sandoval," I said, handing her my card.

"He's not here right now," she said, shuttling the card back across the counter as she wiped the corner of her mouth.

"Do you expect him back soon?" I asked. "I've called a number of times. I'm certain we've spoken. Perhaps you could tell me where he is. I'm happy to meet him at a job site if that would be easier." I smiled at her, again hoping the helpful approach would break down some of the annoyance I could feel emanating from across the counter.

"Well, he doesn't like to be bothered when he's at a job. I'll let him know you stopped by," she said, apparently unmoved.

"Perhaps I could get some basic information from you," I said, changing tactics. "I'm sure you'd like to have the confusion over your company's relationship with Alderman Flores cleared up. Get people like me to stop interrupting your lunch," I said. "That really smells good. Did you get it around here?"

Not even a hint of a smile. The charm offensive didn't seem to be working.

"I'm curious about how many projects, I guess you call them jobs, you have going at any one time? And would they also be city contracts?" I rattled on, throwing out questions that should be devoid of controversy.

"Look, I'm not supposed to talk to reporters," she said, closing the Styrofoam takeout box, her gold bangles jingling.

"Is that right? Have a lot of reporters been calling?" I wasn't the least bit surprised the staff had been given tight marching orders, but depending on their loyalty, or their personal risk assessment, those orders could be worked around *if* I got to the right person. And occasionally a little empathy was all it took to loosen someone up.

"It's hard to get any other work done with the way you guys are hounding us," she said. "I'm fielding ten to fifteen calls a day. Isn't there something else happening in Chicago? How many times do we have to say 'no comment' before you people get it through your heads that we've got nothing to say?"

Rookie mistake. If she thought the guilt trip was going to work on me, she hadn't had much experience with reporters. *Please* and *thank you* only got a journalist to the easy stories, and when politeness didn't work, being as obnoxious and persistent as possible was the next level up.

"We're just trying to do our jobs, as you are. And some reporters are, I'll be blunt, more obnoxious than others."

That got me a half smile.

"Obviously you guys don't have to talk if you don't want to, but in reality, that just makes people more curious," I said, laying down my own guilt trip. "If no one's done anything wrong, why not put the facts on the record. Let the public decide what they believe. Frankly, stonewalling makes people seem guilty of something, whether it's true or not. And impressions can have a long-lasting effect on a company. The way I look at it, it's better to talk than not."

I could see by the look on her face that I had her thinking, if not about the company's future then at least her own, and that was the first break in the ice.

"Whether I agree with you or not, this isn't my decision to make." She shrugged. "The boss said don't talk, and I want to keep my job, so that means you'll have to speak to him."

"Okay, I understand." I looked up directly at the security camera, then back at the receptionist. "Well, I'll leave my card in case he has anything to say. It can be on or off the record," I added, hoping she'd get the hint.

"I'll pass it on." She took the card, glancing at it this time before tucking it under her cell phone. Good. It didn't mean she'd call me, but it was something.

As I left the building, I noticed one of the garage bays was now open. A middle-aged man in well-worn jeans and a company T-shirt was walking from the building to the parking lot with a lunch bag in hand. I picked up my pace.

"Excuse me," I said, calling after him. "Do you work here?"

"Yeah? Can I help you with something?" he said, eyeing me as if expecting me to pull out a sales spiel.

"How long have you worked here? Is it a good place to work?"

"About five years, and yeah, it's okay." He shrugged and ran his hand over the scruff on his chin. "Like every job, some good, some bad. Why?"

"I was thinking about hiring you guys. I have an investment property in Humboldt Park and was thinking that soundproofing might be a good selling point when I rent it out," I said, lying through my teeth. Although it always made me uncomfortable, these little stretches of the truth were occasionally the difference between getting information and getting nothing.

"Sounds like a good idea to me. There are these bratty kids living below me who seem to have screaming tantrums all day and night. If I owned the place, I'd be all over that."

"Yeah, I thought it might attract the right kind of renters. But it's a big investment, and with you guys being in the news and everything, I'm just not sure this is the right company. I don't mean to offend you, but I don't want to put down a big deposit and not get anything for it. I mean, if what they say is true, your company might be in trouble."

He nodded, grasping my insinuation. "Well, don't judge the quality of our work by what you read in the papers. They don't always tell the full story."

I smiled and kept my own commentary to myself. That can of worms was bottomless.

"No, I don't imagine they do. Are you worried about this? Could these accusations affect your job?"

He looked at me quizzically, as if starting to suspect that my questions were a little outside the realm of normal consumer chitchat.

"I mean, I just wouldn't want to start the project and find that your company had to lay off a bunch of people in the middle of the job. We all know lawsuits can be expensive and time-consuming."

"I think you should probably talk to the office about this stuff. You're not some reporter, are you?"

My lawsuit reference was backfiring on me.

"Actually, I am a reporter, but a reporter who also happens to have a house to remodel." I handed him my card. "Can you help me out? You seem like a conscientious guy. Like someone who wants to do the right thing. If there are people in this company who don't share your ethics, do you really want to be the one who stayed silent and went down with the ship? I don't want to get screwed over. And I imagine you don't either. If there's one bad apple in the bunch, it doesn't have to taint the whole company."

He looked over his shoulder, then longingly toward the parking lot, probably annoyed that I was cutting into his lunch break.

"The way I look at it, it's never wrong to do the right thing," I said. "You might even be able to help a lot of people stay employed."

He cocked his head, contemplating. "You make it sound like a damned-if-I-do-damned-if-I-don't situation, and way above my job title. I just want to do my job, get a paycheck that doesn't bounce, and mind my own business. This ain't my mess." He shook his head, let out a breath, and crossed his arms. "Okay, Ms. Reporter, here's one thing I will say, and it's the only thing I'm saying, so don't take this as an invitation to bug me again. I don't know much, but from what I hear, this situation ain't no different than any other scheme. The answer is always 'follow the money.' And if I were you, I'd develop an interest in check-cashing shops. Particularly shops on Fifty-fifth Street who employ a guy named Darius. You have a good day, now."

7

I walked into my apartment with two overflowing bags of groceries in hand. Walter met me at the door as he always did, having heard keys in the lock. I set down the bags and scooped him up. In his little mind, nothing was more important than making sure he got the proper level of attention after I had the audacity to leave him for a few hours. I'd been trained well enough at this point to comply, or I'd risk his wrath at 3:00 a.m. The littleneck clams in my bag would have to wait another thirty seconds to get into the fridge. It was a small price to pay for a decent night's sleep.

His affection tank filled for the moment, I set Walter on the floor and picked up the bags, and we proceeded into the kitchen. Next priority, smelly fish mush. With Walter happily lapping up his dinner, I pulled the clams out of the bag and put them in the fridge, along with arugula, endive, and radicchio. I had gathered all the makings for a tricolore salad and pasta vongole. Michael would be here in about thirty minutes, so I had enough time to change before I started the dinner prep.

My condo was a grand old prewar just down the block from the Hancock Building. I'd fallen in love with the large unit at a point when I still believed I was happily married. Unfortunately, I learned shortly after the purchase that my husband was married to the idea of marriage, just not the monogamy part, and I'd fought to keep the co-op during the divorce proceedings. Despite the fact it was four times larger than a single person needed, it was a source of great joy, along with a select number of very painful memories.

Reflexively my eyes were drawn immediately to the spot on the terrace where not even a year and a half ago, my life nearly ended, and my estranged husband's had. I had expected the memory of that night to color my view of the home. After all, I could pinpoint the exact spot where Eric had died, but somehow, instead, I had found myself drawing strength from that knowledge. Eric's corrupt business partner had tried to end my life, but instead he was the one in jail, and I had put him there. I had survived the crisis in my marriage, the trauma of nearly losing my life, and then a second attack by a deranged woman just months ago, and I had come out of those experiences stronger, more appreciative, and more determined to live life on my terms.

Pots of vibrant flowers now filled the spot where Eric's blood had been shed. I looked around at the home I was making, admiring the classic beauty of the herringbone floors, the grand proportions, and the marble mantel of the fireplace. This was home, my home. And Walter was the only one I answered to in this space. Perhaps that was what frightened me about Michael's suggestion that we live together. As I had been doing for several months now, I again set aside those thoughts, unwilling to analyze what I truly felt for Michael and why. Right now the only thing that I wanted to focus on was that I was content with the status quo. He would have to live with that, or...or what? Was I really willing to issue an ultimatum?

We weren't there yet. I shook it off and walked down the hall to the master bedroom, where I changed into a pair of jeans and a lightweight sweater. A shower would have been nice, but looking at the clock, I saw there wasn't time. Walter reappeared, happy and satisfied with his dinner, while I ran a brush through my hair and freshened my lipstick.

"Walter, let's go chop some garlic." He yawned and licked his paw, then followed me back to the kitchen. It would take at least a couple hours of surveillance before he'd be satisfied that I was staying put before he settled in and let me out of his sight.

Clearing my mind of everything other than food prep, I crushed garlic and chopped parsley, organizing them in small bowls, then pulled out the greens and began the process of washing and cutting. Salads done, I put the bowls in the fridge, filled a large pot with water, and set it on the stove, then opened a bottle of Duckhorn Sauvignon Blanc. I poured myself a glass and left the bottle on the counter. Michael alternated in his drink of choice far more than I did, so I pulled out the scotch as well in case he was in the mood.

I was opening the three sets of French doors to the terrace when the bell rang.

"It's open," I shouted, not that he needed to wait for my response at this point in our relationship.

His smile was warm and broad as he put his arms around me and pulled me to his chest, kissing me as if we'd been apart for weeks.

"I've wanted to do that all day," he said. "I take that back. I've wanted to do that since last night."

I nuzzled into his neck and buried myself deeper in his arms, letting the size of him, the warmth of his body, the security of his embrace say everything for the moment.

"Are you okay?" he asked.

"Yes," I said, pulling away, aware that my answer was mostly accurate. "It's not the first dead body I've had a personal experience with, but I'd say this is the first one who's been dead so long."

As a former prosecutor, dealing with the ravages of death had been part of the job, but my exposure had been through photos and crime scene video. Now, as a journalist, I'd become far more intimate—my estranged husband had been shot before my eyes, a source had died in my arms, and most recently a delusional killer had made me a target—it was a distinction that I took no pleasure in. However, well-decayed bodies were another thing altogether, and I shivered at the memory.

Michael looked at me as if he didn't believe me. He knew firsthand how the dead could haunt. I smiled and squeezed his hand. "Why don't you get a drink, and then we can sit outside."

"You go ahead. I'll be right out," he said.

As Michael walked into the kitchen, I grabbed my glass and went to the terrace. The air was clear and warm for an early May evening. I settled onto one of the chaise lounges, Walter at my feet, and leaned back, appreciating the light breeze and the setting sun, which was giving the Hancock Building a gorgeous pink glow.

Michael returned, having decided on scotch, and sat on the chaise next to me while Walter gave him the evil eye. He still hadn't warmed up to the idea of "strangers" in the house. We raised our glasses in a silent toast, not saying anything more for a moment, simply enjoying the beauty of the evening.

However, dozens of questions were now running through my head, starting with the cryptic lead I had gotten from the employee at the soundproofing company. But my thoughts wouldn't stay focused, and I bounced over to wondering who the dead woman was and why she might have been missing and left undiscovered for so long. Had neighbors been aware of her presence? The smell of death surely had to arouse someone's attention.

"I was surprised to see Janek today," I said cautiously, watching Michael's face for reaction. "I didn't think you guys investigated routine overdoses."

"Well, we don't really know it was an overdose," Michael said noncommittally. "That's certainly one possibility, but it's better to gather the facts while they're fresh and let the ME tell us if we've got something else here."

"What makes you think there might be foul play?"

"I didn't say that." Michael raised his eyebrows in one of those you're-pushing-me-Andrea responses and swirled the ice in his glass before taking a sip of the amber liquid. "What I said is that until we determine cause of death, we're keeping all of our options open."

"Does Janek have some particular interest in this case? He seemed tight, for lack of a better word."

This time Michael squirmed. It was as if I could see the gears in his mind willing me not to go there. Too late for that. I'd hit a nerve.

"Nothing out of the ordinary. You know Janek, he's always a little uptight."

I stopped mid-drink, put my glass on the coffee table, swung my feet over to the ground, and looked at Michael.

"You're lying to me," I said. "I can see it in your face. I can hear it in your voice. What the hell is all that about?" I couldn't decide if I was reacting as the annoyed girlfriend who didn't appreciate being lied to or intrigued because my reporter antenna was picking up a signal.

"No, I'm not lying. I'm just trying not to jump to any conclusions until I have more facts. There are some things about this case that are a little familiar, put it that way. I don't want to jump ahead of my skis."

"Michael, come on. What was familiar? The circumstances? The setting? The victim?"

I stared at him. My eyes locked on him, watching his body language and not liking what I saw. If he had been a defendant in one of my cases, I would have been pushing a full-court press for answers.

"Andrea, cool it. This is just part of the deal we have. You know I can't talk about every case and you can't talk about every story. Don't turn it into something more than it is." He picked up his scotch and took more than a sip, in what I viewed as a manufactured attempt to look casual.

"Okay, I'll leave it alone for now. That part, anyway." I took a drink from my own glass before hitting him up with something less sensitive. But I wasn't done. "What did you make of the smudge stick? And those rocks or crystals or whatever they were?"

"Nothing really. It's basically incense, right? Maybe she was trying to cover up the smell of whatever she was using?" He shrugged.

"But if she was there to get high, why didn't we find drug paraphernalia? Did you see track marks on her arms? Any signs she'd been shooting up? Smoking something? Popping pills, any bottles, baggies?"

Michael was quiet, squirming again in his chair.

"I certainly didn't," I said, since Michael wanted to pull the silent act on me. "And so far, that's the biggest hole in your friend Bernstein's theory. Smudge sticks aren't incense. You said it yourself—they're used in cleansing rituals. What bad energy was she trying to get rid of? And how does one overdose without leaving any telltales signs of drug use? Unless she wasn't alone."

8

Who was calling at 7:00 a.m.? I could hear my phone ringing as I opened the shower door and reached for a towel. With the mood of the evening a bit fragile, Michael had decided to head home after dinner rather than spend the night, and my immediate thought was that he was calling to tell me he'd had a crappy night of sleep and regretted the decision. I quickly dried off, grabbed my robe, and wrapped the towel around my wet hair. The ringing had stopped by the time I reached my nightstand, but I saw a voicemail notice on the screen from a local number I didn't recognize. Hoping it was the receptionist from the soundproofing company, I tapped the screen and listened.

An accented male voice said, "I was told to call you about opening the house on Pierce. I'm on my way to start demo. Are you going to open up for me, or do you want me to cut the lock? Call me back."

What? Dammit, Lane. Did the woman have no common sense? These guys might be walking into a crime scene, and she didn't have the decency to ask them to hold off or to pick up the phone and let me know?

I hit redial as fast as my fingers allowed. Of course the call went directly to the caller's mailbox. Mailbox full. Shit! Contractors! I threw on clothes as quickly as I could, every plan for my morning now completely thrown out the window.

Five minutes later I was in the car with hair drip-drying onto my white shirt and calling the contractor back every few minutes. I didn't know if he was working his way through the overflowing mailbox or having a complex phone fight with his wife, but every call I made now got me a busy signal. Knowing traffic would be a mess on North Avenue, I drove west on Grand and maneuvered north to the home from there. I screeched up behind a beat-up white van top-loaded with ladders twenty minutes after I'd gotten the message, pleased with my navigation skills.

Two guys were pulling equipment out of the back—sledgehammers, shovels, a large box of contractor-size black trash bags —while another was heading up the walkway. Didn't he see the crime scene tape?

"Stop!" I yelled at the men before they could take out the power tools.

"You Andrea?" the taller guy asked.

"Yes. You can't go into the house," I said quickly, my voice a bit shrill.

"But Miss Lane said we have to start right away." He looked at his partner, then pushed aside a strand of slicked-back hair that had fallen over his forehead.

"I'm sorry. Change of plans. You can't go in. The police haven't given the all-clear yet. This is a crime scene."

The men exchanged confused looks. "Crime scene? Miss Lane don't say nothing about cleanup. We don't do that."

He yelled something in what sounded like Polish or Czech to the guy standing on the walk, who grunted back an angry response.

"No, you don't need to clean up the crime scene. That's not what I meant," I said, realizing I was adding to their confusion. "I'm just saying that I don't know if the police are done with their investigation. So you can't go in until they say it's okay. I'll talk to Lane and explain things to her again." I emphasized "again" a little more harshly than I intended to. It wasn't the guys' fault they didn't know what was going on. "The police have to tell her that they're done with their work before you can start. I'll speak to Lane, and she'll reschedule."

The man shrugged. "Okay, we'll go, but she gotta call the boss."

The men moved their tools back into the van, laughing in Slavic at the foolishness of the situation. Or at me. It didn't matter. While they worked, I stood on the sidewalk furiously texting Lane. My first thought had been to wake her ass up to tell her what she'd almost done, but a night of drinking would silence a ringing phone. Maybe I should have let the guys go in, and the cops could've dealt with her idiocy after the fact. But I hadn't held back because I was being nice to my sister. I wanted to know what the hell had happened to this poor woman, and flying sledgehammers weren't going to help.

As the van drove away, I stood on the sidewalk staring at the home, noting the proximity of the neighbors. Homes on both sides appeared to be occupied. Had they seen anything? The image of the basement was sharp in my mind, particularly the position of the chair and the items assembled on the dresser. I wished I'd had the foresight to photograph them. CPD had likely removed them last night.

Opening the gate latch on the chain-link fence, I walked around the right side of the home. Cement pavers rimmed with out-of-control weeds were wedged into the dirt. As I reached the back corner of the building, I noticed a basement window boarded on the exterior with a piece of plywood; its dirty beige coloring told me that it had been there for months, not years. I continued toward the back door, eyeing the grass as I walked. Whatever sod or seed might have once existed had succumbed to the intrusion of weeds and neglect long ago. I saw nothing resembling obvious footprints, and the fragments of trash embedded in the foliage could have blown over from anywhere.

I stood in front of the back door glancing up at the second-floor windows, then ran my eyes along the back perimeter of the house. Nothing I saw foretold the vignette I'd found in the basement. The excruciating loneliness of her dead body splayed in the chair haunted me, taunted me.

After one more look around the yard, I put my hand on the knob and turned. The kitchen bore the marks of last night's police investigation. Black fingerprint powder dotted cabinet doors and laminate counters, creating a record of CPD's work. The door to the basement remained wide open. Steeling myself, I tapped on the light on my flashlight app and continued down the stairs. Any cobwebs that had spanned the space yesterday had been brushed away in last night's police activity. The air still held remnants of the dank and musty scent, although it was lighter now. The maze of boxes still lined the room, but it appeared CPD had opened several. A cursory look showed kitchen utensils and plates inside. The body, of course, was no longer present, nor was the chair she had sat in. But I could feel her presence.

A new thought crossed my mind. Had she been placed here after her death? Images flashed into my head—the chair centered in the space, her body slumped against the wings, highlighted by a single bulb, the altar-like arrangement of items on the dresser. If this was a drug overdose, it was unlike any I had come across in my legal career.

I stood on the perimeter of the space, uncertain whether CPD had finished processing the rug for evidence. The dresser was still in situ, although the items from its surface had been bagged and removed. Again, the evidence of fingerprint analysis was evident on its surface, as well as on the attached mirror. Curiosity drew me. I stepped over, leaning close, trying to determine any particular area of police interest. As I would have expected, the remnants of fingerprint powder were clustered most heavily in the spot that had held the items. The victim, or perhaps someone close to the victim, had handled these items frequently.

The mirror, too, displayed remnants of a former life. Not as many here, but black smudges trimmed the edges. I moved my flashlight closer, noting the clusters of marks. Standing in front of the glass, I observed a light trail of powder that hadn't been obvious at first glance. Tilting my flashlight at an angle, I saw a trail through the dust on the mirror's surface. Someone had dragged their finger down the glass, forming a cross. I took photos of the markings, as well as the surface of the dresser. Instinct pinged caution deep in my brain.

Turning back toward the center of the room, I looked at the spot on the rug where the chair had been, focusing more closely on the pattern in the wool than I had last evening. I saw no obvious signs of blood, nor had any wounds been apparent on the body, but given the state of decomposition and my own shock, I could easily have missed something.

Everything I knew so far was that a life had been lost tragically to drugs. Yet her story seemed unfinished. I wasn't entirely sure why the initial explanation of an overdose was leaving me unsettled. Perhaps it was nothing more than the remnants of a tortured soul left to die alone.

I stood re-creating in my mind every item I had seen—the position, the texture, the scale. The smell of the sage smudge stick. The glint of the light off the crystals. The position of her body as she slumped against the wings of the chair.

The lack of drug paraphernalia also seemed to be stuck in my head, as it was inconsistent with the crash pad--overdose theory.

I stepped over to the open boxes and lifted the flaps. The handful I peered into revealed nothing more than an assortment of kitchen paraphernalia. Dishes, cups, silverware, utensils, a can opener—all loose, as if simply tossed in quickly. One box containing an assortment of dietary choices that made my stomach churn. Store-brand SpaghettiOs, baked beans, beef stew. All items that, in a pinch, could be eaten right out of the can, disgusting as the thought was to my inner food snob. Then again, I imagined that, given no other choices, I too would gladly eat canned goods. The privilege of my life with fresh vegetables as often and as frequently as I wanted was staring me in the face. This was her pantry. Two boxes of baby wipes topped off the collection along with a spray can of dry shampoo. All the basics.

I wasn't a believer in the supernatural, nor was I religious, but there was a heaviness that pressed on me here, a sadness, as if her desolate spirit still remained. With an ache in my heart, I turned and left the ghost behind. Once upstairs, I walked through the kitchen to the front of the home and made my way to the second level, wishing I had done so last night. The stairs creaked, and a different type of musty scent assaulted me. Mothballs and dust. From the landing, I could see three small bedrooms and a bath. The two rooms at the front of the house were empty of furniture and contained closets holding nothing other than dust bunnies. Working toward the back, I did a quick check in the bathroom medicine cabinet, found it empty, then entered the bedroom at the back of the house.

It was a decent-sized room with a set of windows overlooking the backyard. I stepped over to the windows, curious about whether a neighbor might have been able to notice lights. At some point, the long-neglected yard must have been lovely.

Orange tiger lilies fought their way up stubbornly through the weeds along the back fence, as did a few spindly peonies.

This room was also stripped of furniture, but I could see the history of a rug in the faded wood floor. I opened the closet door and initially saw nothing other than some lonely wire hangers. I stifled a sneeze, the dust equally thick here. Swinging my flashlight first around the floor and then up to the shelf above the hanging bar, I caught a glint of red in the light. As I reached up to retrieve the item, a shower of dust fell onto my hair. No longer able to hold back the assault on my nose, I sneezed and brushed the debris off my face. In my hand was a small bundle of brochures secured with a rubber band. Simple two-sided glossy cards identifying an addiction support group.

Had these belonged to the victim or the homeowner?

9

"Lane! What the hell were you thinking?"

I had just pulled open the door to the Link-Media office significantly later in the morning than I'd planned, dressed in jeans, a white blouse, and black loafers. No one would be calling me a fashionista today, and this conversation with Lane could not be shuttled politely to the sidelines. I wouldn't typically be airing my personal dirty laundry within earshot of my coworkers, but I had her on the phone and I wasn't letting her off until I was done vomiting out my frustrations.

"Did you think your contractor could just walk in the door and start trashing evidence before the cops have finished their work? I told you this might be a crime scene. And on top of it, you didn't even have the courtesy to let me know that these guys expected me to give them access. At 7:00 a.m., I might add."

I switched the phone to my other ear and shot a glance at the surprised eyes trained on me. I shook my head and shrugged.

"Hold on a minute," I said as Lane started in on her whiny sob story that was supposed to counter my objections. I marched through the space, flipped a hand at Brynn, and tried to keep my emotions in check now that I had an audience.

"Enough of this, Lane. You've stepped way beyond a simple favor, and I'm not going to get in the middle of you and a fight with the Chicago police force. So I suggest you pick up the damn phone the next time they call or, better yet, get on the next plane. I'm removing myself from your latest mess."

I hung up feeling just as annoyed with my sister as I had before we spoke. I was done with her. This was the last time I'd let Lane involve me in the endless drama that was her life. The cops could deal with her on this problem from here on out.

I tossed my bag on the desk, then flopped into my chair with a sigh before logging in to email to try to reschedule the two meetings I had missed this morning because of the contractor.

"How nice of you to grace us with your presence." My boss, Art Borkowski, stood in the doorway, arms crossed over his chest and a disapproving scowl on his face. He looked me up and down. "What's with the jeans and no-makeup thing? You sick or something?"

I probably looked like I'd spent the morning cleaning the garage. Under any other circumstances, I wouldn't leave my apartment wearing clothes meant for yard work, let alone without properly applied lipstick.

"Yeah, I know, I look like hell. I had a little family emergency this morning," I said. "Sorry to blow you off. Things were crazy, but I should have called in. Are you ready to reschedule our budget meeting?" I asked, reaching for my file and hoping he'd give me a minute to prep a desperately needed cup of tea.

"Reschedule? This is the second time you've been too busy to meet. So that means you lose your ability to vote. It's done." He shook his head as he looked at me again. "You got a little blush or something in that bag? You're going to scare the staff." He tossed a folder on my desk and left.

Thanks again, Lane. I threw the folder in my tote bag to read at home later tonight, then rummaged for a mirror. Flu victims looked better than I did right now. I ran a brush through my hair before pulling it back in a ponytail, dabbed a little concealer under my eyes, flicked some blush on my cheeks, and swiped on some lip gloss. It wasn't my normal full treatment, but it might prevent people from thinking I was contagious.

There wasn't much I could do about my ensemble other than top it off with a black cashmere cardigan I kept in the office for chilly days. I slipped it on, turned up the cuffs on my white shirt and tried to channel Audrey Hepburn. Turning back to my computer screen, I quickly scanned the email addresses and subject lines looking for anything that couldn't wait. And hoping that one of my leads on the alderman story would come through.

"I've got some stuff on the auction process. Do you want to talk about it now?" Brynn asked from the doorway.

"Yes. Anything to distract me from how annoyed I am with my sister." I motioned her in and flipped down the lid on my laptop.

"I hear you. Family has a way of being complicated. We all have at least one relative that we want to forget we know or never hear from again." She said it as if she had a story of her own to tell.

She came into the office and settled herself into the chair, pulling her legs up under her like a little girl, as she tended to do. A notepad was in one hand and the largest mug of coffee known to mankind was in the other. I couldn't think of a time when I'd ever seen Brynn without coffee. How she got any sleep at night with all that caffeine was a mystery to me. But then again, did anything affect your system when you were twenty-five?

"Okay, so I talked to that woman at the auction house, the

one you met," she began. "Well, she passed me on to the office manager, and according to her, they worked this specific deal for Driscoll Community Bank. Driscoll sends over a list of foreclosed properties quarterly, and Higgenbotham & Hudson conducts batch auctions. The bank has anywhere from five to twenty properties at a time in various stages of foreclosure. She didn't know if there were other auction companies involved or if they were the exclusive service provider for this bank."

"And what's the process for unloading the real estate? I can't imagine the bank wants to be in the flipping business."

My exposure to the foreclosure world was cursory at best, but banks weren't generally known for their facile, speedy processes. I didn't imagine the real estate division functioned any better. Visions of antiquated computer systems, miles of red tape, and employees whose customary response amounted to "We'll get to it eventually" filled my thoughts. No surprise that they outsourced the sales transactions.

"The process is pretty straightforward, at least after the bank passes the property off to the auction house. All the hard work—nasty letters and evictions—has been done. The homeowner is basically out of it at that point. The auction house simply has to get the specs into their system and tee it up into the sales schedule. Potential buyers preregister with the auction house and can then submit their bids for individual properties either online or in person, the day of the auction."

"And do these buyers know what they're getting?"

The shaky porch and rickety windows of the property on Pierce came to mind. As did the dollar signs that came along with extensive renovations. Every penny gambled on the purchase, and subsequent repairs, mattered if a quick profit could be made.

"It doesn't sound like it," Brynn said. "At least not in the same way most people go about buying a property. I haven't been down that road myself, but I do know about inspections and nervous insurance companies. Anyway, the potential buyers know the address of the property and the minimum opening bid, which has been determined by the bank. They know if there are back taxes to be paid, but beyond that, it's pretty much buyer beware. Most of the time, sales are to professional investors or flippers. There's not enough hand-holding for the average homeowner."

A satisfied smile on her face, Brynn took a swig of her coffee. We were opposites in so many ways—her utilitarian wardrobe of Oxford shirts and chinos versus my penchant for obscure designer labels, her close-cropped hair and Chapstick compared to my need for a flatiron and lipliner—at least on the surface. But in this relationship, it was the difference in how our minds worked that made us a great team. Nothing delighted her more than rolling up her sleeves and getting dirty with research; even boring stuff like this made her eyes shine. It was exactly the help I needed to keep my focus on the broader issues.

"So buyers are taking a bet with an ultra-low price and hoping that they're not walking into a chemical dump site or something," I said, imagining any number of nasty surprises that might be in store for the purchaser. If you weren't keeping up with your mortgage payments, it was unlikely you were keeping up with maintenance.

"You've basically summed it up. Cross your fingers and hope you hit the lottery." Brynn took another big swig of her coffee. "The properties are sold sight unseen, although I suppose someone could drive by if they wanted. They just can't go inside. Oh, and the buyer has to pay with cash. Usually a percentage down the day of the auction and the balance within days."

"Do we know anything about the bank's process?" Even though it was technically none of my business, I couldn't help but wonder where Lane had gotten that kind of cash. My firsthand history was of her shuffling bills and asking for loans when she got in trouble, usually from me. Our balance sheet was zeroed out at the moment, other than the locksmith reimbursement, so it really was none of my concern, but it struck me as being unlike her.

"I've got a call in to the REO officer," Brynn said. "He hasn't had time to talk in any detail, so I don't know when this property was vacated or when they first started the foreclosure process."

"Is he stonewalling?"

"I wondered about that, but basically, I think he was just too busy to talk to me. Or just didn't find it important. So I upped the pressure a little bit and let him know he had a dead body in one of his properties. That got his attention." She chuckled. "But I think it also moved him into CYA mode and he's probably consulting with their legal team before he says anything else. These guys are pretty risk averse." She shrugged. "I know, it's not much."

"It's a start. Do you have a time scheduled to talk to him again?"

"He wouldn't commit. Like I said, I think he's calling in legal. Oh, the one thing he did let slip was that the home was not owned by an individual. It was owned by a corporation. When I pressed, he clammed up, but that shouldn't be hard to unearth."

"That's interesting," I said, recognizing that new tidbit of information might complicate tracing the ownership of the property. Shell companies and complex holdings were a big part of the investment game. "Even the small-time investors form legal entities to hold assets for liability protection and tax benefits. I suspect you'll be able to get a name. It just might not be attached to a real human being."

My phone flashed an incoming call. Michael. "I need to take this, but stay here," I told Brynn, then answered the call. "Hi, I was just about to call you. Can you guys turn up the heat on my sister? I had to rush over to the house on Pierce this morning and stop a guy with a sledgehammer from busting up the property before you gave the go-ahead. I don't know if you're done with processing, but Lane isn't listening to me at all, so I thought it may be a good idea if she starts getting some stern phone calls from CPD."

"Well, coincidental timing, then. I only have a minute, but I wanted to tell you that we've identified the body." His voice was stiff and fraught with pain, and I felt my body tighten with expectation.

"It's Janek's niece," he said, his voice cracking.

The phone nearly slipped out of my hand. "His niece?" I choked out, staring at Brynn and shaking my head as she mouthed "What's wrong?"—I couldn't find words.

"She ran off about two years ago," Michael continued. "Her family hasn't seen her since. At the time, she had a pretty serious heroin problem. We're still waiting on the tox screen to know if she overdosed."

10

The late-morning sun beat down on me as I walked south from the Link-Media office in River North toward the Loop via Wells. I should have been working on the Alderman Flores story, harassing his office or the owner of the soundproofing company, but the news about Janek's niece wouldn't relax its grip. My head was swimming with sadness and questions.

Brynn had gotten the basics on the auction process; however, the specifics on Lane's property were thin. I needed a distraction and had decided a visit to Higgenbotham & Hudson was something that might serve both purposes. As I was the person who had found the body, they might be more willing to give me details they would hesitate to share with Brynn.

I also needed the fresh air. Janek's niece? I shuddered again at the thought.

I was struggling to process it. And the sight and smell of her well-decayed body refused to leave my head. I was nauseous all over again and heartbroken for Janek and his family. The news was crushing, even when drugs and a long-term disappearance had likely prepared them, to some degree, for bad news.

The walk was only a fifteen-minute trek, but between the sun and the movement, I didn't want to stop, hoping the activity would shove aside some of the frustration and confusion that had filled the early part of my day. I moved past the River North art and furniture galleries and over to Clark Street before again turning toward the river.

Although early in the season, people were beginning to gather on the Riverwalk, craving the sun after the dreariness of the unending Chicago winter. While the tourist boats transported visitors along the various architectural tours, a handful of kayakers inched lazily along the banks, avoiding the larger boats. Crossing the bridge, I was tempted to sit along the steps lining the water below and to try to regain my footing, but my foray over to Lane's property had consumed enough time this morning.

I arrived at the glass office tower on Wacker, my mood improving but my heart aching for Janek's loss. It was hard to conceive of a family member, let alone a child, stepping out of one's life for years. I searched my memory but couldn't recall Janek or Michael ever having mentioned the young woman or a family member with a drug problem. It made me realize I knew little about Janek's family, other than being aware his ex-wife had run off with his ex-partner. Guilt washed over me as I wondered if I had missed opportunities to inquire, or if Janek had simply kept his personal life so close to the vest that it was impossible to really get to know that side of him. The one thing the news of her identity did seem to confirm was that an overdose was certainly a reasonable assumption. What wasn't clear to me was why she had been able to hide in the home for so long without being detected. And why this particular home?

I took the elevator up to the thirty-second floor, where the same receptionist from the other afternoon greeted me.

"Hi. I don't know if you remember me," I said, trying to find a smile. "I picked up a deed to a property on Pierce from you on Monday. I was the one who looked dumbstruck over the lack of keys."

"Yes, I do remember. Were you able to access the home?" she asked, a small smile turning up the corners of her mouth.

"I followed your instructions and called the locksmith immediately. Thank you for the tip."

"Was there a problem?"

"Um, well, more of a surprising find. I was wondering if it would be possible to speak with Sylvia Dunham. I'm a journalist with Link-Media," I said, handing her a card. "I believe she spoke with an associate of mine earlier this morning, and I have some additional questions."

The smile left her face, but she nodded quickly and reached for the phone. Word of the body must have gotten around. "Yes, of course, let me call her. We heard about the death. I'm sorry I didn't make the connection right away that it was your property. It's so disturbing. Just one moment."

As she dialed her boss, I thought about what other morbid surprises owners of foreclosed properties had discovered along the way. Just as there was dark legal humor, there had to be some of the same in this industry related to oddball or gruesome discoveries. Laughter was life's great stress reliever.

"She'll be right up. Would you like coffee while you wait?"

"No, thank you. I'm fine."

She nodded and gave me a weak smile.

Moments later a woman in her midfifties was at the door. She was impeccably dressed in the way women in male-dominated industries often were. Simple navy suit, low heels, and a thin gold chain at her neck. The only obvious sign of wealth, if you didn't recognize the beauty of her Italian tailoring, were the substantial diamond studs in her ears. Gray hair streaked the temples of her chin-length bob, contrasting attractively with her tawny skin.

"Ms. Kellner?" she said, extending a hand. "I'm Sylvia. Shall we go to my office? I think we'll be more comfortable there."

I nodded and followed her down the hall. Her office was small but tasteful. Classic furnishings. It spoke of a company that knew how to balance authority against the bottom line.

"I have to say I'm absolutely shocked by this discovery," she said. "Please, let's sit by the windows. No need for the formality of a desk between us." We stepped over to two small club chairs, where I could see a tiny sliver of the Wrigley building across the river and an even tinier sliver of Lake Michigan beyond that.

"I understand you spoke to my associate, Brynn. As you can imagine, I have a long list of questions. Would that be okay? I believe you were aware that it was my sister who purchased the property. I'm just the one who made the unlucky discovery."

"Yes, of course. I really don't know much, but if I can help in any way, I'm happy to do so."

She twisted an emerald cocktail ring on her right hand as she waited for me to dive in. I found myself wondering if it was a habit or a nervous response.

"It's my understanding that this particular property came to you through your connection at Driscoll Community Bank," I began.

"Yes, that's correct. Banks often find themselves in positions where they end up with real estate on their books as assets due to foreclosure. Obviously, real estate is not part of their business model. By that I mean owning or buying and selling directly. Since they don't have the ability or interest in functioning as Realtors, nor do they have the patience to list properties individually with the Multiple Listing Service or to deal with individual purchasers, they typically avail themselves of services such as ours."

"So they do bulk selling because it's less of a hassle."

"That's what it comes down to. As I'm sure you know, selling properties one by one would involve a number of parties—Realtors, mortgage applications, inspections. By the time these distressed properties make it through the foreclosure process, quite a bit of time may have passed. The conditions of the buildings are generally poor, and back taxes are almost always an issue, making any negotiation an unmitigated nightmare. Auctions of as-is property smooth out the bumps for everyone."

I pictured the real estate auction industry as one that was fast and aggressive, filled with what was basically legalized gambling, each transaction a calculated risk on the future money-making capability of the property. I wondered how such an elegant, poised African American woman had ended up in this cutthroat business. And what the heck Lane thought she was doing dabbling at the fringes.

"The process of selling foreclosures can be quite complicated," she continued. "The buyer has to be willing to take on the property in as-is condition. There are no inspections. There are no loans. The buyer is banking on a good value, and hopefully the lender recovers some of the money that they were entitled to or lost due to default. We simply manage the sale process, receiving a small fee from the bank for coordinating. Everybody wins. In theory."

The sparkle in her eye told me she had stories to tell, and images of some of the HGTV home-flipping shows I'd watched came to mind—vandalism, critters, mountains of trash. I enjoyed remodeling, but this world was too rough and tumble for my tastes.

"What information is available to you when you take on a property?" I asked.

"Address, of course, parcel number, all those things that make identifying the legal description of the property possible," she responded. "These are the essential bits of information that allow us to transfer the deed once the purchase has been completed. We do conduct a search of property tax records and perform a cursory search for outstanding liens against the property. Often from contractors who weren't paid. However, we don't always find every encumbrance, and to be clear, nor is it our responsibility to do so.

"Property taxes are easy since we're dealing with a government agency," she continued. "But if there's an old lien to a contractor that might have been sitting for years, we wouldn't necessarily find that. By purchasing, the new owner is signing up to take over any and all obligations related to outstanding liens or claims—financial, environmental, it doesn't matter, that is all on the purchaser's shoulders. We do everything we can to make that clear. The smart ones who've done their research know this. But every now and then we do get a first-time purchaser who is shocked to discover a thirty-thousand-dollar tax bill is now his obligation. Goes with the territory."

And where did my sister fall in that spectrum? Again, not my concern. And right now financial obligations were the least of the problems.

"And have you ever had a situation where a body was found in the property?" I asked, watching her flinch at the question.

She paused but looked at me directly before answering.

"In all my years in this business, it's only come up once before," she said. "An elderly homeowner, without family, who died peacefully in his bed. We have had a number of 'good find' stories. Just last year a purchaser found a lovely painting left in an attic. It appraised at nearly half a million dollars."

Her face lit up, the story seeming to strike a little amusement in her. Perhaps she was a gambler at heart herself.

"That's a very nice lottery win," I said, wishing I'd been the one to find art instead of a decaying corpse. "And how long have you worked with Driscoll?"

"I developed the relationship with them eight years ago. We started with two properties. They were happy with how smooth the transactions went, and business has grown from there. Now we handle roughly fifty to sixty transactions a year for them."

"Would I be correct in assuming that you have no information on the financial history of the property? Such as when the initial default occurred or what efforts were made by the lender to bring the mortgagee back to the table?"

I was mulling over the timing, trying to imagine how Janek's niece might have remained unnoticed in the basement and for how long.

"Yes, that's accurate. The name of the property owner is available, but we have no direct knowledge of what played out between the two parties."

"Would it be possible for you to share your contact at the bank with me? I'd really like some understanding of the timeline for this property."

"Certainly." She opened a drawer and rifled through a stack of cards.

"And do you invest yourself?" I asked.

"I hate to admit it, but no, I don't. One, it seems like a conflict of interest, and two, I'm not very adventurous with my financial decisions. Here you go," she said, handing me the card. "Phillip Byrne is the REO officer I work with. Please mention my name, and if he is at all reluctant, let me know. I have some experience with arm-twisting." She laughed.

"I imagine you do."

11

"A green goddess avocado salad, please. Skip the beets."

It was nearly two o'clock and I hadn't put a thing in my stomach since last night. Even my morning Earl Grey hadn't happened, and my battery was flagging. Normally I kept a packet of almonds in my purse for food emergencies such as this, but apparently, I had used up my stash. Rather than succumb to the temptation of a Stan's Glazed Pretzel Twist donut, I'd popped in to sweetgreen after my visit to the auction house to regroup.

As I took my tray over to a seat at the window counter, I was regretting my restraint and trying to convince myself the best-donut-in-life wasn't nearly as outstanding this late in the day, anyway. Spearing a piece of avocado, I debated my plan of attack for the balance of the afternoon.

A voicemail notice appeared on my screen. Damn, Vanessa from Impact Soundproofing. Her message simply said she'd call again later. After downing a few more bites, I then phoned Cai. I felt guilty for not giving her much of an explanation when I'd canceled our dinner plans. It had been several days since we'd spoken at any length, and it felt so foreign that it unsettled me.

Another call straight to voicemail. At least I knew this call would be returned.

The Driscoll Community Bank administrative office was only a few blocks south of where I had camped out for lunch, so I finished up my greens and decided an impromptu visit was in order.

Standing in front of the address listed on the banker's business card, I double-checked the name of the officer I was about to burst in on. The high-rise was just another glass-and-steel structure lacking architectural distinction. One of many that could make the Loop seem like a skyscraper cavern. As a local community bank, they weren't a large enough organization to have possession of the entire building, so I stopped at the directory before hitting the elevators. With any luck, I would catch the guy in his office.

I stepped off the elevator to a sea of beige and brown. Obviously the offices had not been chosen for their luxurious appointments. Vinyl lettering on two glass doors to my right told me I'd arrived. I pulled open a door and approached the front desk, asking to see Phillip Byrne. After punching in a few keys, the young receptionist promptly told me that she didn't see my name on his calendar before inquiring about my appointment.

"Tell him I'm from Link-Media, and it's about the body I found at the property he sold my sister," I said, sliding my business card across the counter and suppressing a smile. Over the past year and a half, I'd been able to use a number of dramatic lines to get a source to speak to me, but none as dramatic as this.

She mumbled something unintelligible as her eyes got wide but promptly picked up the phone.

"He'll be just a moment," she said.

I had a feeling his schedule would suddenly clear. I sat in the nearest chair and waited for the next guy in a conservative suit to come through the glass doors. A few moments later a balding middle-aged male exited and looked at me. His pale skin was tinged with blotchy red marks covering his boney cheeks and trailing up to his unusually prominent ears. I hoped he wasn't a poker player.

"Ms. Kellner?" he said. "I'm sorry to have kept you waiting. Sylvia just alerted me of your conversation. I understand you spoke with her earlier today." I imagined she had phoned him moments after I left her office. His speech was rapid fire, showing his nerves. "Kathy," he said, turning to the receptionist. "Can you log me in to conference room three?" She nodded.

"Ms. Kellner, follow me."

We settled into chairs flanking a Formica-topped conference table big enough for ten or twelve. Bland, generic, mass-produced landscapes that looked like they'd come from a one-day sale at an airport conference center decorated the walls. I tried not to cringe.

"I'm quite beside myself after hearing about your discovery," he said. "I can't imagine how this could happen. Surely there is a reasonable explanation. People die of natural causes all the time. It must've been quite a shock for you."

He ran through his speech so quickly I could practically see the thought bubbles above his head—*bad press, lawsuit, what will it take for her to go away?*

"It isn't an experience I recommend," I said, noting the beads of sweat forming on his forehead. "What can you tell me about the history of this property?"

"I'm sorry, you'll have to tell me which property this was. We handle so many."

At least he looked sheepish when he said it. I rattled off the street address, which he promptly scribbled down on a yellow legal pad. His ears were now the color of a pomegranate, and pink was beginning to seep up his neck above the collar of his white poplin dress shirt. It wasn't a good look for a grown man.

"I'll need a minute to place it," he said. "I'm sure you understand. I can't keep them all top of mind. Properties come across my desk when the owner is unable to keep up with their mortgage commitments. Eventually, if they are unable to bring everything up-to-date, the property moves into foreclosure and the asset then becomes the property of the bank. That's when I get involved."

He was stalling, trying to make up for the fact that he hadn't bothered to look up the details by distracting me with process steps.

"Yes, Mr. Byrne, I'm familiar with how this works," I said, trying not to sound patronizing. "Sylvia was kind enough to bring me up to speed. What I'm looking for is specific information. Who owned the property? What was the date of the initial default? And what interactions did the bank have with the owner of this property through this process?"

"Well, um, I don't really know. I can't keep all of that in my head. I'd have to look that up," he said, seemingly surprised that anyone would ask.

"Then why don't you?" I said, smiling at him, my tone that of an elderly kindergarten teacher.

"Oh, yes, sure." He moved to the computer station at the head of the table and punched in whatever codes he needed to get access while I pulled out a notebook.

"Okay, here we are. The property was owned by Quantum Holdings, LLC. They opened the mortgage with us in 2012 and officially went into default in October 2017."

I got up and pulled a chair closer so I could see his screen. He shifted uncomfortably as if I had breached some type of rule about banker space.

"I'm sorry, but this is personal information."

I ignored him and leaned closer to look at the screen, trying to make sense of the numbers and dates and codes I was seeing.

I jotted down the name of the LLC, date of the mortgage initiation, and what looked like the date the company was officially notified. "And how does the bank define default?"

I scrolled the screen as I asked, looking for a contact name and address, but Byrne shifted the screen to minimize my view before I had decoded what I was looking at.

"Um, it's bank policy to initiate foreclosure after four months of missed payments. In this case, we initiated after three months because there was also a substantial outstanding property tax bill that had been due last August."

"And what notifications or contact did you have with the homeowner prior to beginning foreclosure?"

"We contact them initially through US mail and email, if we have one on file, then phone calls prior to initiating bankruptcy. Once the mortgagee hits that default threshold, all communication is then sent via certified mail." He seemed to be relaxing a little as we discussed the process, which was more comfortable territory.

"And do you have any record in your system of whether you got any responses from the homeowner to those communications?"

"According to what I see here, the mortgagee was nonresponsive."

"Did they sign for the certified mail?"

"No response. The notification was returned to us as undeliverable."

Perhaps the owner had been long gone by that point, having abandoned the property or was simply ignoring reality, playing the odds just to buy a little time. A new thought crossed my mind.

"In those communications, the mailed communications, were those sent to the property address?"

He punched a few keys. "We have two addresses in our

system. The property address and then another at a secondary location. Communication was sent to both via certified mail."

"And may I have that address?"

"Excuse me? This is quite extraordinary. There are rules about these things." He reached up and turned the screen further out of my view.

"Mr. Byrne, you've already provided me with the name of the LLC that owned the property. That mailing address is most likely on file with the Secretary of State's office. I'm just trying to save us both some time. I wouldn't want our readers to conclude that you didn't make a concerted effort to track them down before you foreclosed," I said, staring at him hard.

He clenched his jaw but read off an address on Broadway with a 60657 zip code. I wrote it down and ran through what I remembered of that intersection, thinking the address sounded like a strip mall.

"The name listed as the contact is a Stephan Reda. I do see a note that the phone number on file appears to have been disconnected."

"Convenient," I said, not hiding my annoyance. I also knew from my previous work that the guy could simply be a service provider, set up to receive legal notices with no other association with the company. Perfectly legal, it was a common practice when the entity was out of state or just wanted to keep a little cloud cover between owner and company. It could also be stage one of complicated ownership subterfuge.

"As you can imagine, we do try every possible avenue to recover funds," Byrne added.

I bet they did. However, I let his comment slide. Based on some of the work I'd done in the past on predatory lending, that was a can of worms not worth opening now.

"So once you've served notice of the foreclosure, I assume you don't immediately take ownership of the property. That there is a process, a certain amount of time, if you will, for that homeowner to come forward and rectify the situation, even if you believe they've likely abandoned the property."

I was getting curious about the time frame and wondering if Janek's niece had died before or after the property went into foreclosure. Perhaps she had even used the place prior to foreclosure. I wasn't sure if it mattered or added anything that explained the tragedy, but if her family had not had contact with her for quite some time, there were bound to be others with questions about the last few months of her life. I was also struggling to understand how she could have gone undiscovered for so long.

"We continue to make contact attempts with the mortgagee using the information that we have available, but yes, at some point, if there is no response, we really have no choice but to take possession of the property."

"And how long would that process take from notice of foreclosure to the bank repossessing the property?"

"In this case, as I said, the mortgagee was officially in default as of October 2017. We repossessed the property in November 2018."

"And that's when you turned the property over to the auction house. Correct?"

"The banking world, as you probably know, is rather slow. According to the notes, we added the property to our auction list in February of this year, and it got slotted into Sylvia's schedule. I believe you know the rest of the timeline."

"The only other thing I'm curious about, Mr. Byrne, is whether or not anyone from the bank ever physically visited the property. Do you have that information?"

"Let me check." He shifted in his chair but scrolled down the page. I could see from the corner of my eye that the screen was filled with a number of boxes marked with codes that I couldn't immediately decipher.

"It isn't a standard part of our practice to visit the site, but I do see that we attempted service of the final notice directly before we took possession."

"And when would that have occurred?"

"Also in November 2018."

Six months ago. It hit me like a slap in the face. Had Janek's niece been dying in the home while the bank rep was knocking on the door?

12

Dying alone in a cold, dark basement. My stomach was still knotted with the thought, and my head was stuck in a loop wondering what had happened to her. I couldn't come to grips with it and didn't know if I was obsessing because I had been the one to find her, because she was Janek's niece, or because I was a single woman living alone and her isolation was hitting too close to home.

I left the bank feeling I understood the foreclosure process a little better, but the time frame was loose and gave me no indication of how long Janek's niece might have been staying in the property. And why no one seemed to have known she was there.

Exiting the elevator in the lobby of the now bustling bank building, I stepped over to a quiet corner and called Michael. He answered on the second ring.

"Hey, how are you holding up? How's Janek?" I asked, listening for the emotion in his voice that would tell me what he was really feeling.

"I'm okay. Shocked like everyone," he said flatly. "Janek, well, he's pretty much a mess. He just refuses to admit it and won't go home. He's angry. Mad at himself. Flailing. I've never seen him like this. And I'm not sure how to help."

Confusion, frustration, and hurt bounced back at me as he spoke. Reading between the lines, it seemed Michael should have been taking his own advice and set work aside. I didn't imagine either one of them had been productive today, but sometimes going through the motions with things that were routine and familiar was therapy in its own right.

"Did you know her?" I asked. Something I hadn't remembered until now flashed back into my head: Michael kneeling next to her body, noting the tattoo on the inside of her wrist. He had known then or, at the very least, known it was a distinct possibility she was Janek's niece. The weight of that suspicion, as her identity was now confirmed, had to have been unbearable.

"No, we'd never met. I knew *of* her. Knew she had struggles. Janek has a photo of her and her mom on his desk, so I recognized the tattoo. But before this week, the only other thing I knew was that she'd run off and that the family had been frantically searching for her. But I didn't know the half of it. You know Janek. He doesn't talk much about his personal life, unless there's a reason."

Like all cops, I wanted to say. Michael sounded drained, even a bit forlorn, and my heart ached for him. I looked at the time. It was almost four.

"Do you have time for coffee or a beer? It might be a good idea to talk or just sit with me for a little while."

"Yeah, that sounds good. I could use a break. Where are you?"

"I'm in the Loop. Can you meet me at Free Rein? It's in the St. Jane Hotel on Michigan and Wacker."

"Sure. I need about half an hour."

"Okay, I'll see you in a little bit, then."

The restaurant was only a ten-minute walk, and I found a

quiet window table near the bar where Michael and I could speak privately—that is, if he was in the mood. My own emotions could only be described as flat and confusing.

I perused the creative cocktail menu, amused by concoctions titled "What Would Jane Do?" and "The Devil in Blanc," which paid loose tribute to Chicago icon, Jane Addams, the hotel's patron saint. The unusual drinks were too complicated for my mood today, so I stuck with one of my go-tos, a Sauvignon Blanc from New Zealand. I was tempted to order a scotch for Michael —he sounded like he needed it—but I didn't want to make assumptions in case he had to go back to work.

As I sipped my wine, I Googled Quantum Holdings but found nothing in Chicago, so I plugged the mailing address into the search bar. The listings that came up included a Chinese takeout joint, a nail salon, and a dry cleaner. Was one of these businesses doing real estate investment on the side? It wasn't clear, but nothing that came up initially looked like it had any connection to a real estate investment company. Then again, businesses and websites changed frequently and weren't always up-to-date, so it was possible that the information in this top-level search wasn't current. Next, I opened Google maps to see if I could get a street view. Although challenging on my small phone screen, I panned across the image.

Interesting. The end unit appeared to be an independent pack-and-ship location, or had been at the time of the photo. Perhaps they also offered mailbox services? As long as there was a legitimate street address and not simply a PO box, a registered agent could get away with listing a mailing service as a property's address.

Cai phoned as I scrolled through the search results, letting me know she was deep in a case and couldn't swing a free evening. However, we tentatively planned for the following night.

I saw Michael across the room before he saw me, and I found myself smiling. It was always a delight to catch him when he didn't know I was watching. It felt like a moment of secret admiration for those broad shoulders and that chiseled jaw. I stood and waved. He broke into a broad grin and picked up his pace as he crossed the room.

"Hi. It's been the longest forty-eight hours of my life," he said, pulling me close.

I took a deep breath, inhaling the sandalwood scent of the soap he favored, and hugged him back hard. If Janek was hurting, so was Michael. That was their relationship.

"I'm drinking wine but thought I should wait to order yours in case you're going back to work." I clasped his hand and held on as he settled in next to me.

"I'd better stick with coffee."

I flagged over our server and ordered his coffee and a cheese and charcuterie plate, imagining that food hadn't been on his priority list today either.

"Has the funeral been scheduled yet?" I asked. His eyes were tired, and his chin hadn't seen a razor today. It didn't take much insight to glean that he was emotionally drained.

"It's set for Friday."

"Send me the details. I'd like to be there."

"Will do. By the way, I called your sister four times."

"Let me guess, she's ignoring you too." I shook my head and lifted my wine glass to my mouth.

I didn't have the energy right now to worry about Lane's inability to take this situation seriously. CPD's handling of the property was her problem, and I wasn't going to mother her into responsibility. She'd been advised to deal with them herself. I also knew Michael and I were ignoring the obvious, getting minutiae out of the way before getting to the tough stuff.

"This has to be devastating news for Janek," I said. "What

was her name? I was so shocked earlier, I neglected to ask," I said, realizing that I didn't even know the most basic information about the young woman.

"Her name was Zoe Symanski. She was barely twenty-two. Janek and I had a long talk this morning, and he filled me in on the family history."

The waitress returned just then with coffee and the appetizer plate. I smiled and thanked her, but Michael couldn't even pull his eyes up from our clasped hands.

"Apparently she'd been in rehab at least twice, once in her final year of high school, and then again her sophomore year of college," Michael continued. "It's been a really rough road for her family. She flunked out of college after the second rehab attempt, moved back in with her mom, who is single. The drugs didn't end and money kept disappearing from her mom's wallet, so they were at each other's throats constantly. A few months later, the kid took off after yet another big fight. That was two years ago. They haven't seen or heard from her since."

"They've had no idea where she's been?" I said, incredulous. Michael shook his head. "That's heartbreaking. I can't imagine how that must feel. What about friends? Or was there a boyfriend?"

She most likely had help from someone, even if it was just a couch to sleep on occasionally, but that didn't mean those friends had shifted loyalties and talked to Zoe's mom, regardless of how misplaced those loyalties were.

"There was a boyfriend all right," Michael said, finally looking at me. "But he was just as much of a doper as she was. He's the guy who introduced her to the stuff. And was probably her dealer. At least that's what Janek believes. Sounds like it was one of those on-again, off-again relationships. The kid got picked up coming off a plane from Mexico, trying to import his own personal stash." He paused, pain filling his eyes. "I understand he was pretty physical with her. I'm not sure how far he took it, but he laid a hand on her. One black eye is all it took for Janek to go off on the kid."

With everything he had seen during his years in the police force, there was little that got to Michael the way that abuse of women and children did.

"Did anyone speak to him while she was missing?"

"Loud and often. Apparently Janek had at least one run-in with the guy. Bumped into him on the street one night, picked him up on possession with intent, and hauled him in. Don't know if Janek went looking for him or just got lucky, but it sounds like he got a little hot. That didn't play out too well in the courts. The kid's attorney argued that it was a false arrest, that Janek planted the smack, basically, that he had an axe to grind because of the niece. It created just enough doubt to get the kid charged with possession, but they couldn't make a stronger case. He paid his fine, was put on probation, and life went on." Michael shook his head and looked at me. "Let me tell you, that sure didn't help Janek warm up to the kid."

"Understandable." I'd never seen him lose control, but the Karl Janek I knew was capable of a simmering, controlled rage, the kind of rage that would only be expressed when someone near and dear had been hurt badly. "I know you don't believe Janek planted the stuff, but did he go overboard? Did he get too rough with the kid?"

"Maybe," Michael said, after pausing to think about it. "He's like a pit bull when it comes to protecting his family, so who knows. I've never seen Janek step over the line, but in this case, I have to say, it's possible. She was his only niece. It's a tough thing to watch your sister's kid deteriorate like that, particularly when you know who hooked her in the first place."

I squeezed Michael's hand tighter, feeling his pain. Knowing the only thing I could do to help was simply to listen.

"I can't say the family took it very well—the fighting, the blame, the boyfriend receiving no consequences. It wasn't long after that Zoe ran off. I don't know how Janek reconciles everything that happened after, but I know his sister blamed him, at least for a while. In her mind, if Janek hadn't gone after the boyfriend, maybe Zoe wouldn't have left. It's pointless to speculate about what might have happened, but that's human nature. She was dealing with her own guilt. Anyway, I get the sense that with the passage of time, they both understood that Zoe was running away from, rather than dealing with, her problem. The bigger issue became their anger with this boyfriend. They believe he conspired with Zoe, helped her hide from her family."

"You said she'd been in treatment. Do you know where?" I asked, thinking about the pamphlet I'd found at Lane's property.

"No, but she had a couple goes at it. Didn't seem to work, but you know how that is. Someone's really gotta be ready before they face the hard work. That stuff isn't easy. And it sure ain't easy when you're twenty-two and still think you're invincible."

"And this boyfriend, you said that the family thought he might have been helping her hide. Could he have been staying with her at the house?" I asked.

My gut told me she'd been there alone, but new questions were forming in my mind about the boyfriend and what he knew. And I couldn't shake the feeling that there was a staged quality to Zoe's death, at least when it came to how and where she was placed.

"We didn't see any signs of anyone else staying at the house, and it didn't appear, to me anyway, that she had been there long," Michael said, giving me a long look. "I know where you're going with this. Aside from Janek being this kid's worst enemy, I'm not sure anybody knows where he is or has been in contact with him since he and Janek had their run in-in court."

Michael knew my instincts were to process the events as if this were a problem to solve, a series of clues that would build the picture of how and why Zoe had died. He knew my thinking because it wasn't that much different from his own thought process. Be suspicious of everyone and everything until proven otherwise. Some thought it was a tough way to go through life, that it made me jaundiced. I just saw it as practical.

"It's so hard to think of anyone down in that basement all alone for so long," I said. "And I've got to imagine the neighbors were wondering what the hell was going on."

"You know how people are. They may have wondered, thought there was a dead animal somewhere, but nobody was concerned enough to try to find out what was happening at the house. The old not-my-problem. Sad stuff."

"How close are you on cause of death?" I asked.

"While the ME hasn't come to any official conclusions yet, as you'd imagine, overdose is the baseline everybody's working from. We're basically just waiting for the autopsy to confirm it."

"Any guesses yet on how long she's been dead?"

"Cold basement, nobody around, obviously all of that slows down the rate of decomp, but it sure looks like months to me. It's hard to gauge yet. We're really going to need to rely on the ME to see if he can get a range. As you know, cold temperatures can really make it hard to assess. She could have been down there all winter."

13

Tarot & Crystals.

The flashing neon sign distracted me as I drove south on Ashland toward Alderman Flores's office. I was heading to his office this morning hoping a surprise attack would get someone in the office on record. Polite phone calls certainly hadn't done the job.

I'd left Michael outside of Full Rein at around six last night and gone home to a quiet evening of restless alone time. His desire to go back to work after seeing me likely had more to do with feelings of impotence than with any pressing work activities. He and Janek were cut from the same cloth in that regard—time off was for sissies, even if all you could manage at the moment was shuffling papers.

Crystals had held enough meaning for Zoe that despite her homelessness, they were some of her few precious possessions. I made an impulsive decision, pulled over, and parked. The store was in older building with a bowed bay window that hadn't seen a paint job or a window squeegee in way too long. Overgrown plants, macramé hangings, and large purple amethyst geodes served as advertisements. Talk about fitting a stereotype. A bell rang as I opened the door, and the scent of something sweet, yet musky, hit my nose.

It took a minute for my eyes to adjust to the low light. Music—chanting, really—played from somewhere in the back through a tinny sound system. It was a language I couldn't identify, but the rhythmic repetition seemed to fit every bad Hollywood movie image I had of this type of establishment.

The center of the store was a series of waist-high tables laden with bins, each containing rocks or crystals of different shapes and colors and sizes. The perimeter shelving housed candles, incense, oils, and books, along with a bevy of things that I couldn't identify, things foreign to my non-metaphysical life experience.

A woman who I guessed to be in her seventies, wearing a flowery caftan and with long salt-and-pepper hair piled high on her head, nodded hello but made no effort to engage me. I wandered through the space, overwhelmed by the colors and the scents of the items around me, but I couldn't make much sense of any of it. Small hand-lettered signs identified the contents, but telling me I was looking at tourmaline wasn't the education I needed.

A display of bound leaves, similar to what I'd seen on the basement altar, was in front of me. Michael had called it sage. Finally, something I recognized. I picked up a bundle and took it over to the counter.

"Hi, I'm a complete novice. Can you tell me what this is used for? I've heard it called a smudge stick. Is that accurate?"

"Yes, that's exactly right," she said, taking the bundle from my hand and raising it to her nose. "Smells wonderful, doesn't it? The stick is a bundle of dried herbs, usually white sage, but it can also include lavender or yerba santa. It's bound with twine. Burning the bundle is an ancient practice and was part of Native American ceremonial rituals. See? Like this here." She lifted up a large flat shell, its pearly interior full of ash. It was just like the one I had seen at the house.

"And what is it supposed to do?" I asked, smiling. "See, I told you I was a novice."

"Don't worry. Many people come to us at all stages of knowledge. We are just as happy to educate as we are to sell. Smudging is a cleansing ceremony. The sage is lit, then using a feather, or your hand, you walk around the room you want to address, stating your intention to clear the space of the negative energy, and then fan the smoke into the crevices."

She spoke to me seemingly oblivious that anyone would find directing smoke with feathers odd. In her world, perhaps it was downright logical, but in mine, scorn and laughter would be the prevailing response if I started waving my hands above burning weeds. If you believed it to be true, I guess it was. Hopefully my skepticism wasn't showing too badly, or perhaps she was long past the worry of judgment.

"And you must speak your intentions, as well as distribute the smoke, is that correct?" I was confused by the whole concept, and under normal circumstances the language alone would have had my eyes rolling. Setting your intentions, places holding energy, wafting smoke into corners—it was all far too woo-woo for my analytic brain.

"Yes, smudging a room is one of the basic principles of cleansing," she explained patiently. "Some will smudge their home when they first move into it to remove any negative energy from the prior occupants. Some will smudge a room after someone has been ill or angry to help move those negative forces away. Here in the store, because we get so many people who are bringing with them their own troubles, we are cleansing on a continual basis."

If her calm, patient demeanor was any indication, something was working for her. Maybe I needed to be more open-minded?

"And are there other items or processes that people use for this purpose?"

"Well, that would depend on what you're trying to accomplish. Some prefer palo santo for its scent, or they find it more effective for their needs. It too is burned, although it's available as an essential oil formulation that can be diffused."

She stepped out from behind the counter and walked over to a nearby shelf, a heavy stack of brass bangles clacking as she walked. She picked up a package of small brown sticks that reminded me of fire starters. I recognized them from the dresser. Tearing open the plastic, she handed me a piece and allowed me to smell the aroma. It was both woodsy and citrusy and quite pleasant.

"Individuals have different opinions on the effectiveness of sage versus palo santo, or even the type of sage. It can get complex, if you want it to, but it doesn't have to be. I advise customers initially to simply choose the product that they prefer the scent of or that they find easier to use. The sage creates a lot of ash and not everyone appreciates that, but it would be entirely your choice."

"And what about the crystals? How are those used?"

"Again, one must know what you want to accomplish. Every crystal has a quality, a vibration or frequency to it, and these frequencies can communicate in a way that we can't see. If you're highly attuned, holding one in your hand will allow you to feel some of the vibrational energy of the stone, but that is a more advanced way of using the stones. In guiding customers toward crystals, we really have to have a conversation about your life. Are you looking to bring in more prosperity? If so, then agate and citrine are wonderful crystals to have where you work. If you are looking to bring love into your life, I personally like carnelian and rose quartz."

She walked over to the center bins and pulled out a beautiful pale pink specimen, then handed it to me. Its smooth surface was cool and glossy, sparkling in my hand. I didn't know what it was or what it was supposed to do, but it was beautiful.

"Close your fingers around the crystal, then close your eyes, and raise the stone to your heart. Clear your mind and feel the vibration."

I did as I was told, feeling nothing other than silly, but like anything, belief was required. I opened my eyes and shrugged.

"Perhaps we haven't chosen the right crystal for you," she said slowly, watching my eyes. "Or perhaps your heart hasn't healed enough to receive its gifts?"

I stared back at her, feeling that she had just looked into my soul and seen my vulnerability. I flinched, handed her the stone, then moved closer to the bins so as not to see my past reflected in her eyes.

I was in awe of the beauty in front of me, but so far I had not been convinced the stones were anything more than pretty to look at. A number of the larger specimens would look beautiful artfully arranged on one of my bookshelves, but decorating inspiration wasn't what I was here for. Walking along the table, I looked over the items, hoping I could recognize the crystals I had seen on the basement dresser. I pulled three different stones from their bins and held them in my hand.

"And what about these? What would these be used for?"

"Oh my, how interesting that you're drawn to these crystals. This is a very powerful combo." A crease formed on her brow.

"What do you mean by that? What are these stones used for?"

"While there can be a number of interpretations and uses, this combination together is useful for someone very concerned about keeping evil at bay. It's very serious stuff. Looking at your selections, I'd say you're looking for protection. You must be scared to death."

14

My mind was tangled with thoughts of death and loneliness.

My plan to ask Alderman Flores some uncomfortable questions had been a bust. As usual, the guy never seemed to be in his office, and the primary qualification of his frontline staff seemed to be their skill at shooing away pesky people like journalists.

Feeling frustrated, I now found myself back in front of the home on Pierce, standing on the sidewalk and consumed with dark thoughts. Why was I feeling this compulsion over Zoe's death? Of course it was tragic, but I hadn't even known she existed just days ago.

This young woman's death wouldn't leave my mind. I couldn't put my finger on it, but there was something stuck there for me. The image of her decaying body spotlighted in that dark space was ever present in my mind. Was it the cross drawn on the mirror? The smudge stick? Or the sheer tragedy of self-destruction? My therapist would probably tell me it was my own subliminal fear of dying alone, but I wasn't willing to write it off that easily.

Everything I knew at this point told me the facts of the case were likely going to conclude this poor young woman had tragically overdosed, perhaps even been helped along by a little fentanyl. But there was something about the space, the place that she had died, that felt staged to me, for lack of a better way to explain it.

Someone had to have seen or heard something, even if they didn't realize its significance at the time. The immediate neighbors flanking Lane's property were the obvious starting points. The boyfriend Michael had mentioned would also need to be located. Lifting the latch on the gate, I moved toward the house, pausing on the walkway to look more closely at the surrounding homes. They were showing their age—a roof past its prime, several in need of a fresh coat of paint— but they were generally tidy. Developers had not yet infiltrated this particular stretch of homes, knocking down the old three-story structures in order to build some silly glass box that had no connection to the history of the neighborhood.

Given the faulty lock on the back door, Zoe would have used the more hidden access point to come and go. I followed the path around to the back of the building, curious about who might have been able to see her movements. I stood surveying the space, calculating the sightline from the back door to nearby properties. Garages, tall trees, and an alley added to the distance between buildings and the obstructed view. Anyone could have come and gone largely unseen via the back door.

The lock was a cheap piece of garbage that most ten-year-olds could pick with a light jab of a screwdriver. One more item for Lane's to-do list. I let myself in, wondering why scavengers hadn't stripped the home of its copper pipes or everything else of salvage value.

Drawn again to the basement, I stood in the dank, depressing space feeling the tragedy of Zoe's death, feeling her young, sad spirit crying out in pain as if she were calling to me. Or was it just me projecting? Wondering how long it would be before anyone came looking for me if I were in trouble?

As I'd noted on my last visit, many of the boxes contained the essentials of life without a kitchen or shower. But there were far too many boxes unless Zoe had been running a food pantry out of the space.

I retrieved house keys from my bag and began slicing open some of the additional boxes. The first was heavy and the light was dim, so I dragged it over to a spot where the light from the single weak bulb was more direct. Lifting open the flap, I found bundles wrapped in cellophane. Pulling one out, I tore open the plastic. A stash of brochures from a place called the Renacido Center stared back at me. Brochures that matched the one I'd found in the upstairs closet for the addiction treatment support group. Ten boxes in total, thousands of brochures. Why were they here?

The answer wasn't obvious, nor was any rationale for a young woman overdosing alone in a chair in a basement with no drug paraphernalia to be found. All the more reason to find the boyfriend.

I left the basement and went outside, planning to knock on doors of the surrounding properties, hoping someone had seen Zoe's movements. If I could put together a timeline of when she had started squatting in the home, maybe I could ease my own mind about her death.

The boarded-up basement window well was ten feet in front of me and fairly concealed. But the weak illumination of the light coming from below might have been visible at night. I bent down, noticing textured glass through the makeshift plywood covering, which only hid part of the window. The boarding appeared to be a homemade job. The cuts on the wood were rough and the board imperfectly attached. As I looked closely, I could see the pane of glass was broken beneath and a crack ran from the upper edge, but the glass was fully intact.

"You looking for something?"

I jumped at the unexpected voice, then turned to see a man, well into his seventies, watching me over the chain-link fence separating the adjoining properties. His white T-shirt was stretched out at the neck, and his baggy jeans were supported by Chicago Bears-themed suspenders. Thin white hair barely covered his scalp on top but brushed the edges of his shoulders, as if he couldn't be bothered with a trip to the barber.

"Oh, I didn't see you there," I said, getting to my feet. "I was checking on the window. My sister just bought this property. She's out of town, and I'm helping her out a bit." I wasn't sure how much the man knew about the recent police activity, so I kept my response vague.

"And what's she going to do with it? Knock it down?" he asked, his tone indicating his low opinion of the idea.

"I'm not entirely sure, but I believe she has plans to renovate it and then rent it out."

"I guess that would be okay." He nodded, considering the idea, setting the rake in his hand against the fence. "As long as she ain't going to knock it down. We don't need any more cement block hipster pads around here. This was a family neighborhood before all these kids started coming in with their tattoos and their pot."

"So this is a pretty quiet neighborhood, then?" There was nothing like nosy neighbors when it came to sources. Their conclusions weren't always accurate, but if something suspicious was going on, the nosier the neighbor, the better.

"Yeah, it is. And she better keep it that way," he said, giving me a look that told me Lane was in for some challenges with this guy. She might be able to sweet-talk a potential buyer into a deal by playing fast and loose with information, but a guy like this, set in his ways, was a phenotype Lane would have a hard time finessing. I chuckled to myself and smiled back at him.

"What do you know about the previous owners of this house? I understand my sister bought it at a foreclosed property auction." I brushed the dirt off my hands and shoved them in my pockets, preparing to keep this conversation going for as long as the guy was willing to talk.

"It's been sitting empty for a couple years. Every now and then I'd see somebody poking around. Always looked like contractors or developers, those types. They wander around with their digital measuring devices and cameras, like they was trying to figure out a plan. Based on what's been going on around here, I always assumed they were another one of those predatory developer types."

"Why do you say that?"

"Those guys have been flooding the neighborhood the past year or two. I get at least one flyer slipped under my door every week saying they'll pay cash for real estate, as if I'm some crotchety old daft-in-the-head idiot who doesn't know any better. Those guys are just trying to line their own pockets."

He humphed and shook his head, galled by the vultures looking for deals.

"I take it you have no interest in selling."

I couldn't help but glance at his property, one of the hazards of my remodeling hobby, curious about the upside potential. His backyard was well kept, if uninspiring, and the windows were in need of replacement, but overall the exterior wasn't in bad shape. Doing a rough calculation in my head, he could probably sell for enough to make his retirement dollars stretch for quite a while.

"Hell no, I'm not selling. I lived in this house for forty-five years." He nodded his head at the clapboard three-story behind him. "The only way I'm going out is in a box. But these developer types, they don't care about any of that. And what gets me the most is they all think we're just a bunch of stupid old people. That we don't know what our property's worth. They think they can come in here and dangle a couple hundred thousand in front of our noses and we'll take the money and run because it's ten times as much as we paid for it originally. While that may be true, some of these guys just come in, slap some paint on the place, spruce up the landscaping, swap out the kitchens with granite and stainless steel, then turn around and flip it for two million, and I'm supposed to be happy with two hundred? I may be old, but I didn't get old being dumb."

Not only was this man not dumb, but he knew enough about the real estate game to understand the flippers' playbook.

"It must be difficult to see your neighborhood changing around you. Aside from the contractors you've seen poking around, have you seen anyone else? Maybe somebody staying here for a while? Any signs of lights or people coming and going?"

"This about that body they found?"

"Oh, you heard about that." I should have known. He'd probably been watching out the window the whole time CPD was onsite.

"Course I did. We all did, at least those of us that are still part of the old guard. The new ones, they just keep to themselves, go about their business, hanging out in their coffee shops and their music clubs. We don't exactly mingle."

"Did you ever see anyone? Did you ever see the woman who died?" I asked, hopeful that a piece of the timeline could be confirmed.

"No lights or anything, if that's what you mean. I noticed that broken window a while back and I boarded it up. Didn't want any critters or hoodlums taking advantage of the break. Did smell pretty funky, though. Thought maybe there was a dead animal back in the bushes. You know that stink. Something rotten but you can't quite place where it's coming from. Called animal control out a couple times, but they never found nothing either."

"Do you remember when that occurred, when you called?"

"Let's see." He ran a hand across his chin, contemplating. "That broken window, I'd say that was back in November. We'd had that early cold spell, and I thought it would be good to take care of it before the snow got started."

"Is that when you called animal control?"

"Yeah, probably, the first time was around then, but I called after that too. Never thought it was anything more than a dead rat or maybe a raccoon. Never imagined," he said with a sigh. "I just never imagined. They know what happened yet?"

"No. They're still working on it," I said, seeing no reason to share any of the details with the man right now.

"Okay then, I better get back." He picked up his rake and turned toward the house. "Oh, wait. There was this one guy poking around out back. Saw him once or twice walking through here, probably last December. Twenties. Had a backpack and ripped jeans. Couldn't see his face much because of the hoodie. Figured he was looking for a place to get his fix. So tell your sister to watch out for needles."

15

Had the guy with the backpack been Zoe's drug-dealing boyfriend? If so, she'd been alive in December.

I'd knocked on the door of the neighbor to the west, striking out, as the owner was an elderly woman so blind she could only tell I was female from my voice. With overgrown foliage and garages blocking the view, the backyard wasn't visible to anyone other than the two immediate neighbors. That left me with the information I'd gleaned from the guy who lived on the east side of the property.

The brochures I'd found in the house for the addiction treatment center indicated a weekly open house. I had no idea how old they were or if the information was up-to-date, but the card said the meeting was every Thursday. So I'd left the home on Pierce and was now driving north to check out the business.

I pulled up to the building in the Buena Park neighborhood, parked across the street, and stared. It was stunning. The property was an enormous red sandstone Victorian with narrow windows, a turret on the right corner, and a deep arched portico that graced the front of the building. A driveway ran to the back on the left side of the building, and I could see a large multi-bay coach house at the end of the lot. The building spoke of history and the grand lifestyle of a long-gone era. It had been built in the days of servants, horse-drawn carriages, and heat provided by fireplaces or maybe coal furnaces. Buildings like this, although occasionally still configured as single-family homes, more often than not had been broken into multi-unit rentals or condos.

I glanced around at the surrounding structures, and while the buildings here were certainly large, none matched the grandeur of the property in front of me. I looked again at the brochure I'd pulled from the closet to make sure I had the proper address, as there was nothing about it visually or in signage that identified its purpose.

Taking the brochure with me, I got out of my car, crossed the street, and walked up the steps. A small brass plaque above the doorbell read *Renacido Center*. The interior door was open, leaving only the decorative wooden screen door as a barrier. I could see a round pedestal table in the center of a wood-paneled foyer decorated with a tall vase of silk lilies and stacked with literature. A center hallway appeared to run front to back through the building. I paused, looking again at the brochure. In big, bold letters it said, "Open House Every Thursday from 3:00 to 5:00." Footsteps on the brick behind me drew my attention. A woman with a sullen-looking twenty-something trailing behind her approached. She smiled weakly at me, while he refused to lift his eyes from his feet, then opened the door. The family dynamic playing out between them was likely not an unusual one.

What the hell, I was here. I followed them into the foyer, stopping to look at the literature and giving myself a chance to get my bearings while the two continued into the meeting. The room on my right opened to a large parlor beyond it. Ten-foot-tall doors separated the first room from the next, and elaborate fireplaces graced both. Rows of folding chairs had been arranged in the adjoining space. Between the two rooms, about two dozen people were milling around. They spoke in low tones and clutched plastic cups of water or what looked like weak tea. Plates of cookies and pre-poured drinks were laid out on a buffet.

Given the small size of the group, there was no way to hide myself in the back to observe. However, looking at the faces around me, discomfort with the gravity or foreignness of this unknown next step seemed to be the common denominator. Checking out another newcomer was the last thing on anyone's mind.

I remained at the table in the foyer, busying myself with pamphlets as I stole glances at the attendees and wondered about their stories. I could see the mix of fear and hope and desperation in their faces. How many had been down this road before? How many were facing their first public acknowledgment of their struggles with substance abuse?

As I perused literature with taglines such as "We can help" or "When you have no other options," the screen door opened again and a gruff-looking man in his forties came in, followed by a girl of about sixteen who was his spitting image. He took hold of her arm and nodded toward the parlor. She glared at him and pulled her arm away, quickly heading for the table I was standing at. The man I assumed to be her father scowled and proceeded to the other room, where he stood alone, busying himself with a cup of coffee and checking his phone.

One of the staff stopped, handed the girl and me name tags and a Sharpie.

I gave her a weak smile, scribbled my first name on the sticker, then concentrated on the flyer in my hand. The language of desperation ran throughout the sales pitch, coupled with photographs depicting people in emotional agony. I flipped the trifold card to the back, where the photo was now a beaming couple, their arms around each other, a happy teenager at their side. The business of selling hope.

The teenager next to me seemed to be more interested in being away from her father than the promises on the page, but she complied and slapped a tag on her shirt that read "Kendall."

"I hope it gets easier," I said to her, "because this first step is a bitch." I hadn't known what I was walking into, and it now appeared I would need a personal backstory to explain my presence here. I was also starting to think acting classes would be a good investment.

"They'll tell you it only gets easier when you decide to surrender." She shrugged, rolling her eyes and fiddling with the charm dangling from the leather choker at her neck. "Surrender? To what? The fact that your life is shit? To God? At least the idiots around here don't make you pray. My last gig was the fire-and-brimstone folks. They never could answer why God would let people get hooked on shit in the first place. What kind of God does that? But those are my dad's beliefs, not mine."

"It sounds like you have a little more experience at this than I do," I said, playing my role and disturbed by the thought that this pretty, young woman was facing such a monstrous challenge far too early in life.

She smirked. "Don't worry, it won't take you long to get the hang of it. Just smile and sound agreeable." She tucked a strand of hair behind her ear, accenting the two-tone dye job—dark layers under platinum. Although intended to make her look tough, as was the heavy eye liner, the effect instead increased her vulnerability. She looked even more like a little girl trying to play dress-up in big girl clothes.

A man near the refreshment table was calling for the meeting to get started.

"I'd better go." She walked off sullenly to join her father, who had been glaring at us from the other room. I could feel his frustration and annoyance from here. I followed them and took a seat a few rows back where I could make a quick exit if I needed to. I looked again at Kendall, wondering about her struggles, comparing the little I knew about Janek's niece and this young lady. Would she be one of the resilient few who made it?

As the attendees settled in, a round-faced woman stood near the podium at the front of the room, smiling and welcoming the group.

"Thank you all for coming. We know all too well how difficult it was for each and every one of you to come here today. For many of you, your struggles with addiction have been an ongoing battle over many years. You are to be applauded for your bravery, and yes, it takes bravery to combat a force as serious and as relentless as addiction. I won't take up much of your time. My name is Francesca, and I'm the office manager here at the center. If you have any questions later about the admission process, just flag me down and I'll be happy to help. Now, I'd like to introduce Dr. Troy Wykell, our program director, chief psychologist, and the man who developed this highly successful treatment protocol."

A tall, thin man with a close-shaven beard, who I would've pegged as a therapist on sight, stepped over to the podium. *Bookish* was the single word that came to mind to describe his appearance. I could picture him in a cardigan with suede elbow patches, loafers, and corduroy pants in cooler weather. Yet, despite the horn-rimmed glasses and gentle features, his gaze was cutting. He swung his green eyes around the room, person to person as he spoke, as if able to separate the addict from the non-addict via some kind of telepathy. A chill ran through me when his eyes met mine. My instinct was to turn away, but I held firm until he moved on to the next person. If this was the guy charged with one-on-one treatment, he wasn't making me feel warm and fuzzy.

"Yes, you are to be commended for the bravery you're demonstrating," he began. "You've all heard some version of the sales pitch for twelve-step programs, prayer therapy, just-say-no, yet here we are, fighting this disease still, day in and day out. Some of you have been told that it's just a flaw in your character. That if you only tried a little harder, you would be successful. Bullshit, I say. That's right, *bullshit*. And I'm not going to apologize for my harsh language. Although well-meaning, most of these programs are simply a version of a hope and a prayer. Most of you are here because you've been through it all already, yet still your struggle continues."

He spoke with the authority and presence of a preacher, and I found myself listening for an "amen" from the crowd.

"Here, there are no twelve steps," he continued. "Or any other kind of steps, for that matter. Here we use science. We use science to understand, and we use science to treat."

I watched many of the attendees nodding their heads. They understood this cycle intimately. A few mothers dabbed away tears as their sullen adolescent children sat next to them. The slumped posture of their charges was always impossible to gauge. Others clung to their partner's hands, hoping beyond hope that this would be *the* thing to end the agony and the war in their relationships.

"Let's get to the heart of why you're here," Dr. Wykell continued. "You're here because you're ready to put this behind you and rebuild your lives. That's our mission. That is our goal. That is our record of success. An eighty-five percent success rate, I might add. Yes, you heard that right.

"Our program is not for people unwilling to be open-minded, unwilling to try new things, even when they might not make sense. We are not talk therapy, linking every trouble in your life with some long-held childhood belief. We will not blame you for where you are, and we will not blame the parenting you received. None of that matters. None of it matters while you are in the throes of battle. Here, we don't care about the why. We care about getting you sober. If why matters to you, the yellow pages are full of other people who can help you work through those struggles. But unless you are sober, and unless you stay sober, does the why matter?"

Parents and partners in the room seemed to collectively relax. The months, or years, of the battle feeling less daunting when hope was presented. But wasn't hope the cornerstone of every treatment program? Or was hope simply what all these people had left after ongoing fear and struggle had drained them of everything else?

"Our program is highly effective," Dr. Wykell said. "It is unconventional, and yes, it is expensive, but so are years of your life lost to drugs and alcohol. Think about the time and money lost over years as job performance suffered, raises were denied, jobs were lost, heartbroken families were pushed to divorce or worse. Is there really a price one can put on the destruction of a life?"

Despite his mousy appearance, Dr. Wykell delivered his speech with a passion I wouldn't have predicted. I could feel the glimmer of optimism spreading around the room as possibilities for a different outcome entered people's minds. People sat up a little straighter in their chairs, eyes were brighter. The man hadn't actually outlined a single detail of his center's protocol, yet the energy in the room had changed.

"I know that you are all anxious to know more and anxious to find out what we can do to end your suffering. Due to the unique nature of our program and the personal customization, we find it best to meet one-on-one. We like to understand a little bit more about the specific challenges in your life and your recovery goals before getting into the details. Francesca will coordinate individual consultations, so you'll be able to set that up with her in a few moments. If you have any high-level questions, I certainly can answer a few of those now, but please don't be offended if my response is to suggest that your issue is best discussed in private consult."

A man in his thirties raised his hand. "I hear that psychedelics are being used these days for addiction treatment. You do any of that here?"

"While there is some literature to that effect," Dr. Wykell responded, "I prefer not to discuss any of the specific techniques we use, other than to say again that we allow science to dictate our treatment protocol. We also believe that no one modality is a single answer. Each person's addiction history and physiology will shape their protocol. We find that it is the combination of protocols delivered in precise sequencing that is the key to our success rate."

He nodded to a woman in the front row. "Is this stuff covered by my insurance?" she asked.

"No. Excuse me for being blunt, but our medical system is not set up to understand or accept treatment protocols that don't fall within tight parameters. I'm sure many of you have had difficulty getting medical coverage for conventional rehab or found that the treatment was restricted in a number of ways. We would rather spend our time treating our patients, rather than building in layers of expense and arguing with some insurance clerk—who only understands billing codes—about the validity of our treatment. In order to provide the best level of care, we are a cash-only facility."

I noticed an intake of breath here, could see a grimace there, as the group grappled with the financial reality and calculated what the hit to their family finances might be.

A commotion in the back of the room pulled my attention. A

young man in his twenties stormed in, oblivious to, or perhaps because of, the audience. His long hair fell in clumps, clinging to the sweat dripping down the side of his face.

"You told me this wouldn't happen!" he screamed at Dr. Wykell. "What did you give her?"

I swung my head from the young man to Dr. Wykell. He'd lost the passion of the preacher, and in his face, I could see his therapist hat was back on. He smiled calmly at the crowd. "Thank you all for coming. Please enjoy your refreshments. Francesca's here to answer any of your questions and to set up your consultation."

With that, he stepped away from the podium, exiting the room through a side door as the angry young man plowed after him.

16

What did you give her?

The young man's question to Dr. Wykell echoed in my mind as I left the property, as did his anger.

I was confused about what I had witnessed and had no better idea what the unique protocol of the Renacido Center consisted of than I had before I walked in the door. Given Zoe's drug history, it was easy to imagine that she may have received treatment there, but why tuck the pamphlet on the top shelf of an upstairs closet if she'd simply been using the basement as a crash pad? And what was the explanation for the thousands of brochures boxed and left behind?

Sitting in my car, I stared out at the building, running through what I knew of addiction treatment protocols and the sad, tragic end to Zoe's life. How many others who had walked through these doors had lost their battle?

I reached for my phone. "Where are you?" I said the moment Michael answered the call.

"Well, that's a nice hello."

"Sorry, I got a little overly enthusiastic. I have something I want to talk to you about. Can I stop by?"

"I'm working a scene up in Lakeview. Can it wait?"

"I'm not far away. Text me the address. I only need a minute or two."

"Okay, see you in a few," he said, but his normal enthusiasm was lacking.

Fifteen minutes later, I got out of my car to a scene that was now familiar—four cop cars and an ambulance, police tape surrounding the building, and clusters of onlookers speculating about what had happened. I walked over to one of the cops, a guy I recognized from my legal days, and asked if he would let Michael know I was here. As I waited, I watched the officers corralling the crowd and listened to the buzz from the bystanders around me. The commentary seemed to focus on one local gangbanger apparently taking out a rival who'd made moves on his girlfriend, and to hell with them both.

Moments later Michael came out of the bodega. He'd removed his jacket and rolled up his shirtsleeves, which meant he was in the thick of it all. Karl Janek followed behind him. What was he doing here? They walked over to the perimeter where I stood and motioned to the attending cop that it was okay to let me pass. I ducked under the yellow tape and walked toward the men.

"Karl, I'm so sorry about your niece," I said immediately. "The funeral is tomorrow, isn't it?"

"Yes, thanks, Andrea." His voice was hollow and flat. He had that robotic demeanor I'd seen in crime victims when all they were capable of was rote execution of tasks. Shutting down prevented us from focusing on the unfaceable. "The service is tomorrow at 11:00 a.m."

This was one of the few times that I ever recalled the two of us addressing each other by our first names. Janek had saved my life the night Eric's business partner tried to toss me off my eleventh-floor terrace, having decided I was an obstacle to his corruption. Janek and I had a complicated relationship, given his dislike of journalists in general and his disapproval of Michael dating one, but we'd forged a respect for each other over the past year. I didn't always understand him, but he was the kind of man I'd want at my back any day.

Janek wasn't warm and fuzzy on a good day, but if there were any more tension in his face, his skin would crack. The man should have been home with his family, but who was I to advise him on his coping mechanisms? Then again, I knew nothing about his relationship with his sister, and he had been divorced for a number of years; perhaps work was simply better than being alone to face the pain.

The clang of metal pulled my attention toward the bodega. I leaned over to look around Janek's shoulder as the medical team brought out the first gurney. We all watched in silence as the body bag was lifted into the ambulance.

"One fewer piece of shit in the world today," Janek said. "Couldn't have happened to a nicer guy." Janek's voice bristled with disgust and hatred. It was hard to imagine that he was able to separate his personal life and his professional life on a day like this. The business of rounding up gang members, who often made their living by selling dope or guns, had to be hitting close to home.

"And the other guy?" I asked.

"Off to a term of fifteen to twenty, if I have anything to say about it," Janek added.

Michael looked at his partner, his faced etched with concern, before turning to me. "So what brings you over here?"

"Well, it's about Zoe." I couldn't see Janek's eyes through his dark aviators, but there was no mistaking the raised eyebrows.

"I found a pamphlet in the house," I said. "It's for a drug

treatment center called the Renacido Center. Does that ring any bells?" I looked at Janek.

"She did a couple of stints in rehab, saw a shrink, made a half-assed attempt with some support groups—I don't remember the names of any of them. I doubt she did either, since she was high most of the time. What about it?" He crossed his arms over his chest, already irritated with my interruption.

"Well, I found it odd that this pamphlet was in the house, but it was up on the second floor tucked away on the top shelf of a closet, and there are also thousands of them in the basement."

"I'm not following you, Andrea. What were you doing back in the house?" Michael said, with a look that wasn't tough to decipher. "What's this about?"

"I'm not sure. This program, it's unusual, I'll put it that way. They claim to have an unconventional but highly successful protocol. I don't know any of the details, but there was this vibe about it that's a little off, and it has me wondering if Zoe might have participated."

Between Janek's irritation and Michael's "what the hell" tone, I was feeling foolish for even bringing it up. At the rate Janek's jaw was tightening, he'd be needing dental work by Monday morning, and Michael was giving me that "what can of worms are you opening now" look.

"What do you mean *it has this vibe*, because that sounds like you've done something," Michael said.

"The brochure indicated that they have an open house every Thursday. So I went."

Michael opened his mouth, probably to give me shit, but Janek jumped in before he could get the words out.

"As in, investigative journalist wants the behind-the-scenes dirt? Maybe watch an overdose up close and personal?" Janek's voice dripped with sarcasm. "Did you get all *60 Minutes* on them?"

"It wasn't that dramatic," I said, immediately regretting my timing and feeling the full brunt of Janek's displaced pain. "I didn't go in microphones blazing. I sat in the back and listened. But there's something that isn't sitting right with me, and I was curious if you've ever heard of the facility, and if maybe Zoe had sought treatment there. That's all."

"Jesus Christ, Kellner!" Janek exploded. "I know it's your damn job, but can't you just let this dead kid rest in peace? She's dead because she put a needle in her arm one too many times. That's the story. You want to go after somebody, go after that creep who got her hooked. He's the one to investigate. Where the hell did he get his supply? What are they cutting it with? The synthetic crap that's coming out of China is laced with all kinds of things. Things we've never even heard of before. They've got labs that do nothing but fabricate a bigger, better, cheaper high. None of them give a shit whether anybody lives or dies. They just want poor slobs hooked so that the money river keeps flowing. She could have been shooting up with rat poison, for all we know." He wiped his mouth with the back of his hand. "Concocting some stupid story about one of the few places that try to help only takes the pressure off the real problem."

I listened to Janek rant, watching veins throb on his temples and wishing I'd kept my damn mouth shut. Michael looked at me, shaking his head, and Janek stormed back toward the crime scene.

"Your timing is shit," Michael said when his partner was out of earshot.

"I'm sorry. When I called you, I never imagined Janek would be with you. Any sane grieving person would be home with his family. What the hell is he doing here?" I was mad at myself and looking for a way to blunt my insensitivity.

"Key word *sane*. And right now, sane isn't how I'd describe Janek. We all process grief differently. And for Janek, the only thing that's going to heal his grief is nailing the goddamn dealer who gave her the smack."

"Has the ME confirmed this was an overdose?"

"Sweetheart, time to find another story to chase. Leave the man alone."

17

"Dinner? My place or Nico?"

After leaving the bodega, I had parked myself at a small table in the first Starbucks I'd come across as I'd driven south on Clark Street toward downtown. I'd pissed off Janek, insulted Michael, and accomplished nothing. Which meant I needed moral support from my best friend, Cai.

"Let's make it Nico," Cai said. "I've been home with takeout sushi, since you blew me off the other night—home alone, in case you're wondering—and I need to get out and remind myself there are human beings in the world who aren't attorneys. I also desperately need a proper drink. I can be there in twenty minutes."

"Well, *I* can't," I laughed. "It's not even five and you need a drink already?"

"Don't pretend this would be the first time we've started drinking before five."

"You go over if you need to, but I won't be there until closer to six."

"Party pooper. Well, then, drink alone I must. Meet you at the bar."

I switched off the call, grateful for our long friendship. She was always able to ground me in reality or, at the very least, remind me of the absurdity of situations. There was no one I trusted more.

Looking at my watch, I took a sip of my Earl Grey and was reminded that I'd accomplished nothing on the Flores story today. It was too late in the day to expect the alderman's office to answer the phone, but check-cashing shops were always open.

I pulled my iPad and a notebook out of my bag and did a search. The guy at the soundproofing company had said Fifty-fifth Street and the name Darius. He shouldn't be too hard to find. I scanned the locations mapped out on my screen. Two locations hit the mark with a third that was a maybe. I zoomed in, seeing it was a corner location and could be construed as on Fifty-fifth, even if the mailing address was actually Archer. I added it to the list.

My second call hit pay dirt. After a short pause, a male voice mumbled back, "Yeah, this is Darius. Can I help you?"

"My name is Andrea Kellner. I'm with Link-Media. I'm doing a story on Impact Soundproofing and their contracts with the city. Can I ask you a few questions?"

"I don't know anything about that, and I ain't never met Mateo Sandoval. Don't call here anymore."

With that, he hung up. I stared at my phone and smiled. Interesting. Volunteering the answer to a question I hadn't asked was a sure way to let a reporter know he *did* know something.

I'D LEFT my car in the garage at my apartment and walked the four blocks to the restaurant. The fresh air had felt amazing, as did getting out and moving my body. After the darkness of the last few days, the gentle breeze of an early May evening was a much needed respite. Clearly I wasn't the only one reveling in the weather. Even though it was early, the outdoor patios at the Rush Street restaurants were starting to fill with patrons overly anxious to believe summer was around the corner after the long winter.

Despite concentrated effort, I'd been unable to conjure up much of an explanation for the boxes of brochures for the Renacido Center at the Pierce Street house. The only thing that seemed logical was that someone associated with the property also had an association with the treatment center. But who or why eluded me. It was conceivable that the corporation that owned the property prior to foreclosure had been renting it out to an employee of the treatment center. Which might explain Zoe's presence, but it was a guess at best.

Cai was waiting at the bar when I arrived at Nico, chatting up one of the cute but way too young bartenders. Boy toys never moved beyond the flirting stage with Cai, but she sure did enjoy the game.

She had a martini in hand when I settled in next to her, and her jacket was draped carefully across the back of her stool.

"Whoa, this looks like it's going to be a rough night," I said. "Please tell me that's your first."

"Of course it is," she replied, feigning outrage. "I've been holding back until you got here. Do you want one right away, or should we go to our table?"

"Table. And I'm not drinking those." I laughed. "I also suggest you get some food in you before ordering another."

"Ugh, there you go again, being a Debbie Downer." She smiled and gave me a hug. "Boy, do I need girl time." She grabbed her bag, a Stella McCartney tote I'd lusted after myself, and we walked back to the hostess desk to let them know we were ready for a table. She led us outside to a prime people-watching spot on the sidewalk patio next to a heat lamp. A server appeared immediately, inquiring about our preference for still or sparkling water.

"I'll have another of these," Cai said to the server, ignoring his question and my disapproving gaze.

"Pellegrino with lemon. And I'll have a glass of the Nebbiolo. Oh, if you could also bring us the Hamachi crudo to start. I need to get some food in my friend before she slips under the table," I said, smiling at the young man, recognizing him as someone who'd waited on us a number of times in the past. Nico was one of our go-tos. The food was good, the atmosphere lovely, and the location convenient for both of us.

"You really need to lighten up. Have a martini." She smiled at me over the rim of her glass. "What's the worst that could happen?"

"The list is too long to answer." I grinned. "Besides," I continued in a more serious tone, "I need to go to a funeral in the morning, and I shouldn't go stinking of stale booze."

"Who died?" Cai asked, her expression immediately somber.

"Karl Janek's niece. It appeared to be an overdose."

"Oh my God, that's awful. He must be crushed."

Although Cai and Janek had met several times, I wouldn't describe them as having a relationship. However, she did know Michael and understood the deep connection between the two men.

"And if that weren't enough, she died in the basement of an investment property Lane just purchased. I had the pleasure of finding the body."

Cai nearly dropped her drink. "What?" she said, dabbing the spilled alcohol off her hand.

"That's why I had to beg off on Monday night. I was too overwhelmed to go into it then. It was gruesome and sad and flat-out disturbing." I shuddered again at the image my mind refused to let go of. "It's been one hell of a week, and tomorrow isn't going to be any better."

"My god. How awful. How did Lane react? She came back on the next plane, didn't she?"

"After all these years, do you really have to ask?" I tipped back my glass, then speared a piece of fish. Wine snobs would be horrified by my pairing of the rich red wine with the delicate fish.

"No, ignore the stupidity of my question." Cai shook her head in disgust. "Silly me, I applied logic and responsibility to your sister's behavior. I should have assumed she's still in Mexico, hanging by the pool, expecting someone else, namely you, to deal with this trivial inconvenience."

Just as I opened my mouth to respond, my phone rang. Brynn. "I need to get this," I said, tapping the screen.

"Sorry to bug you after hours," she said.

"Brynn, you have to stop apologizing. I tell you all the time that the workday doesn't end at five o'clock. You can call me twenty-four-seven."

"I know, but it feels wrong. Well, anyway," she trailed off. "So, I'm digging into the foreclosure, that property your sister owns, and well, I just found out something interesting. I don't know what to make of it, but it seems odd. Okay, so we know the company is Quantum Holdings, and we know the address. Right?"

"Yes, and it looks to me like that address is a mailbox at a pack-and-ship place," I added.

"Well, it turns out that the same company purchased one of the properties two doors down the block, and that too has gone into default."

"Do they still own it, or has the bank taken possession?" I asked.

"It's bank owned. I checked with the auction house, and they have it scheduled for auction next week."

"Shoot me the address. I spoke with one of the neighbors earlier today, and he mentioned that developers have been trying to acquire properties. Apparently, he had been approached several times. Sounds like they smell profit. He assumed the developer's plan was to flip, which is what most of the small guys are doing."

"If Quantum is having financial trouble, it wouldn't be surprising that the developer would lose multiple properties," she said. "I tried to do some digging on the investment company, see if I could go a little deeper. But I'm not finding a lot of information, so this can't be a very big organization, or I suppose they could also go by another name. You know how sometimes one company is a division of another and you can't connect them right away."

"Usually that's a legal or tax strategy, a way of protecting assets," I said.

"But I also saw the company had filed a zoning application on your sister's property. About a year ago. Never got approved, but it looks like these investors had plans to do something unusual with the property."

"Why do you say unusual?"

"Well, I don't know the area, but these two properties they owned are both residential, and single-family at that. As you said, a small developer coming in would want to either fix them up and flip, which doesn't require a zoning change, or renovate and rent, again no zoning change needed. The other option would be to convert it to multi-family, so we're talking condos or apartments."

"Yeah, this is a pretty typical residential neighborhood, so those are the options. Are you saying that they wanted to do something other than the standard conversion to a three-flat?"

"They submitted an application for a change from residential to business zoning. They were asking for both properties to be converted to B2, which does allow residential usage but only above the first floor. What kind of commercial use would you pop into that location?"

I paused, my mind running through the options. "It could only be something that doesn't need parking or walk-in traffic."

18

My heart in my throat, I took a deep breath, then let it go, moving toward the funeral home.

Janek stood just inside the open door, his arms around a woman sobbing into his chest. His eyes were closed as he held her convulsing body to his shoulder, allowing her the space and the comfort that she needed in this moment. I froze, watching, not wanting to interfere, but feeling their heartbreak and humbled to be part of their grief.

I hadn't been to a funeral since Eric's, and my chest was tight not only with Janek's grief but with the memories that were surfacing. For a half second I had the urge to flee, to protect myself from the pain—theirs, and the remnants of mine. I stood on the sidewalk, statue-like until they moved further inside, then closed my eyes, pulling in more deep, slow breaths until I found the courage to follow them.

Inside, the elegant stone building featured a central parlor carpeted in a deep burgundy. Bland instrumental music played softly from a built-in speaker system hidden somewhere in the back, chosen for its ability to be unobtrusive. On my right, a sign directed visitors straight ahead to a room further down the hall.

Janek, and the woman I assumed to be Zoe's mother, had moved just outside the room and were greeting visitors as best they could.

Friends and family stood with the two, speaking in low tones the way people did when there were no appropriate words. I knew I needed to approach them, to offer my condolences, but the moment seemed so raw, so personal, that I hesitated, feeling torn between the intrusion and my own memories of standing where they stood, a moment that would forever be a blur of pain.

"Good morning." Michael had come in behind me and was now standing at my side. I turned to him, reached out and wrapped my arms around him, knowing that words were virtually useless right now. He was pale and his eyes were flat. The hurt he was feeling for his friend was unmistakable, and my heart ached for him. I wanted to hold on for as long as he would let me, to hold on until his pain no longer felt like a cattle prod to the heart, but now wasn't the time. Janek needed him.

"I should go over and offer my condolences," I said, nodding toward Janek and the woman. "I assume that's Zoe's mother?"

"Yes, her name is Theresa, and she's a mess."

I could feel the devastation emanating from the core of her soul. She seemed barely able to stand without support. "How is Janek holding up?"

"He's focused on his sister, but underneath that, I would describe him as a pissed-off bull, out for blood. Although that's not how he sees himself. He's trying to be strong, to pretend he's got his act together, but this has brought back feelings that he should have been able to get the boyfriend or the dealer or whatever the hell he was off the street. Right now he's blaming himself and covering it up with anger."

Michael's voice was soft, his emotions blunted, and all I could think about was the desire to protect him, to make *his* pain go away. What did I feel for this man? I'd been pushing him away when he was someone who cared so deeply. Now wasn't the time to answer the question, but deep, unexpected emotions of my own were bubbling to the surface. Was there any truer indication of love than the desire to save someone else from pain?

"How awful to carry around guilt like that," I said, not trusting my voice, "particularly when it's misplaced. I'm sure he knows, at an intellectual level, that if she hadn't bought her stash from her boyfriend, she would've found it from someone else. There is always someone else."

"It's easier to be logical when you're not the one in the middle of it." He looked at me as if wanting to say more, as if wanting *me* to say more. Instead he turned back to look at Janek. "It looks like now's a good time. Do you want to go and say hello?"

I nodded, and the two of us walked over. I extended my hand, introducing myself to Theresa and offering my condolences.

"Thank you," she said, dabbing at the tears that refused to stop.

I turned to Janek, started to say something, but words failed me. I embraced him instead. "I'm so very sorry," I mumbled, squeezing his hand. He nodded, his eyes saying everything. I gave Michael a weak smile and then stepped away, leaving the three of them to continue to greet the mourners.

Knowing no one other than the men, I took a seat near the back, feeling lost and empty myself. The group was small. Primarily young people about Zoe's age. People I assumed to be friends, or perhaps college acquaintances. From what Michael had told me, the family was small, just Janek and his sister. Their parents had passed away long ago, and Zoe had been the only child. Zoe's father had never been part of her life. It made her death all that more poignant.

I watched as a pastor entered, speaking with Janek and Theresa before moving off to attend to the preparations. As he left, a couple of cops, clearly friends of Janek's, stopped to pay their respects. They were followed by a group of five women, friends of Theresa's, I assumed, who immediately attached themselves to her. I sat quietly, deep in thought, my own past coming to my present. The casket loomed large, and I couldn't pull my eyes from the plethora of photos of Zoe, which had been placed on the stands nearby. The images of a young, vibrant, happy child and then woman bore no resemblance to the remains I had discovered. It was impossible not to wonder about her life, and her choices, and the agony she must have endured to keep coming back to this demon.

As I sat with my thoughts, a man walked past me and took a seat across the aisle and three rows in front of me.

Startled, I looked at him a second time. It was Dr. Wykell from the addiction treatment center. Why was he here? This had to mean that Zoe had been a patient of his, that she had received treatment at his center.

I turned toward Janek and Theresa, watching for a reaction, but I had no sense that they were aware of him. Then again, in the middle of grief, it was difficult to be aware of much of anything. Dr. Wykell sat quietly, hands clasped in his lap, eyes on the floor as if in prayer. The boxes full of pamphlets for his center immediately flooded my mind. If Zoe had been working for the center, that might explain why the stash of pamphlets was also in the house.

He made no attempt to approach Theresa, to offer his condolences, which was in itself interesting. I could only assume they hadn't met. But why not acknowledge her? It was certainly obvious who the family members were. And how had the doctor known of Zoe's death?

The pastor had returned and now stood at the front of the room beside a large photo of Zoe. The room quieted in preparation with visitors taking their seats. I looked for Michael, wondering if I should make him aware of this new visitor, but instinct told me it was better that Dr. Wykell didn't notice me. I couldn't identify the ping in my head that told me I was missing something.

As I debated, another attendee came through the side door. Although he had cleaned up considerably—running a comb though his hair and now wearing an ill-fitting but clean sport coat—I recognized the young man as the same individual who had made the outburst at the open house. Dr. Wykell caught his gaze immediately and visibly withdrew at the sight of him. Was he expecting another outburst? The young man's words came back to me. *What did you give her?*

His jaw clenched, and he shot a look of hatred at the psychologist before starting to turn away, but he seemed frozen by the reality in front of him. His eyes were now glued to the casket. He was visibly shaking, and tears ran unapologetically down his face. The boyfriend?

I stood to make my way toward Michael, wanting to tell him more about the details of their interaction before something erupted between the two. I'd only taken three steps when Theresa, now moving toward her seat in the front row, let out a scream. Her tear-streaked face was red with rage. Janek looked at her, then over at the young man, and his fury matched hers. Janek reached out to take her arm, but she pushed him away, charging forward.

"How dare you show your face in here!" she screamed. "This is your fault! This is all your fault. She's dead because of you! How can you live with yourself?" She lunged toward him, eyes wild, and Janek was right behind her, equally enraged. The room erupted as Theresa came at the young man and those around her struggled to restrain her.

He stood rooted in place, letting her wail, shaking his head and sobbing. "No, I loved her. I loved her! She was off that shit. She didn't deserve this."

"Love? You know nothing about love," Theresa yelled back. "You poisoned her. Stole her life. You did this to her!" Theresa threw off the arms that held her back and ran at him. All of her grief was directed at this young man, who simply stood waiting for her wrath. She reached him seconds later, hauling her arm back to strike him. But Janek got to her first, pulling her away as she screamed and fought into his chest, releasing pain that refused to be contained.

Janek's eyes blazed, but the young man didn't see him, simply shook his head and continued to sob as the fight left his empty shell of a body. Then with one last look at Zoe's coffin, he turned and left quietly, the way he had come in. With Michael and Janek occupied consoling Theresa, and the room abuzz, I slipped out after him.

19

"Hey, can you wait a minute?"

I called after the young man, but he had maneuvered out of the building at a pace I was struggling to match in heels. Organ music drifted out from the building as I picked it up to a jog, reaching him after he'd turned onto the sidewalk. "Wait. Please, can I speak to you for a minute?"

He stopped. Facing me, his cheeks were wet with tears and his eyes bloodshot. He looked at me blankly.

"I'm sorry about what happened in there," I said. "Everyone is hurting. And I can see that you are as well."

He nodded but stayed silent, his eyes on my face, tears still flowing uncontrolled.

"I'm the one who found her," I said. "My name is Andrea."

He stepped back, drawing in a breath, his jaw dropping. It was almost as if I'd slapped him in the face. "That must've been awful," he mumbled, his lips trembling. He'd gotten so pale that I wondered if he was on the verge of collapse himself.

"It's obvious, to me at least, that you loved Zoe a great deal. How long had you been dating?" I asked. He wore the pain of her death like a shroud. Regardless of what Janek and Theresa had said or thought about the young man, his grief could not have been more real. He had loved Zoe and loved her deeply. "I'm sorry, I don't know your name."

"Levi," he said, sniffing and wiping his eyes with the back of his hand. "Levi Vinson. We were together about three years. We met in school."

There was a fogginess about him even through the tears—a delayed, sluggish movement of his body—which made me wonder about his current drug use. Although his eyes were certainly red, his pupils reacted normally.

"How long had it been since you'd last seen her?" I asked hesitantly.

A flurry of questions were running through my head, first on the list the veiled accusations he'd directed at Dr. Wykell, but pressing him on it when he was so fragile seemed to cross the line. Obviously, there had been some messy aspects to their relationship, and he may have been her dealer, but it was also possible that he had been the last one to see her alive.

"About nine months ago, maybe ten," he said, pulling a wadded-up tissue out of the pocket of his jeans. He dabbed his nose and continued. "We both had some shit going on. We were trying to get clean. She was doing good. Me, I was having a hard time of it. And she couldn't stay clean if I wasn't." He paused and tried to fight the tears welling again in his eyes. Looking at the ground, he said, "She told me we couldn't be together anymore if I was still using."

"And still dealing?" I added softly.

"Yeah." He nodded. "It was just as hard to get out of selling the stuff as it was to stop using it. Once people know you can help them score, they hound you until you hook them up. The suppliers, they aren't any better. They'd just as soon take an organ as give you a break when money's involved. And it's not like there are a lot of other ways to make that kind of money after you've dropped out of college."

His voice was still flat, filled with resignation. The reality of the choices he'd had to make loomed large, and I could sense his regret. I looked closely at his face, wondering how drugs fit into his life now, wondering if he held any feeling of guilt for Zoe's outcome.

"So, as far as you knew, Zoe was clean? At least when you last saw her?" The image of her body was filling my head again. It wasn't an image anyone would want burned into their memory.

"Yeah, as far as I know. We exchanged texts every now and then, but eventually that stopped too," he said, looking forlorn and unfocused. "I tried to call a couple times after but got a message that the phone had been disconnected. I assumed her mom had gotten tired of paying the bills and cut it off."

I wasn't sure what to make of Levi. His anguish was raw and real. But then again, if he had been her dealer, I couldn't exactly trust him to not be protecting his own interests. And Michael's comments about a black eye he'd given Zoe didn't help. We still didn't know if he had supplied the product that killed her or if it had been tainted. Drug dealers weren't known to be any more reliable sources of information than drug users. Yet, I didn't question his love.

"Did you know where she had been living?" The time frame was still confusing, as was the venom Levi had directed at Dr. Wykell.

"After her mom kicked her out, we got a place together. Just a little shit hole in Logan Square, but it was ours. We both had bartending jobs then. Made enough money to manage a dumpy, roach-infested studio apartment. Then I went to rehab, and she couldn't afford the rent on her own. She crashed with friends for a while. I did the same after I got out. We were saving up for a place of our own, but the rehab, well, it didn't take."

That phrase "it didn't take" was something I'd heard for years as a prosecutor. It confused me as much now as it had then, since it suggested that this process was completely outside of individual control, something done *to* them. Intellectually, I understood it was far more complex than simple free will, but the ravages of addiction were beyond my personal experience.

"Do you know who she was staying with? I mean, after you guys broke up." I'd gotten the impression that Zoe had been alone at the house on Pierce, but I was looking for a connection to the stash of rehab center pamphlets in the basement.

"Not really. Like I said, she broke up with me, so it isn't like I got the download. She just said she was back to hitting her friends up for favors, a few days here, a couch there, someone who had a cousin who was leaving town for two months. There are a lot of compromises you make when your head's all fucked up."

"So you don't have any idea where she'd been staying when she died?"

A shadow crossed his face with the question. "No, I didn't see her again after we broke up."

The kid was lying to me. I didn't know why or what about, but it was there in that moment of vulnerability. He had seen her and may have known exactly where she had been staying the last days of her life.

"Did the two of you ever crash in a house in Humboldt Park? A house on Pierce?" I kept my eyes trained on him as I asked the question, my prosecutor background instinctively watching for the tell.

"No, that doesn't ring any bells. I was pretty fucked up sometimes, but not that I remember."

There it was again, the lie—eyes that shifted away from mine, the withdrawal of his body. What was he hiding?

"Was Zoe spiritual? You know, into sage, amulets, crystals—

any of that stuff?"

Voices to my left caught my attention. The doors of the funeral home had opened, and a handful of people were beginning to leave. And Levi would be gone the minute any of the immediate family stepped outside.

"Yeah, she was into that," he said, nervously looking at the building. "Didn't make any sense to me, but she was always lighting incense, chanting. Clearing the bad energy, she called it. She had these rocks, crystals, I think. I don't remember their exact names, but she told me every stone meant something. She said they had powers and if you held them and kept them around you, they could protect you. I thought it was all a bunch of bullshit, but hell, if she wanted to believe in the tooth fairy, it was her business. Sure wasn't my job to tell her any different."

"And what was she protecting herself from?"

"She said they kept away the evil spirits. I always thought she meant the horse, you know. That they could protect her from the addiction. Doesn't seem like it worked."

Or perhaps she was using the phrase *evil spirits* as metaphor for something else dark in her life.

"How do you know Dr. Wykell?" I asked, my eyes still studying him like a prosecutor. I threw it out there, assuming I only had moments before Levi would be scared off, or run off, by Janek. My inquiry seemed to startle him. He jolted as if he were stunned by the question or uncertain of how to answer. It only lasted a moment, but it was long enough to have registered with me before his fogginess was back.

"I don't know who that is. I gotta go," he said, looking over his shoulder and moving further away from the building as more of the attendees left.

What was *that* lie about? It seemed pointless. Which is exactly why it meant something.

20

"Look, I can't stay here and face these people again," Levi said as he backed away, looking at the trickle of people leaving the funeral home. His body was in nearly full-blown spasm in anticipation of another conflict with Zoe's mother or with Janek. As if on cue, Janek and Michael exited the building, and Levi took off in a sprint.

Janek, ever the cop, had of course caught sight of Levi and was shooting daggers in my direction. If he hadn't had an arm supporting his sister, he would likely have taken off after the man. He, Theresa, and Michael had planted themselves outside the door, saying their goodbyes to guests who were not continuing to the cemetery.

I scanned the faces leaving the funeral home, looking for Dr. Wykell. I hadn't made any headway into understanding the connection between Levi and the doctor, but Levi's odd response was notable and not explained by a stint at the Renacido Center, if that had been the rehab he'd mentioned.

Janek had left his sister with her girlfriends and was barreling my way, Michael at his heels.

"What the hell was that all about?" Janek asked, his voice full of disgust. "You and Levi. Are you coddling that piece of shit?"

Accusation burned in his eyes and his voice. He was pushing for a fight, although I knew deflection when I saw it. Hatred of Levi oozed from his body like a fish rotting from the inside. He didn't see Levi's pain, didn't see his love for Zoe. He was blind to everything but his own grief. Michael lifted his hand to his partner's shoulder, trying to defuse the tension.

"Coddling? No, of course not," I said calmly. "Levi clearly was in love with Zoe. Whatever happened between them, whatever his role may have been in her addiction, he's reeling. And for all we know, he may have been the last person to see her alive."

"Yeah, when he gave her her last hit." Janek's voice was tight and unyielding. It was the pain talking. He wasn't capable of being convinced of anything that didn't fit the narrative he had already built in his mind, certainly not today of all days. I wasn't sure if Levi had had anything to do with Zoe's death, but assumptions weren't going to help us figure out what had really happened.

Michael's gaze told me he wanted to ask me something, to know more about the conversation and ask questions his partner couldn't right now, but this wasn't the moment to question anything.

"We're going over to the cemetery now," he said instead, giving me a long look. "Let's talk later."

He gave me a quick kiss goodbye, and I turned to Janek. "I hope you can find some peace." I squeezed his hand and watched the men walk off to their cars for the funeral procession.

KICKING OFF MY HEELS, I plopped into the desk chair in my office at Link-Media, crossed my arms, and laid my head on the desk. The morning had drained me physically and emotionally, but it had also deepened the knot in my stomach that told me something was not as it seemed. Levi was lying. Wykell was suspect. And the circumstances of Zoe's death felt staged. My first and only thought right now was to wonder if Levi had been present when she overdosed, gotten scared, and placed her in the chair before he took off to save his own ass.

Frustration was building in my mind instead of clarity, so I lifted my head, shook out the cobwebs, and opened a new document on my laptop. I laid out everything I knew, every thought I had, every question that came to mind in bullet points without any thought to their importance. Somewhere in here was a pattern, a spark. One thought would lead to another, and another, as the tapestry was woven thread by thread.

So much had happened in the past few days that I was having trouble processing. I needed to see the physical manifestation of events, so I struck the keyboard with every ounce of energy I had to get a version I could print and evaluate.

"I didn't think you were coming back today?" Brynn was in my doorway, her shirtsleeves rolled up and looking a little worse for wear herself.

"Neither did I," I said, motioning her in. "I'm going to need some help with this Flores story. You game?"

Guilt was eating at me that I hadn't been putting in the time and effort the story needed, but my heart wasn't in it, not with Zoe's death gnawing at me. Brynn was ready for a break. She'd moved past the community service fluff given to the new kids in the newsroom but had yet to tackle a story with real meat. If she could do the legwork, I could supervise from the sidelines. It would help us both out and keep Borkowski off my ass.

"Absolutely!" Her face lit up as she took a seat. "I'd love to help knock this guy down a few pegs. What do you need?"

"Work a lead for me." I jotted down the address and phone number of the check-cashing shop. "There's a guy named Darius who works here. I've been told he has some inside knowledge of the scheme. Near as I can tell, he's just a clerk, but I'm wondering if maybe the check-cashing shop served as a pseudo-bank to handle the payoffs and he's getting a cut of the transaction. He hung up on me when I called, so maybe if you go in and flirt with him, he'll be more talkative."

Her face fell. "You want me to flirt? Like a pushup bra and a heavy spray of Obsession? I think I'd rather donate a kidney."

"I'm joking. No cleavage required." I laughed. "Just see if you can get him to talk to you."

She leaned back in the chair. "I really want the chance, but man, not if it means I have to go all bimbo to get the story." She looked positively nauseous, and I had to stifle another laugh.

"Hey, are you forgetting who you're talking to? Do you see me running around with my boobs hanging out just to get a story?" This time I did laugh. "Although, if you think about it, it seems a small price to pay in the right circumstances." I pretended to ponder the idea.

"Cut it out, or I'll start taking you seriously. You're playing with a neophyte, and this conversation is downright mean." She smiled but was obviously relieved. "To change subjects, how bad was the funeral?" Her young face twisted with expectation, as if she weren't sure she really wanted to hear my answer. "It's so hard wrapping my head around someone younger than me dying. Janek's gotta be in a whole heap of pain."

"Well, I'll put it this way, for a moment I thought we were going to have more bloodshed. It could have been a *Doctor Phil* episode, complete with a brawl. The dead girl's mom went after the boyfriend. Apparently, she and Janek blame him for getting her daughter hooked. He was her dealer, so they nearly came to blows. Janek had to physically separate them, and if there hadn't been an audience, Janek would have taken the guy out himself. Family justice minus a trial. It was just flat-out ugly." I shook my head and hit save on my document before I distracted myself and lost the work.

"How awful. I can imagine Janek leading the charge. In fact, I can't imagine him not adding his two cents to the fight."

"Frankly, I don't know what Janek would do if the two of them were alone in a back alley. But I'm also not sure they're barking up the right tree."

"What do you mean?"

"I don't know exactly." I sighed, wishing for some explanation that told me I wasn't just indulging my active imagination. "There's something funky going on here. I don't think this was a straight-up overdose. The boyfriend is lying about something. I spoke to him today. It's just my gut instinct, but I think he knew Zoe had been staying at the house and is pretending otherwise for some reason. I'm not getting a good vibe from him. He's hiding something. I can't tell what, but I think he knew she was at the house and is denying it."

"Could he have given her tainted product?" Brynn asked. "After all, so much of that stuff is cut with mystery crap. There aren't exactly Yelp reviews for the drug trade tracing the purity of the supply chain. There are a lot of ugly stories about manufactured drugs. Is it possible he knew? Or figured it out later and is nervous about being charged now that she's dead?"

"You might be right. That's certainly possible. The ME will have something to say on that," I said, reflecting on the idea. "I do think he loved her and would never have intentionally hurt her—if you can set aside the harm heroin does—but he's covering up. Or protecting his own ass. The other weird thing is that the therapist that runs the treatment center I told you about, the one from the pamphlet? He showed up at the funeral too."

"Had she been a patient?" Brynn asked, looking at me quizzically.

"That's my question. What other reason would there be for the man to show up at Zoe's funeral? He didn't approach Zoe's mother, or anyone else, for that matter, to offer his condolences. It's odd. When I went to the open house, I thought he was being really vague about his process. Claims these astounding success rates, yet he was cagey about what makes his program different and how he's getting those kinds of results. Something feels off. I just can't put a finger on it. Can you look into their ownership history? When they were founded. You know the drill."

"Of course. But people can create any kind of statistics they want," Brynn said. "Maybe he's lying. Or manipulating the time frame or defining success as staying off the shit for two weeks. It's marketing, right?"

"Marketing." My brain was buzzing with a new thought. "The core of marketing is brand recognition, right? So why do people choose one addiction program versus another? It all starts with awareness."

"Plus the price-to-benefit ratio," Brynn added. "Whether anyone realizes it or not, we all make decisions like that, even if we're not aware that we do when we buy something. And this is a product that is being bought. Consumers decide whether they perceive the benefit of the product to be in line with its cost."

"As far as I know, other treatment centers aren't quoting success rates," I said. "I understand why people would want them, but that almost becomes a guarantee. And how in the hell is curing someone of addiction something you can guarantee?"

"You can't. Can you?"

"I don't see how. I'll need to find someone else to talk to. Someone who can educate me on what standard protocol is these days."

"Wasn't there a forensic psychologist who specialized in stuff like this? I'm thinking about a case you told me about from back when you were an attorney. He comes up in the news now and then because he does the expert witness thing."

"Yeah, Dr. Franklin Lecaros. He gets called in a lot to testify. I think he makes more money as an expert witness than in private therapy practice. But he would know what's considered the gold standard in current treatment."

"Sounds like a starting point. It would at least give you a benchmark. And if this guy really is an expert in current thinking, he's probably heard of the center, or the doc."

"Yeah, I'll give him a call. But just imagine if Dr. Wykell is right and he really does have an eighty-five percent success rate."

"The world would beat down his doors."

21

Zoe had been scared. Scared of her addiction or of something else?

Levi's accusation hadn't left my head since the funeral yesterday, his angry words—*What did you give her?*—reverberating against the denial that he even knew the doc. I'd spent the balance of the day and into the evening trying to formulate a legitimate explanation for the exchange, but I could only conclude that Levi had been talking about Zoe.

Consumed with the thought, I was now sitting in my car outside the Renacido Center trying to figure out what I was going to do about it. As of yet, there had been no confirmation on the cause of death. So was I making assumptions, letting my journalistic desire for a story falsely conclude crime and deception? Maybe, but until the ME told me otherwise, I was going to press forward.

It was clear that there was some kind of connection between the doctor, Levi, and Zoe. Their lies had a purpose.

A text pinged in from Michael as I plotted my strategy. *Need to see you. Are you at home?* After the emotional drain of the funeral and what I imagined were equally draining hours afterward for him, Michael and I had only exchanged a couple of texts. My heart tugged. I reluctantly sent him a note that I was following up on something at the treatment center and would call him as soon as I was done. For the moment, anyway, I decided to hold back on the details. It was our version of *don't ask, don't tell* in our complicated work lives, but a day wrapped in his arms would do both of us good.

As on my previous visit, the door to the center remained open, except for the screen. I hit the buzzer as a courtesy and then stepped inside. Francesca, the office manager who'd kicked off the open house, appeared in the entryway a moment later.

"Good morning," I said. "I'm here to see Dr. Wykell."

She looked at me quizzically but said nothing, suppressing the question that was clearly formulating in her mind.

"You were here at the open house, weren't you?" she said, remembering my face. "Just a moment, let me see if he's free."

I nodded and smiled. No reason to add comment when none was necessary. Better to let her form her own assumptions about the purpose of my visit.

She walked down the hall toward the back of the building while I waited in the foyer. As I perused the beautiful Victorian architecture, I looked again at the pamphlets still arranged on the foyer table, apparently a permanent part of the fixtures. I picked up a couple and put them in my bag. I had yet to see or hear anything that explained what this treatment protocol entailed, but perhaps that was typical. I imagined it was hard enough to get an individual to seek treatment in the first place, so why scare them off with details? Kendall, the young girl I'd spoken with at the open house, popped into my mind, and an uneasy feeling settled into my chest as I replayed Levi's accusation.

Low voices bounced down the hall from the back of the building, bringing my attention back to the present. Somewhere out of sight, a heated conversation was occurring. It was too distant to make out who was speaking or what was being said; however, the angry tone of two male voices was unmistakable. A few moments later, Dr. Wykell appeared at the end of the hall, having walked away from the conversation. He hadn't noticed me yet, as the faux flowers partially obscured my presence. As I watched through the foliage, he shook off whatever had irritated him and put on his game face. In my experience, therapists were quite skilled at masking their emotions, probably even more so than attorneys.

"Hello," he said as he reached the table, extending a hand. "I'm Dr. Troy Wykell. I understand you joined us earlier this week for our open house. It's lovely to have you back. How can I help you?"

He wore khakis and a button-down shirt, its collar open, and the sleeves were now rolled tightly above his elbows, a look that seemed to be his uniform. Clearly my vague request had worked and Francesca had formed the conclusion I wanted her to.

"My name is Andrea Kellner," I said, shaking his hand. "I'm here to talk to you about Zoe Symanski. You were at her funeral yesterday."

A slight shadow crossed his piercing eyes, but for the most part, his mask didn't slip. Impressive.

"Yes. Yes, I was. She had been a patient of mine for a brief period of time. Her passing is such a tragedy. Addiction ravages far too many of our young people."

He contracted his brow and shook his head in an appropriate level of concern. But his body language showed tension.

"I'm the one who found her body." I said it straight out, figuring his response would be telling. This time he couldn't keep the mask in place.

"Oh!" Shocked, he stared at me for a moment, and I could

see questions were forming in his mind. "That must've been awful for you. It's so terribly sad. How did you know her?"

He was deflecting, trying to take control of the questioning and shift it back on me, a legal technique I was quite familiar with. Professional habit? Or was he just uncomfortable being the one on the other side of the couch?

"I didn't know her. I simply found her body," I said. "My sister purchased the property where Zoe died. I was helping her out and found Zoe alone, dead in the basement."

I watched his face as he replied, reading it like a truth map.

"Addiction is so devastating. There are people we can help and people we can't. I do have to say it's some of the most gratifying work I've ever done, but on those occasions when you just can't break through, it can be quite distressing." He sighed and again shook his head.

I didn't doubt for a second that he was disturbed by the limitations of therapy. His tone was authentic and I believed he was committed to his cause, but that didn't mean he wouldn't protect himself in the event of a mishap.

"You said she was a patient. When was that?" I asked, needing to get the conversation back on Zoe.

"Let me think. Perhaps nine months ago, possibly longer," he said, absently tugging on his beard. "To say she was a patient might be a stretch. She started the treatment but had a hard time committing to the rigor that our process requires. It isn't for everyone. It takes many individuals quite some time to come to grips with not only the extent of their problems but also the hard work required to really get to a permanent solution."

"And Zoe wasn't ready? Wasn't fully committed?"

My read on him was that his empathy for those struggling with addiction was real, as was his commitment to a solution, but there was something about his demeanor that suggested he was holding back. One of the side effects of my legal career had been the development of an internal truth-divining rod, and this guy made mine quiver.

"I really can't discuss her treatment." He smiled at me condescendingly. "We take our requirements of confidentiality quite seriously. As I'm sure you can understand, not only do we have legal responsibilities to our patients but also moral and ethical responsibilities for their privacy. I can't go into the details of individual treatment plans for Zoe, nor anyone else's, for that matter."

"Yes, of course I understand."

His statement was certainly true, but I hadn't asked because I expected him to spill her private medical history. Alarm bells had been ringing in my head ever since he'd identified Zoe as a patient. She and her mother had been estranged for two years. Where had Zoe gotten the money to pay for a center such as this, even if her stay was short-lived? I made a mental note to follow up with Janek, but the timing was awful. It would mean adding undue burden onto Theresa just as she buried her daughter. However, even if Zoe had backed out of the program early, somebody had been prepared to foot the bill.

"Tell me about your treatment protocol," I said, moving to more neutral subject matter. "I've looked over your literature, and it contains some amazing claims of your success rate." I was curious but also trying to keep him talking, and I had a feeling that this was a guy who would respond to having his ego stroked.

"Yes, we've developed an extraordinary protocol." His eyes lit up with pride as he spoke. "It took quite some time and a number of patients willing to make the commitment, but we couldn't be more pleased with where things are headed. I'm not sure if you are familiar with this industry, but it is notoriously difficult to get any sense of success rates from other programs. And as a scientist at heart, I find that quite disturbing."

"Disturbing? In what way?"

There was an energy and passion in his voice that hadn't been present earlier as he spoke about what he had accomplished. His face was animated, and he'd finally pulled his hand away from his beard.

"Just think about the number of people who are suffering with this terrible disease. Think of the lives lost needlessly. Think of the money invested into twelve-step programs with no guarantee that an individual won't be right back where he started less than a year later. How can we live with those odds? That uncertainty?"

"So you believe treatment should come with a guarantee?"

"No, I wouldn't go that far. After all, so much rides on the individual's readiness and willingness to commit to treatment. I'm simply responding to the 'black hole,' as I call it. Treatment is an investment in your future. An investment in your life. How does one turn over tens of thousands of dollars of hard-earned money to individuals who won't, or can't, provide data on their track records?"

"Probably because there are no other options. Medical treatment, regardless of the type, never comes with promises. The best we get is rough odds of success."

"Exactly. *We* have another option. And an option with proven success."

"And how do you measure success?" I asked. I was no expert in the area of addiction, but even I could comprehend the variabilities in acquiring the data. Methodologies would need to be in place that kept track of or monitored an individual over a period of time in order to claim success, unless weekly drug testing was part of the program. Self-reporting was hardly a rigorous testing standard. Was this guy full of BS, or was he on to something new?

"Well, we keep our data confidential, just like our protocol.

But I can assure you we have the most successful program available. When we have the right individual and the right motivation, lives are changed."

"That all sounds pretty amazing. If what you've said is accurate, this could be groundbreaking."

I watched the glow settle over his face. The man wanted validation. Needed it, even. From my past experiences as an attorney, I knew that many individuals in the mental health profession entered the field altruistically, their desire to help others a core element of their being. But there were some who sought it as a career because of past trauma, a doctor-heal-thyself experience. What personal need did the work serve for this man?

Dr. Wykell's arrogance was beginning to annoy me, but the good thing about arrogant men was that if you kept the praise coming, they would share information they didn't even realize they were sharing. As long as it made them look good.

"Can you tell me about the types of tools you use in treatment? I understand that many therapists in this specialization rely on cognitive behavior therapy or other redirection therapies."

My repertoire of psychological buzzwords had its limits, but I was hoping I only needed to throw out a few terms to get him talking. Before he could respond, the office manager, Francesca, rushed down the stairs. Her face was flushed, and a bead of sweat clung to her upper lip. She paused when she saw me, shooting me a look that told me exactly how unwelcome I was at that moment. Dr. Wykell turned when he heard her and, seeing her distress, hurried forward to meet her. I watched the two huddle, Francesca speaking in low tones but clearly upset. Dr. Wykell's face was tight, but he maintained his calm. Francesca nodded her head, seemingly relieved to have someone else give direction, then hurried back upstairs with another cutting glance at me.

"I'm sorry, I'm afraid we're going to have to cut this off. I have something I must attend to. You'll need to excuse me." He placed his hand on the small of my back, guiding me toward the door. His touch felt invasive, unnecessary, and I tensed.

"Yes, of course, I understand. Thank you for your time," I said, before opening the door.

As I stepped back onto the porch, the heavy wooden door was closed firmly behind me and I heard the lock catch. Whatever emergency had arisen apparently required his full attention, and I couldn't help but think of Zoe. I walked across the porch and down the steps, moving toward my vehicle and feeling uneasy. As I reached my car, I turned and looked back at the house. A curtain moved on the second level. Francesca stood in the window, watching.

22

The hairs on the back of my neck were standing at attention as I watched Francesca stare at me, her face twisted with disgust—or was it anger? It suddenly felt like a scene from a bad horror movie as I looked up at the second floor of the old Victorian. As I pulled out my keys and unlocked the car door, movement at the end of the long drive caught my attention. A man dressed in nothing but gym shorts stumbled as he tried to cross the blacktop. He appeared to be walking from the center—if you could call it walking—to the carriage house at the back of the lot. A patient who'd wandered off? I watched for a moment, wondering if he was inebriated. I looked from the man back up to the second-floor window where I'd seen Francesca, but she was gone.

The man stumbled yet again, going down on one knee. Hesitating for only a second, expecting someone from the center to rush out to assist him, I ran forward down the drive toward him. Before I could get close, he regained his footing, stood, and moved unsteadily toward the coach house. By the time I reached the spot where I'd seen him fall, he was no longer in sight, having disappeared into the outbuilding. Concerned for his safety, I followed. On the right side of the building I found a door with a "No Admittance—Private Property" sign prominently displayed. Where the hell was the staff? I looked back at the house, but no one seemed to be coming out to help.

My choices were to go back to the main building and tell them they were missing a patient or ignore the warning sign and enter. A loud crash behind the closed door made the decision easy.

Inside was a set of stairs on my right that rose toward a second floor. A hallway straight ahead was flanked by a series of doors. The light was dim, and the space wasn't what I'd expected. The interior of the coach house had been chopped up, reconfigured way beyond its original purpose. There were no signs of the young man. I scanned the nearby walls for a light switch, but none were apparent. Illuminating my phone, I stepped up to the first door in the hallway, then put my hand on the knob and turned. Light washed over what appeared to be a large storage closet. Boxes and bottles were stacked floor to ceiling on the shelves. Beyond their shape, it was too dark to make out any details. Medical storage? I closed the door and moved to the next one. It too opened freely, this time into a larger room. A row of chairs were arranged in front of a hospital bed, and several supply carts lined the far wall. What was this?

As I stood contemplating the function of the room, a loud, guttural wail came from the upper level. I raced up the stairs only to find yet another hallway lined with a series of doors. These, however, had been outfitted with glass windows.

I couldn't see the man, nor did I hear him any longer, so I quickly stepped to the nearest door and peered in. Inside was a hospital bed, a cabinet, and an IV stand next to the bed. Were patients receiving medical care here? Thoughts of licensing requirements ran through my mind as I viewed room after room, finding more of the same setup.

Another wail, this one closer, louder. It was the sound of agony. But was it emotional agony or physical? I rushed to the end of the hall where light from a clerestory window illuminated a larger open space. The young man I had followed was on the floor, thrashing, scratching at his forearms and his neck.

I rushed to his side, scanning his body for obvious signs of injury, but nothing was apparent.

"Can you speak? Where are you hurt?" I asked these things as I tapped open my phone. He threw his head and shoulders side to side, clutching at me, his long hair tangled over his face as I dialed 911.

Giving my name and the address, I asked for an ambulance while the man groaned and flailed against me. Whatever agony he was in had no visible physical manifestations. I searched again for signs of blood as the operator asked me to stay on the line, doing what I could to calm him down but to no avail. He was sweating profusely, and I brushed the hair off of his face.

"What the hell are you doing in here?" a male voice behind me boomed.

I looked up to see Dr. Wykell barreling toward me, a nurse in blue scrubs right behind him.

"He's in trouble. I called an ambulance. They're on the way," I said, ignoring his accusatory tone. This was hardly the time to be worried about a trespasser.

"You did what?" he shot back.

Pulling the man from my arms, he then shoved me away with one firm jab. I fell against a medical cart, sending the clanging metal into a bed and my body to the floor. Shocked, I sat against the cart, trying to understand his response. The nurse stood behind him, her brown eyes wide, but she did nothing to assist, seemingly waiting for Wykell to issue an order.

"Do something!" I yelled at her. "He's in trouble. Look at

him. I saw him fall in the driveway. He was clearly in serious trouble, so I followed him and found him like this."

She stared at me, pain in her eyes, but hesitated half a second before stepping forward.

"You're trespassing on private property. You need to leave immediately," Dr. Wykell shouted at me. His nurse froze, and whether it was out of fear or needing his permission to proceed wasn't clear. "How we handle our patients is none of your concern."

Wykell motioned for the nurse. She moved to his side, checking the young man's pupils and pulse. Locking her eyes on Wykell, she opened her mouth to say something, but he shook his head, silencing her.

What was happening?

"Look at him," I said again. "What the hell is wrong with him? Do something!"

The nurse looked nervously from me to the patient, then back to the doctor, grappling with her medical duty and the parameters Wykell was placing on her.

"Please," I said to her. "Help him. Don't let this kid die when he doesn't have to."

"We need to get an IV into him immediately," she said, her slightly accented voice wavering. After one more check of his pupils, she took hold of his wrist, turning the arm to expose the veins. Small dark bruises dotted his pale skin. She was a sturdy, big-boned woman and probably could have tossed her patient over her shoulder if needed. Her stick-straight hair was pulled back into a ponytail, and she wore a name tag that identified her as Darna.

Wykell ignored her demand. As she shifted, presumably to reach for supplies, Wykell pushed her arm away.

"I said, get out!" he screamed at me instead.

"I'm not going anywhere," I shot back, getting to my feet. Still on a live connection, I could hear the operator again. I pulled the phone back up to my ear. "Yes, I'm here." She told me the ambulance had just pulled up.

"I'm not leaving until I know he's okay," I repeated to Dr. Wykell. Whatever calm the young man had felt for a moment was gone and he beat his hands against the doctor's chest, pushing him away, his head still thrashing. Wykell moved behind him, pulling the man's arms across his body as if he were a human straitjacket, forcing him to become still. This man needed medical attention, not a straitjacket.

The nurse had stepped over to a nearby cabinet and was pulling out a syringe and a vial.

"I'm telling you to leave," Wykell repeated as the nurse handed him the injection.

As she swabbed a site with alcohol, two EMTs rushed in. "Hold on. We've got it from here," one of the technicians said. "Step aside, sir," he ordered, this time more sternly. Wykell no longer had a choice, and he released his grip on the young man, handing the syringe quietly back to the nurse.

The young man's body still twitched as the EMTs quickly assessed his dilated pupils. Wykell stood to the side, glaring at the technicians as they worked.

"Do we know if he's taking anything?" one EMT asked, directing his question at Dr. Wykell. He mumbled no, but I didn't believe him. The nurse stood mutely next to the supply cabinet, but her eyes told me she was as frightened as I was. As the medical team worked, the young man began to clutch at his chest, taking loud, raspy breaths. A moment later he was convulsing on the floor, his body rolling in waves and foam coming from his mouth.

I watched in horror as the EMTs seemed unable to stem the pain wracking their patient's body, and Wykell and his nurse refused to offer any assistance.

"Time to fess up, people," the EMT said, this time urgently as the two technicians struggled to stabilize the man. "What is he on?"

Silence from Wykell. With one loud gasp, the young man's body shuddered.

"We're losing him," the EMT said. "One of you had better start talking!"

"Dr. Wykell," I screamed. "Stop the goddamn stonewalling. What is this kid taking?"

23

Raspy, gasping breaths echoed in the room as the young man's body shook and fought to stay alive. Wykell and his nurse stared silently at their patient while the EMTs' frantic efforts at resuscitation were failing.

Trembling in disbelief and anger that this man was dying before our eyes while a supposed medical professional and his nurse said nothing, I also stood by helpless, shocked into silence by Dr. Wykell's refusal to open his damn mouth.

As the EMTs prepared the defibrillator, Francesca entered the space. She stared in horror at the scene, her hands over her mouth when the reality of the situation began to dawn on her. She rushed toward Dr. Wykell, who raised his palm and stopped her with barely a glance.

"Go back downstairs and attend to the others," he said.

She looked at him, disbelief blazing in her eyes, and then toward the scene on the floor, before turning and following her orders. The nurse shot me one more pleading look, then followed Francesca down the hall.

The medical team was doing their best, but by the sideways glances they were giving each other, I could tell the outcome would be bad. A clomp of footsteps in the hall caused me to turn. Two CPD officers had arrived, with Michael right behind them. The officers quickly surveyed the scene, stepping over to the techs while Michael came to me.

"What happened?" he asked, looking from me to the activity on the floor in front of us. Somehow his spy system within CPD seemed to have me on a tracking device, and I generally had mixed feelings about it. Right now, however, it was a good thing.

"What happened is that *this* woman is trespassing," Wykell retorted, his voice tight with accusation and face flushed with anger. "She had no right to enter this property. She has no right to be here now. She is interfering with this man's treatment. I want her arrested!"

"Arrested? What?" Michael gawked at the man, just as stunned as I was at Wykell's bizarre response. His patient was dying in front of his eyes and the guy was focused on my trespassing?

"Your patient doesn't seem to be doing so well. Why don't we deal with that first," Michael said, somehow managing to keep the sarcasm out of his voice.

Administering one last unsuccessful jolt from the defibrillator, the EMT looked at us and shook his head. All eyes were now on the lifeless body on the floor. As the EMTs moved from lifesaving maneuvers to processing the death, the officers shifted their attention to me and Dr. Wykell.

Michael stepped over toward Wykell as the man turned toward me, his face red and clenched. Sensing another outburst was building, one of the other officers led me down the hall away from the doctor.

"You're Andrea Kellner, aren't you?" he asked. He stood, looking at me squarely, thumbs tucked nonchalantly into his belt. It was the stance of an officer who'd done this far too long and seen far too much to ever be surprised.

"I am." I shot a glance at his name tag. Wrobleski. It was vaguely familiar.

"Yeah, I thought so. I remember you from a couple years ago. You prosecuted one of my cases. I thought you were a tough broad back then. I wouldn't want to get on your bad side."

"And?" I said, my tone harsher than I had intended.

"Hey, that's a good thing. Trust me." He chuckled, raising a hand in surrender. "Particularly when we're dealing with scum. You want to tell me what happened here?"

I filled him in on the erratic behavior I'd seen outside before following the now deceased man inside the building.

"The kid was clearly in trouble," I said. "And it didn't look like there was time to go hunting down whoever the hell is in charge of patients around here, so I followed him inside. I found him here, upstairs, convulsing on the floor. Called 911. And then screamed at these so-called medical professionals to do something until you guys arrived."

Shock and anger and adrenaline were still coursing through my body, and I found myself unable to stand still as I relayed the information.

"And what is this place?" the officer asked, looking around.

"A drug addiction treatment center," I said, doing the same, this time noting every detail.

There seemed to be an awful lot of medical equipment, but then again I'd never been inside a facility such as this. Perhaps the building was used for detoxing. Again, I didn't know enough about the process to know what to look for. But the bigger question was Dr. Wykell's odd reaction. At the moment, I had far more questions than answers.

As I spoke with the officer and continued filling in the gaps that I could, I watched Michael and the other officer across the room speaking with the doctor. I could see Dr. Wykell was getting agitated again—excessive gesturing, the inability to stand still, the raised voice—but it wasn't clear if he was upset about the death of this patient or upset that he was being challenged at all.

The officer finished his questioning and instructed me to wait downstairs but not to leave the property, in case there was any additional information needed. I caught Michael's eye as I turned to leave, hearing Dr. Wykell lament, "This is going to ruin everything, all the progress we've made. We have a breakthrough here and *you* want to ruin it in one fell swoop."

The storage room beckoned as I reached the main-floor landing. Silently, I twisted the knob and opened the door, swinging my phone's flashlight over the boxes and bottles stored here. The IV stands I'd seen upstairs were on my mind as I snapped photos, focusing on the labels. Whatever was stored here sure wasn't cleaning supplies.

Hearing footsteps, I put my phone back in my pocket and stepped out onto the driveway. Francesca stood next to the back porch of the main house, speaking to a few individuals. She appeared to be trying to calm them down, however unsuccessfully. Others stood in the lawn watching from a distance, surprise and concern on their faces.

Wykell's nurse stood alone at the side of the building, a tangle of emotions etched on her face. Her arms were crossed over her chest, and she chewed the end of a nail. I started toward her, but she shook her head when she saw me coming, then turned and went back inside the center. Was she afraid of Wykell or just frightened by what was happening to her patient?

A second death. What was going on here? I scanned the faces of the group assembled outside, stopping at one I recognized. Kendall, the teenager I had met the other afternoon at the open house. She stood alone, scuffing her motorcycle boot in the dirt and staring at the ground.

She looked up as I approached, recognition spreading across

her face. "What's happening in there?" she asked, fear in her eyes. "I heard that this guy, Paul, died."

"I don't know his name, but yes, a young man died. We met the other day, I think. It's Kendall, isn't it?"

She nodded.

"I'm Andrea. Do you know his last name?"

"I think it's Macanas. But I just got here, so we aren't into the deep connection thing yet."

She said it nonchalantly, but the way she was twisting the metal charm on her choker told me she was spooked. She was a kid who hid her fears and insecurities behind a mantle of projected toughness. A mantle that was more like a spiderweb than metal. I had a hard time imagining the emotional turmoil of being sixteen years old and having a peer die, particularly a peer suffering the same affliction. It would either scare her straight or bolster any nihilistic tendencies she might possess. My heart ached for her.

"But you've met him?" I asked. "He was a patient here too?"

"That's what they're all saying." She shrugged.

"The guy that died, he was somewhere in his twenties, thin, dark hair down past his shoulders. Does that sound like the guy you're talking about?"

"Yeah, he's the only guy I've met with long hair, so that sounds like him. Do you know what happened?"

I shook my head. No reason to speculate and scare the girl. "Any idea how long Paul had been here?"

"Not really. The program is supposed to be thirty days. At least stage one is. Kind of depends on how fucked up you are."

"What do you mean by that?"

"I mean, if you been using hard right up to the day you walked in the door, they might set you up for a longer stint, detox, and all that shit, at least on the first go-around. If you been off the stuff for a while, the hitch is a little easier."

"So how does it work? The process, I mean."

"I don't know it all yet," she said, her eyes locked on the door to the carriage house. "This ain't my first rodeo, but they do things different here. And I only got here yesterday. They keep you in the dark. Probably so they don't scare you off. Easier to wrap your head around small chunks of time, but they told me the first week is the normal stupid stuff. Talking about your problems, confessing every stupid thing you've ever done, as if being publicly embarrassed is supposed to do the trick." She rolled her eyes and stuck her hands into the pockets of her camo cargo pants. "I don't know where they get the idea that this talk therapy stuff actually works. We all take shit for the same reasons. We don't want to think about how fucked up our life really is. We want to numb the pain. Duh, as if this is some big revelation."

"But there must be something more about this program, something that is unusual. Isn't that what they sell? It's supposed to be different than standard therapy. Supposed to offer something unique and unusually fast compared to everything else. Right?"

"Well, whatever it is, I don't know anything yet. They won't tell us in advance. My dad's so pissed off at me that he'd let them drill holes in my skull if they said it would end all this shit. Whatever." She shrugged it off. "Anyway, the rumors are that they use some other drugs. Drugs that are supposed to fix our brains, whatever the hell that means. I heard somebody talking about psychedelics. But I think they were just bullshitting. If anyone let it get out they were using 'shrooms, they'd have a line of people around the block volunteering just for the buzz." The idea seemed to amuse her.

"Do you have any idea what this building is used for?" I nodded toward the coach house.

"No, I haven't been in there yet. I've just been locked in my room. I go to meetings for therapy, I go down and I eat, and the rest of the time I'm supposed to sit and meditate. Never understood why anybody thinks sitting with your eyes closed, saying 'ohm' over and over, accomplishes anything, but hell, if it gets you off, go for it."

As we spoke, Michael exited the coach house, followed by Dr. Wykell and the two cops. Right behind them, the EMTs maneuvered a gurney that held the body bag. A collective gasp escaped. Tears flowed for some, while others stood stony, their eyes the only indication of what they were feeling. Francesca hustled over to Dr. Wykell, and the patients around her did the same.

I watched as Michael began his rounds, questioning the individuals assembled. He furrowed his brow as he caught me deep in conversation with Kendall. I knew what he was thinking, but I didn't care. One woman standing near Francesca seemed particularly distraught. Her shoulders shook as she sobbed, clutching her stomach.

"Do you know who that is? The woman in the blue T-shirt?" I asked, pointing at the woman.

"Her name is Sondra. She's down the hall from me. I think she and Paul are pretty close."

I looked at Kendall, really looked at her, seeing the sensitivity and pain she hid under a tough veneer. Would she be one of the few who found her way? I smiled softly and placed a hand on her shoulder. "I hope you figure all this out," I said. "You're a smart girl, and you deserve better. If I can help with anything, let me know." I handed her my card.

She nodded, a rare moment of vulnerability in her eyes, then tucked the business card in her back pocket. The slam of the ambulance doors shifted our attention back to the body as the vehicle pulled away. With one last glance at Kendall, I moved over to speak with Sondra.

"Hi, I'm Andrea. I'm so sorry about your friend." I handed her a packet of tissues.

"Thanks, I really thought he was going to make it. He was really trying hard." She sniffed and wiped her tear-stained face, but the cascade of grief would not stop. Her T-shirt was dappled with wet droplets, and her shoulders heaved as she struggled to catch her breath long enough to fight back a sob.

"Do you know anything about his family or where he worked?" I asked.

"He mentioned something about a brother, lived in the suburbs, Deerfield, I think. But he and his parents didn't get along."

Another casualty of addiction, but again, I had to wonder who was funding his treatment.

"This stuff can be really hard on families," I said, running numbers in my head on the likely cost associated with inpatient care. "Did they ever come visit? His parents, I mean?"

"No, not that I know of," she said, dabbing at her nose. "I don't think they talked anymore. They'd given up on him. But then what? What did he have if even his family wouldn't talk to him?" Her expression held the pain that only someone on her side of the addiction curve could fathom—desperation, loneliness, hurt, and the fear that standing on the edge of the abyss could bring.

"Did he have a job?" I asked, my mind still on the expense.

"He mentioned tending bar. It was this place in Wrigleyville, The Rusty Bucket, or something like that. We talked about whether working in a bar was a good thing or a bad thing for an addict. He didn't have a problem with booze, but still, being around that lifestyle, well, it's kinda like playing with dynamite."

Similar to Zoe's situation, it was unlikely that a bartender had the resources to manage a bill that had to be in the tens of thousands of dollars. So where were these kids getting the cash to handle the financial commitment of a high-priced rehab center?

"Did you ever meet a girl named Zoe Symanski? I think she was a patient here, around nine months ago, maybe a year?" I pulled out my phone and scrolled to a picture that had been part of recent news coverage and showed it to her.

Sondra looked carefully at the photo, nodding. "Yeah, I'd met her. She was here the first time, the first time I was here, I mean. She was finishing up a six-week stint, and I was just getting started. I didn't last long the first time. I bailed after a week and a half. I wasn't ready then. But yeah, I remember her. Did she make it?"

I paused, knowing that Sondra was asking about Zoe's sobriety, before responding.

"No, she's dead."

24

Paul's twitching body filled my thoughts—the way he had clutched at his chest, the glassy incoherence of someone moments from death—I couldn't let go of the image. Had Zoe's death been equally horrific?

It was barely past sunrise, but sleeping in this Sunday morning was not going to happen. Paul and Zoe had haunted me in my dreams, crying out for attention. With eyes still unfocused from the lack of sleep, I turned over to find Walter sitting patiently on my nightstand, as he did every morning, waiting for me to stir. I liked to think of his morning presence as protective, but in reality, it was just his desire for fresh kibble.

I tossed off the duvet, grabbed my robe, and together we padded down the hall toward the kitchen. He moved into a happy sprint the moment we hit the hallway. I smiled to myself but was too groggy after the pathetic night of sleep to pick up my pace.

Walter's bowl filled and my mug of Earl Grey steaming, I returned to my bedroom and started the shower, my head filled with questions.

Cleaned and dressed, I refilled my tea, then moved to my

office. It was originally a maid's room and I'd expanded the space, combining it with a neighboring powder room I could afford to give up, and I now had a sunny, cheerful office with built-in cabinets, a custom wall-sized tack board, and narrow windows overlooking the building's back garden. I'd been remodeling the sprawling vintage apartment room by room, as time, money, and energy permitted. The seventies kitchen had been the first to see a sledgehammer, followed by the master bath and then the office. Only three more bathrooms to go. I shook the thought out of my head.

Sensing an opportunity to make a few bucks, Lane hit me up at least once a month about selling the apartment, thinking a single woman belonged in a bright, shiny, new construction two-bedroom, provided it had a doorman and a great gym. Her argument that it would be a more practical situation made sense, but I'd chosen the co-op based on emotion and I wasn't giving her up for a bland box, inconvenience and high HOAs be damned.

Post-its and Sharpie in hand, I laid out the facts as I knew them—names, dates, locations—trying to piece together a narrative that might connect these deaths. The treatment center was the obvious starting point, with Dr. Troy Wykell front and center, but there was far more that I didn't know. I added notes until I'd tacked up anything remotely connected, paused for a moment, then added a card for Quantum Holdings to the "Maybe" column. I couldn't imagine that the prior owners of Lane's property had any connection to the deaths, but it was odd that a stash of brochures for the Renacido Center had been in the home, and I didn't have a logical answer for that other than one that connected back to Zoe, so onto the board it went.

Walter, having decided this was the perfect moment to make his presence known, jumped on my desk, sending pens, business cards, and odd bits of paper flying. He parked himself on top of my legal pad, flicking his tail in amusement. I sighed and scratched him behind the ears.

"Feeling ignored, were you?"

He looked at me, then promptly stretched his body out full length on the desk.

Who was I to argue with his nap location? I bent down and picked up the pieces of paper off the floor and looked at the wall. It seemed clear that the first gap I needed to fill in my knowledge was a better understanding of the current standard of care in addiction treatment. Walter's scattered materials still in hand, I reached for my phone, intending to add a note to my schedule about phoning Dr. Lecaros first thing in the morning. Wait. The Nico logo on the pen in my hand stopped me. Paul had worked at a bar called The Rusty Bucket. Maybe Zoe and Paul had another connection? Bars and restaurants were often loose with their hiring standards, and perhaps they'd worked together. Or perhaps Levi and Paul had? I added more Post-its to my "Maybe" column.

My phone rang as I placed the last note.

"Any chance you're at home and sitting around waiting to see me?" Michael said.

"What else would I be doing?" I laughed. "If you're asking if it's okay to stop by, that's an emphatic yes."

"I'll be there in fifteen minutes."

"What? Are you calling from the corner?"

"Something like that," he said, laughing. "See you soon."

―――――

"I TOLD you I was close by." Michael stood in the doorway, takeout coffee in one hand, a small white paper bag in the other. His face lit up when he saw me. Ignoring the potential hazards, he pulled me into an awkward but much needed embrace and kissed me.

"You'd better put that coffee down before one of us is wearing it," I said, taking the cup and bag from his hands and placing them on the nearby console table. "Now, let's try that again." I wrapped my arms around his neck and drew him in for a long, deep kiss.

"Much better. You can have your caffeine back now." I smiled and peeked into the paper bag. "Ohhh, croissants. You've been to Hendrickx." I pulled off a corner of the delicious, flaky pastry and popped it into my mouth as Michael followed me to the kitchen.

"Jam?" I asked. He shook his head. I handed him a plate and a napkin and settled in at the small pedestal table.

"How are you? How's Karl? It feels like a lifetime has transpired in a week. I've been so worried about you. This roller coaster of emotions..." My thoughts trailed off. There was so much I wanted to say, but right now I needed to listen. I clasped my hand over his and waited.

"Janek finally stepped away from the job for a few days. Theresa's a mess and someone needed to stay nearby, so he's hunkered down with her for the weekend. I don't know how restful it will be, but they both need the time to grieve. Or to just cry until there is nothing left." He tipped back his cup. "Me, well, I'm running on fumes."

I could see his distress in the circles under his eyes.

"We cops project all this macho, tough-guy bullshit, as if it's supposed to save us from feeling anything. We're above all the emotional stuff. But when bad stuff hits, when people we love are hurt, we're suddenly shocked that we're not protected from anything. That knife can slice open our hearts just as easily as everyone else's. So what's the point of being a hard-nosed dick if the rug just gets pulled out from under you even harder because you thought you could handle anything."

Tears welled in my eyes. This was the most raw, the most open Michael had ever been with me. There was nothing for me to say. Nothing he needed other than me to listen. I clasped his hand tighter and wiped the tears, honored that he could share his vulnerability with me.

"You're scaring me," he said. "I go to two crime scenes in a week, both involving you."

I opened my mouth, but Michael held up a hand.

"Let me just say this. It doesn't matter if you were in any real danger or not." He stared at our hands as though he'd be unable to get the words out while looking at my face. "I know you were going to explain away my concern by reminding me Zoe was already dead. But that's not what this is about. Seeing Janek and Theresa lose Zoe, I can't stand the thought of you being anywhere near something that could hurt you. I want to wrap you up and lock you away somewhere where nothing can ever hurt you. Not exactly a fine-tuned security plan, but that's where my head is, and it scares me. Seeing you at the carriage house yesterday has had me panicked." Finally he looked at me. "And I don't know what to do about it."

Tears now approaching full-blown faucet, I said, "Perhaps you now understand what goes through the mind of everyone who loves a cop, each time one of you walks out the door. Your desire to wrap me up and protect me is no different than my desire to do the same for you. The difference now is how do we proceed, how do we talk so that the fear doesn't cripple us or our relationship."

He reached over and wiped my tears. "I've been afraid to say this, but I love you. I really love you, and I need you to know that."

I leaned over and kissed him, gently. "I love you too."

"Wow, I hadn't planned on saying any of that, but I'm glad I did." He exhaled, his whole body relaxing, then shifted gears with a much needed swig of coffee. "So what did I interrupt this morning? I don't imagine you were just waiting around for me to have an emotional breakdown."

"I was in the office, playing with a few ideas," I said, feeling giddy and a little nervous and trying to sound nonchalant.

The dance we played with our overlapping work worlds was never easy, and Michael sharing his fears just now wouldn't simplify anything. Most of the time I was the one chomping at the bit to hit Michael up with a barrage of questions. I often felt like the kid whose dad owned the candy store, only to be refused access to the product. Prior to today, Michael and I had settled into a pattern of me throwing out questions and him honoring the cop vow of silence. His two decades of police stoicism were strong obstacles against my thirteen years as a prosecutor. However, my background had given some fuel to my nonverbal decoder. Would today's true confessions change anything?

He cocked a brow. "Sweetheart, I know that tone. Come on. You may as well show me."

"Bring your coffee. You might need it." I winked and tilted my head toward the hallway.

Michael planted himself in front of the tack board, his eyes scanning the bits of paper I had assembled. I parked myself on the front edge of the desk and watched him process.

"What are you doing? Seriously, Andrea, are you trying to create a story here?"

"You saw how Dr. Wykell behaved," I said. "You saw the setup in that coach house. Can you really tell me you don't find the situation odd? Aren't you wondering if Paul would have survived if Wykell hadn't obstructed his care?"

"Of course I find Wykell's behavior strange. He had a patient dying on him and he was more concerned about you trespassing than his patient. But we're talking addicts here. They don't all make it. That doesn't mean it's some nefarious scheme, just that the doc is a royal dick. And it's up to the ME to decide if that extra time would've made a difference in his survival."

"Okay, here are a couple things you don't know. Whatever he *is* doing at the treatment center, Dr. Wykell believes his treatment protocol is a game changer."

Michael rolled his eyes.

"Just listen before making faces. It's a cash-only facility. No insurance coverage at all, and he's closemouthed about the treatment plans. I haven't confirmed this yet, but there are rumors of psychedelics being used."

"That's suspicious. I'll give you that. Health and Human Services doesn't exactly approve of off-label 'shrooms as a treatment plan. But you said yourself, it's unconfirmed." He looked back at my tack board and squinted. "You don't seem to be going after a regulatory problem. So what's your angle?"

"Did you notice Wykell at Zoe's funeral?"

Michael raised his brows and shook his head.

"I went to the center last Thursday during an open house. Levi came in during the meeting. Of course, I didn't know who he was then, but he was enraged. I heard him say to Wykell, "What did you give her?" Then Friday, after the funeral, he told me he'd never heard of the man. Why would he lie? And who was he concerned about if it wasn't Zoe? Can you explain any of that?"

Michael paused, continuing to look at my board. I could see his mind run through options. He shook his head. "No, I can't."

25

A satisfied smile on my face, I wrapped my hands around a near scalding mug of Earl Grey, inhaling the hint of bergamot and lemon. My computer screen was on, but I had yet to open a single email. Luckily, it was early Monday morning, and there was no one in the Link-Media office to question the Cheshire cat expression on my face.

Michael's breakfast visit Sunday morning had become lunch, which eventually became dinner, and then quickly morphed into a delicious evening of tangled, sweaty sheets before we both woke this morning pre-dawn. I could still feel his hands on my body, and a shiver from the memory ran up my spine. I looked up at the ceiling, let out a breath, and tried to tamp down the post-sex glow. I was never going to get anything done this way.

Looking out at the empty office space, I could feel my present collide with the ghosts of my past. My lusty evening contrasting with the reality that Link-Media had been my deceased husband's business. There were moments when being alone in the office unnerved me, moments when I could still feel Eric's presence—after all, he had founded the company. Link-

Media had been his dream, not mine. However, in the year plus since his death, I had come to feel like its guardian. Not a guardian of Eric's legacy—his legacy was too tarnished for me to honor—but a guardian of the truth. Graft, corruption, greed—there were endless misdeeds to expose, and if I could be responsible for unveiling even a single offense through this media outlet, it was worth every moment of blood, sweat, or tears I could produce.

I scrolled through email since it was too early to hit the phones. The Alderman Flores story was still nebulous, and although I'd handed the bulk of the work off to Brynn, if I didn't have something soon, Borkowski would be handing me my ass. Hopefully Brynn had gotten somewhere with Darius at the check-cashing place, because reading through my notes, I had shit. There was nothing here that hadn't been pounded into the dirt by other journalists. I hammered on the keyboard anyway, filling the page with drivel, falsely hoping that stream of consciousness would lead to a moment of inspiration.

An hour later, I had a rough draft so full of holes and speculation it wouldn't have passed muster with the *National Enquirer*. I wasn't sure if I felt better or worse for having put in the effort.

I printed out the draft and went to see if Brynn was at her desk yet.

"Morning," I said, finding her hunched over her keyboard.

"Hey, how was your weekend?" She sat back and blinked as if her eyes needed to adjust from too much screen time.

"Some good, some not so good," I said, glad I wasn't the blushing type. "There was a death at the Renacido Center on Saturday. A young man named Paul Macanas."

"Oh no. Related?"

"Not sure. But it means I have even less time for this Flores mess." I handed her the draft. "I put some thoughts together. It's garbage, but a start. Let's touch base on the check-cashing situation later, see how it fits in, or doesn't, and maybe we can pull some structure into this thing before Borkowski blows a gasket."

She nodded and took a quick glance at the draft.

"I'm going to try to track down that expert witness this morning," I told her. "The whole situation at the center, and Dr. Wykell in particular, is just feeling off."

"Sure. I'll keep the old man at bay. Just give me a shout when you're ready."

"I need you to work your magic and get personal contact information on the head nurse at the Renacido Center. Her name is Darna Ocampo. My hour of surf only dug up her work info, but I know your techie resources can find it in two seconds. I'd love to speak with her outside of Wykell's supervision. He's got serious control issues."

Brynn turned and let her fingers fly over the keyboard. The nurse's pained face came back to me, but I still hadn't been able to discern its source—conflicted loyalty or patient care.

"You have her direct line at the center, but give me a second," Brynn said. "I should be able to pull that up. Most people aren't buried too deep. Ah, here it is. You ready?"

"Go ahead." I copied down the cell number she gave me, as well as a home address. "Thanks. Once again, I owe you."

"Don't worry. I have the tab running, and review season is just a few months away." She gave me a wink and huge grin.

I laughed, but she was right. This was going to cost me.

I returned to my office, then punched in Darna's cell number. Voicemail. I left a message but wasn't hopeful about a response. It would take serious guilt or personal vulnerability to supersede Dr. Wykell's iron fist.

Dr. Lecaros's office should be open by now. I phoned, only to be told he was in court today and that if I wanted an appointment, he could see me in six weeks. Yeah, right. Instead, I wormed a little information out of his receptionist about his court appearance. Maybe I could catch him before he was called to testify.

I STOOD outside courtroom 304 at the Leighton Criminal Court Building thirty minutes later. Court was already in session, so I nodded hello at one of the security guards and gently pulled open the heavy wooden door and snuck into a seat at the back. Dr. Lecaros was on the stand. Although not a particularly large man, his voice rang with the confidence of two decades of trial work. His bald head, the well-trimmed goatee, the frameless glasses, the impeccably tailored but low-key suit—all told the same story. Authority.

"The concept is known as settled insanity," Lecaros said, speaking to the defense counsel. "It's a permanent condition resulting from long-term, chronic substance abuse in some prone individuals. Psychotic symptoms persist past the stage where drugs can be detected in the body because the brain can no longer function normally. In other words, the drug use has permanently changed the condition and functioning of the brain. Therefore, insanity is not fleeting. It is not an impulsive, uncontrollable, drug-induced action. It indeed has 'settled,' leaving the individual unable to control their behavior or their thinking and therefore unable to know the difference between right and wrong."

Whoa, that was a ballsy defense strategy. *Not guilty because I've done hard drugs for twenty years.* In some rare instances, the settled insanity argument had worked in other states, but in Illinois? I couldn't remember a murder trial that had ever even attempted to make drug use anything more than a contributing factor. I looked at the prosecution table. The lead attorney knew well enough to keep his cool, but a junior attorney assigned to sit behind him and keep him stocked with legal pads was shaking her head and shrugging her shoulders toward the junior associate on her left. I smiled to myself. They'd both get a stern kick in the ass back at the office. Theatrics, if there were any, were the purview of the senior team, not the wet-behind-the-ears legal babies.

The defense continued its line of questioning, pushing Dr. Lecaros on the technical details of how the disorder may have presented. The more he spoke, the more the glow of the expert seemed to bubble up. He sat up straighter, looking down his nose in a way that begged a challenge. I could see this was his ego boost. Lecaros got off on displaying his authority. I wondered how he'd handle the cross-examination?

Expert witnesses were one of those love-them-or-hate-them parts of a trial. They could make your case or do you in if you weren't careful. And a good one charged a shitload of money for the privilege. No wonder Lecaros had turned it into a full-time gig. I looked at my watch, wondering how long he would be on the stand. I'd give it an hour, after which I'd probably need a plan B.

As I listened to the defense counsel work his witness, my legal history had me involuntarily formulating challenge questions and strategizing how I'd move in to neutralize the guy. But backseat lawyering wasn't why I was here.

A Cook County sheriff entered the courtroom, hustling up the aisle toward the judge but motioning toward the defense counsel instead. The attorney stepped over and the two men conferred for a moment, then counsel asked to approach the bench. A moment later the judge called for a one-hour recess. Perfect.

I jumped to my feet, my eyes glued to Dr. Lecaros. After a brief conversation with the attorney, he shuffled out the door, a slim leather briefcase in hand.

I fell into step behind him. "Excuse me. Dr. Lecaros?" I said.

He turned. "Yes?" he said, his eyes narrowing a bit. "You look familiar. Have we met?"

"Only briefly a few years ago. I believe it was the Handforth trial. The charges were dropped as we were about to take your deposition."

"Ah, yes, so it was." He nodded, reflecting back on the fact he'd gotten paid anyway, no doubt. "A brief encounter indeed. I generally remember the attorneys I've had the pleasure of working with," he said, smiling. "Well, it is nice to see you again." He glanced at his watch and adjusted his grip on his briefcase.

"I was wondering if you had a few moments. I have a case I'm working on that I need some insight into, and I thought of you."

"Yes, of course. Just give my office a call and we can set up time for a consult."

He gave me a dismissive smile and kept his eyes trained on the passing attorneys. I wasn't the one buttering his bread unless he had a contract in hand, so I wasn't offended that his attention was elsewhere. Time was money in the legal world.

"Actually, I phoned this morning, and you're booked for the next six weeks. Since you seem to have an unexpected break, perhaps we could speak now?"

"Excuse me? That just isn't how I operate. Send over a brief, and I'll take a look. I'm sure we can find a slot if your matter is urgent."

I'd already spent over two hours waiting for a chance to speak to him, and I wasn't going to give up without another shot. "Perhaps I could ask you a quick question or two now, just to see if I'm in the right ballpark before we schedule, for the sake of efficiency?"

He glanced again at his watch. "Okay, but I may have to cut you off. I do have clients who are expecting me."

"Terrific. Thank you." He hadn't asked for any details about my legal credentials, so I saw no harm in letting him continue to assume there was a paycheck at the end. If the conversation led to a formal meeting, I'd set the record straight.

"The situation I'm researching involves cutting-edge addiction treatment. Perhaps even treatments that do not fall within currently accepted standards of care."

"Alcohol?"

"Opioids, actually. Are there any new drug-based treatments that you're familiar with?"

"Methadone, Suboxone—there are several medication-assisted treatments currently in use. Not that I would describe any of them as new or cutting edge. It's quite the travesty, as far as I'm concerned, that there are so few choices. There is nothing that works fast enough or without quite unpleasant side effects, I'm afraid. Although a number of pharmaceutical companies are working aggressively on additional drugs in the buprenorphine family, they only reduce the withdrawal symptoms. It's not a cure, of course, but simply a transition drug to improve the odds of preventing relapse. The pharmaceutical world—and the FDA, for that matter—is doing a real disservice to the poor individuals afflicted with this disorder."

"What about off-label drugs? Have you heard of any facilities that use protocols that are not approved currently? Rumors, perhaps?"

His brow furrowed as he looked at me. "I get the feeling you have a very specific facility in mind. That's going beyond what we can discuss standing here in a hallway."

"Fair enough. Perhaps if I give you the name of a doctor, you could simply let me know if you're familiar with him? Then we could schedule."

He nodded but looked uncomfortable.

"The psychologist's name is Dr. Troy Wykell. He's the medical director at the Renacido Center. Do you know him?"

Lecaros jolted upon hearing the name but quickly recovered his composure.

"I don't know how you're involved with him, but I'd suggest you stay away. He's dangerous. Flat-out dangerous."

26

"Where are you?" I barked into the phone, hoping Michael would interpret my tone as urgent rather than rude. It was quite a shift from the way we'd said our goodbyes this morning, but my anxiety was ratcheting up.

Although Dr. Lecaros had declined to explain his comments about Dr. Wykell, at least while standing in the middle of a courthouse hallway, his intensity had pushed the right fear buttons in me and I was waiting for a call back from his assistant to schedule a time to discuss the issue privately.

Grilling Michael for answers on Paul Macanas's death suddenly held new importance. It was crossing the line in our agreed-upon boundaries, but I needed to understand where CPD was going in the investigation of the young man's death. And whether Zoe's might be related.

"I'm at the treatment center. Why?" he replied.

"I'll see you in twenty minutes." I heard the word *no* come out of his mouth as I pulled the phone away from my ear but hung up anyway.

Twenty-three minutes later, I was at the Renacido Center.

Michael's SUV sat prominently in the driveway. I parked on the street and saw Officer Wrobleski rooting around the perimeter of the coach house when I got out of the car. It wasn't obvious if he was looking for something specific or if this was a general search. Calculating my odds of gathering information, I headed toward the officer rather than barging up to the front door directly.

"Hey, you doing okay? Saturday was pretty wonky," Wrobleski said, looking me over for signs of instability.

"I'm fine. You have this thing figured out yet?" I smiled at him and jerked my thumb toward the coach house. Wrobleski didn't have a reputation for being a steel trap of information, which was probably why they'd stuck him out here to dig in the dirt.

"Wouldn't it be great if it were that easy." He laughed. "Not exactly a talkative bunch around here, if you know what I mean," he said, nodding his head at the house and hiking up his belt.

"I got that impression too. Any initial thoughts?" I asked, pulling off my sunglasses and tucking the stem into the neckline of my shirt.

"I can't tell if they were letting these kids have a supervised high or trying to bring them back from the brink. Did you see all the IV setups they have upstairs? And there are an awful lot of locked storage cabinets and closets. They won't let me even walk through the place without an escort or a warrant."

That was an angle that hadn't occurred to me, a supervised high. Perhaps it was a method for downshifting tolerance or cravings?

"Is Hewitt around?"

"He's inside chatting up the head doc. I got my crew here in the coach house being led around on a leash by some nurse who won't let them touch anything. You'd think they had the Hope

Diamond stashed out here, as nervous as we're making them while we poke around. I can feel the eyes on the back of my head now. The scary-looking chick has been staring at us from up on the top floor the whole time. I'm expecting to turn around and see her eyes glowing or see her levitating any minute now." He chuckled. "Seems to me, they should all be a little more cooperative after one of their charges croaked. Some lawyer must have coached them."

"It's an odd bunch, that's for sure." I turned toward the house, my head running sprints through the possibilities.

"You should probably wait till Hewitt comes out," he said, watching my gaze. "It'll give them less reason to be spooked, if you know what I mean."

"Sure." I looked back at the house, my eyes drawn to the second-story window. Sure enough, Francesca stood at the glass watching, her eyes in a squint, and sending crazy vibes our way.

"Other than the IVs, have you seen anything else that seems off?" I asked. "What I saw looked like they'd set up as a medical facility, not a support group." I didn't mention snooping in the storage closet or taking photos.

"I don't know what kinda kinky stuff they're doing in there. Maybe scientific experiments or something. But there seems to be an awful lot of little treatment rooms. At least, that's what they look like to me." He leaned in close. "Two of them even have padded walls."

I looked at the coach house one more time. Padded walls? "Maybe it's a precaution for detox?" I said, not even convincing myself.

"I know, right?" Wrobleski said, watching my face. "There's something spooky going on in there. Not that you could tell from the outside. Who knows, maybe they're making smut films. I've seen stranger things. Hidden cameras, chains. I don't make assumptions about anything or anyone when it comes to depravity. Wonder what the neighbors know?"

Movement at the end of the driveway stopped the conversation as Michael came around the side of the building. Janek was right behind him. I left Wrobleski and headed toward them, hoping to have a conversation out of earshot of the rest of his team. Not that I didn't trust Officer Wrobleski, but it was impossible to know who else he was so liberal with in his conversations.

I could see the exhaustion in Janek's face as I neared the men. He was trying to macho through the emotional strain of Zoe's death. Bad move. I knew firsthand how grief had a way of landing on you eventually, usually like a cement truck to the body.

"Was Dr. Wykell cooperative?" I asked, knowing that I wouldn't get a straight answer. It was part of the game. I told them bits of things I'd uncovered, they told me nothing. Our little tango seemed to play out that way on every story that I'd done involving CPD. With a number of less than flattering exchanges between cops and suspects making headline news over the past year, one of the measures the police chief had been drilling into the team was the need for tighter message control. It was hardly his only problem, but I understood his reasoning. Officers had been reminded repeatedly to run everything through the community liaison's office. Michael and Janek both knew me well enough at this point that we understood the boundaries. As long as we kept the one-way street of communication top of mind, everything was cool.

"He is one odd duck," Michael said.

"You mean arrogant prick," Janek added, lowering his sunglasses and shooting me a don't-you-dare-quote-me look.

Janek's true state of mind had been revealed. He would never have denigrated a source publicly under normal circumstances.

"The kid that died Saturday, Paul, does the ME have any idea on the cause of death?" I asked.

"Not yet. But we got the tox report back on Zoe. He's pegged the time of death as roughly the beginning of January," Michael said, looking at Janek, then back at me.

"No heroin in her system, or any other opioids," Janek said.

"Then why did she die?" I asked, my mind running again to Levi's words.

"The ME thinks her heart gave out. Probably damage from her prior drug use," Michael said.

"That damn Levi," Janek spat out. "He got her hooked and didn't give a shit about what happened to her. God knows what she was taking and for how long. That stuff does all kinds of things to your body. Even the straight stuff. Lord knows what it was laced with and what it did to her."

Janek seethed with rage. The veins in his neck bulged, and his jaw was locked down like a vise. This was a man ready to blow.

"Is it possible there were other drugs in her system?" I asked tentatively. Janek was so riled, I was concerned I'd be adding to his burden with the question. "Toxicology doesn't uncover everything, unless you know what to look for. The unusual stuff isn't part of the first pass, and there are a lot of synthetics out there that could be causing all kinds of problems."

"I know how tox screens work, Kellner! You think you need to educate me?" Janek shot back.

"She had a known history with heroin. And the ME looked for all the usual bad shit, fentanyl, etc. He's ready to declare on this one," Michael said, his eyes on his partner.

"How long ago was she a patient here?" I asked.

The men looked at me with confusion, then at each other.

"What?" Janek said. "She was a patient in this loony bin? I don't know anything about that, and neither does her mother."

"How do *you* know that?" Michael asked. "Wait, is this related to that comment you heard Levi make? You don't know he was talking about Zoe. That's nothing but speculation."

Janek swung his head from me to Michael. "Will one of you just tell me what the fuck is going on?"

"Dr. Wykell told me directly that Zoe had briefly been a patient here. He was at her funeral. I'm sorry, but I assumed you knew her treatment history," I said, looking at Janek. "You were occupied with your family and didn't notice, but yes, he was there. He had to have known her or he wouldn't have shown up, so I asked him."

The men were still giving me growly looks.

"Let me back up. A couple days before the funeral I found a stash of brochures for the treatment center in the home where Zoe died. Initially, I was just curious about why they were in the house. Like I told you the other day, I went over and sat in on an open house. That's when Levi stormed in. I didn't know who he was at the time, but I'm certain I heard him say to Wykell, 'What did you give her?' When I later saw both Wykell and Levi at the funeral, that's when I got curious. So I spoke to them both. Levi right after the funeral and Wykell a day later. Wykell told me she had been a patient, and Levi claims he doesn't know who Wykell is. I don't know why, but he's clearly lying for some reason."

Janek seemed to be calming down, but he still had that look on his face that said he was ready to tell me I was full of shit.

"On Saturday, I confirmed it with one of the patients who is receiving treatment now. I showed her Zoe's photo. She said Zoe had been a patient here about nine months ago, maybe as much as a year ago. I would have mentioned it earlier, but it never crossed my mind that Zoe's mom hadn't known. You said there had been a couple of stints at rehab that your sister had paid for. I just assumed this was one of them."

"No, absolutely not." Janek shook his head. "Not a place like this. Theresa is a nurse. She would've never let her daughter hook up with any treatment that didn't have total AMA best practices approval. They did a ton of research before choosing a facility. This never would've passed muster, regardless of how high-and-mighty this guy thinks he is."

"Okay, then Zoe must have done this on her own. Any idea how she would have paid for it?"

It was another question that now connected Zoe and Paul. Neither one of them had the financial resources to swing treatment in this price range.

Janek shrugged, but I had his attention now.

"And the bigger question is, why didn't Wykell tell us himself?" Michael added.

"No," I said. "There's one question even bigger still. Are the two deaths connected?"

27

I stared up at the brick three-flat looking for signs of occupancy. Brynn had tracked down a last-known address for Levi Vinson, but standing here in front of the building, I had my doubts. It had been decades since anyone had put money or attention into this property. Peeling paint, wood rot, a roof missing a third of its shingles—from where I stood, the building looked like it needed to be condemned. Junk mail was piled up on the porch, torn and disintegrating in the weather, and others had been tossed into the scrawny shrubbery by the wind. I saw no signs of Levi's name on the front buzzer near the door, nor did I see the apartment number Brynn had indicated. Perhaps it was a basement unit or had back access. Slimy landlords could always find someone to occupy the most unappealing space if the rent was low enough.

I walked around the side of the building. Finding a path of weeds trampled into the dirt, I continued to the back. There a stairwell descended six steps into a concrete pit. Apartment B1 was scribbled on a piece of cardboard and duct-taped onto the basement door. Dead leaves and standing water littered the foundation. I imagined there was a drain somewhere under the debris that was probably perpetually blocked with garbage and plant material. Apparently the building owner preferred a crumbling foundation and smelly biology experiments.

Oh well, the shoes I'd slipped on this morning were uncomfortable anyway. I looked down into the dark space, took a deep breath, and stepped into the muck.

I knocked hard on the wood and listened for any sign of an occupant but heard nothing. However, a faint light was visible in the glass block window on my left, so I knocked again, harder and longer.

After a few moments, I heard a muffled shout, but the words were unintelligible, so I knocked again. I could hear footsteps now, and seconds later the door opened a few inches. An irritated Levi Vinson stood on the other side of the door, blinking hard to refocus his vision.

He was shirtless, clothed only in a pair of ill-fitting gym shorts. He rubbed his hand over his eyes and then down over his beard.

"What the hell do you want?"

"I want to talk to you about Zoe."

"Jesus Christ! She's dead, all right? What the hell is there to talk about? And why the fuck would I talk to you?" He pinched the bridge of his nose, trying to shake off sleep before looking more closely at me. "You're that woman from the funeral," he said, a scowl quickly crossing his face. "Can't you people just leave me alone?"

"She's dead, Levi, so, no, you are not going to be left alone. Karl Janek isn't about to leave you alone. And it doesn't appear Zoe's mother is going to sit back quietly, either, after burying her daughter. They just want to know what happened to her," I said, softening my tone. "They want to know why she died. Why she died alone in a basement in an abandoned house."

He clenched his jaw and stared at me, anger in his face. Or

was it defiance? Perhaps that was a more accurate assessment. Regardless, it wasn't the emotion I'd seen the other day at the funeral. I couldn't quite get a handle on Levi. His love for Zoe was clear, but there was something else complicating his behavior that I hadn't figured out. Nor was I certain that he could be absolved of guilt.

"Here's what I believe," I said. "I believe that you loved her."

He dropped his head, staring at the floor as if the thought were too much to bear.

"I also believe you may have been the last person to see her alive." I was thinking about his outburst at the treatment center. The vague accusation he'd made and what it might have meant. Levi had been too upset at the time to notice anyone else in the room, let alone me. He blamed Wykell for something. But it wasn't quite time to make him aware that I had seen the exchange.

"We're just trying to figure out what happened to her. Don't you want to know that too? Or do you already know?" My voice was firm. I let the accusation sit there, hoping that his love for Zoe would prevail over whatever battles were going on inside him.

He cleared his throat and opened the door the rest of the way. "Come on in." I followed him in to a concrete room where the scent of mildew and stale cigarettes hit me immediately. A single bare bulb hung over a folding card table. On top of a stash of plastic milk crates, a microwave and electric hot pot filled in as a makeshift kitchen. The floor held a single twin mattress with a stained pillow and threadbare blanket. T-shirts and jeans were piled on a stack of boxes.

He plopped into a folding chair at the card table, and I sat across from him feeling the squish of stagnant water in my shoes and repressing visions of flesh-eating bacteria.

"So, am I right? Did you see Zoe while she stayed at the home on Pierce?"

He chewed on his lip and stared at the table, debating, his internal monologue playing out.

"Look, you either saw Zoe or you didn't. Can you just tell me the last time you saw her?"

"It was the end of last year. Thanksgiving. We didn't have anybody to spend the day with. It's not like our families are inviting us over for their festivities. Easier to pretend we don't exist." His tone was full of resentment. He sighed and leaned back in the chair. "Yeah, I knew she'd been staying over at that house, so I scrounged up a meal and we had our own little celebration. It's not like we had a lot to be thankful for, but there was something about it that made us feel a little more normal. Just some grocery store sandwiches and beer from the Jewel, but that's what we did."

"And she'd been living in the house for a while at that point?"

He nodded but didn't lift his head, seemingly fixated on a hangnail he kept picking at. It was hard to look at him and not wonder about how his life had taken a downward turn, what it would have been or could be without the damage drugs had done. But so far he was doing little to build my trust.

As I waited for him to say something more, a clear plastic tub tucked into a corner on the floor caught my eye. Baggies of brown powder, a scale, a metal scoop. Looked like the kid was still in business, but given the quality of his accommodations, he couldn't be moving much product or was using his own supply. I quickly looked away. He'd never talk if he thought I had caught him in the lie.

"She'd been there a few months, I think," he said. "It's not like she had anyplace else to go. She crashed with me, here, for a while before that, but after we broke up, she found that place."

"And did the two of you get high together on Thanksgiving?"

His head shot up. "No, hell no! We were both clean. It wasn't easy, but we were clean."

His vehemence seemed authentic, but that didn't mean he knew the details of Zoe's habit after they'd separated. Or that he'd stopped dealing. Although there had been no opioids in Zoe's system at the time of her death, we had no real idea of her sobriety.

"How do you know Dr. Wykell?" I asked, deciding to probe for links between them.

He drew back, his eyes getting a little wider. I could see I'd caught him off guard. He checked himself and slouched back into the chair.

"Why do you think I know him?"

"Because I was at the center a few days ago. The afternoon you came into the meeting."

He stared back at me, his eyes shaded, trying to read me. Assessing whether I was telling the truth and how much I had heard. Given his agitation at the open house, he might not even remember exactly what he had said.

"What was all that about? You seemed really angry with him. Were you a patient? Was Zoe?"

He stayed silent, his attention back on his nails. I let him sit, let the silence and his own conscious weigh on him.

"We were both patients," he said, his voice cracking. "At least we both started the program. I don't think either one of us lasted more than a week and a half."

"Why was that?"

"Things just got weird. They control everything. When you woke up, when you ate, talk sessions, rules for everything you did, IV treatments every day. It was like being in jail."

"That doesn't sound all that weird to me, under the circumstances. At least it doesn't sound all that different than any other rehab center."

Patients walked out of treatment all the time, fabricating excuses for why it was just too hard to comply with rules they found onerous. It was common and a sign of not being ready to face the work versus anything inherently wrong with the treatment protocol.

"I got spooked, okay? It was my roommate. He came back from a treatment session, something where they had him in the coach house locked up for two days. When he came out, something wasn't right with him. It was like he'd changed. His whole personality had changed. I thought about that Stepford wife thing, where the women move in and have some weird operation that their husbands secretly set up. Afterward, they're all docile and have big boobs. You know that movie?" He shrugged. "I don't know, but the guy changed. There was just something different about him that I couldn't deal with. It was him, but not him. He was empty inside, like his mind was altered. I kept looking at his head for scars to see if they'd drilled holes in him or something. The staff was so proud of him, thrilled to see how he was afterward. It scared the fuck out of me. I sure as hell didn't want to be turned into some zombie. So I split."

"What do you think they did to him?" The IVs and padded rooms came back into my mind. Levi was making it sound like a chemical lobotomy. It might also explain his accusation.

"I don't know. I didn't see any scars. You can't exactly hide a lobotomy, but somehow they messed with his mind. How do you do that? Drugs? Electric shock? I wasn't going to let somebody put electrodes on my head and turn me into a eunuch. So I got the hell out. There'd been rumors about some experimental drug they're using. Something that might not be legal, but what do I know? Those are just rumors."

"Patients aren't told what the treatment will involve?" My

mind was racing as I watched Levi. His account of the coach house jived with what I'd seen, but the IV treatments could just have easily been nutritional. Every major city had walk-in IV hydration facilities where two hundred dollars could get you a Myers' Cocktail and B12 infusion, not exactly sketchy science. Perhaps Levi simply didn't know what his roommate's personality was like without mind-altering chemicals.

"They keep you in the dark intentionally," he said. "You wake up in the morning and they don't tell you what they're going to do till they're just about to do it. As if that's supposed to make you feel more comfortable." He shrugged again. "They kept talking about the need for secrecy, that there were some bigger plans, that they had an investor who was going to make the place a big deal. I thought it was all bluff. A way to keep us from freaking out."

"And did Zoe leave the center when you did?"

"Not long after. She wasn't as freaked out by what happened to my roommate, but she didn't see him. I think she just didn't want to stay there alone."

"Do you remember when this was?"

"A year ago, maybe even a little more. That's when I got serious about getting myself clean. Didn't want to go back to a treatment center, and if I didn't start taking charge of my problems, I was going to be dead or chained to a bed in jail or running from my suppliers. Figured those were all bad choices. I stopped all the shit and got a job at this club down on Halstead, Rocket Lounge, kind of a dive but they pay cash."

Levi appeared to be sincere about having gotten clean, although the stash in the corner suggested his selling days weren't over. However, all addicts, at some point convinced themselves and loved ones that this time they were serious. I didn't know the odds, but promises made were not the same as promises kept.

"And how did you pay for this? The treatment center, I mean. Excuse the assumption, but it doesn't appear that you are in a financial position to be able to afford inpatient care. I know it's a very personal question, but Zoe wasn't in a position to pay for it either, and I know her mother didn't pay, so I'm curious about the financial arrangement."

"No, I'm not offended. I wouldn't be living in this shit hole if I had another choice. The center has a special program for people who aren't rich. You don't pay anything until you get through the first month. After that, they have some kind of scholarship. I don't remember exactly what he called it. They work some bookkeeping magic to make it all happen. You have to sign some papers saying that you won't sue them, but it seemed like a good deal to me. They told me not to worry about it, that I'd get treatment even if I didn't have the coin to cover it."

"That's a very unusual financial model," I said. Wykell didn't seem to be in the charity business, and without insurance or government agencies to foot the bill, that left a huge question to be answered. And the threat of lawsuits seemed to be the least of it.

"On the one hand, it kinda makes sense, if you think about it," Levi said. "Pretty hard to have a conversation about your addiction when your head is all fucked up. Takes a while for shit to get cleaned out of your system. But I didn't get through the month, so I don't know what kind of quid pro quo they're looking for. Maybe you gotta scrub toilets with a toothbrush for the next twenty years?"

"And how did Zoe stay clean?"

"I guess you have to define the word *stay*. She struggled, like we all do. We were both clean when we left the center, but for Zoe, it didn't last. She relapsed, and when I saw her for our Thanksgiving, she was going to give Dr. Wykell another try. That was the last time I talked to her, because she stopped taking my calls. Like I told you at the funeral, I left a bunch of messages and texts, but she never responded. Then her mom cut off her phone. I went over to the house a couple of times after, but she wouldn't answer. Someone at the center had hooked her up with the place initially. But it didn't look like anybody was living there, so I thought maybe she left, moved in someplace else." He blinked back tears, then looked away.

"Do you remember when you were last at the house?"

"January, I think. It's all kind of a blur. I guess she was just down in that basement dying while I pounded on the door like a schmuck."

28

Guilt could eat away at your insides.

I sat in the car pondering my conversation with Levi. His grief was real, but I still felt he knew more than he was saying. He had seemed so sure of Wykell's guilt when he confronted him that I was convinced Levi had more information about Wykell. Was it torturing him that Zoe had been in that basement dying when he might have been able to help, or because he had contributed to her death through inaction? Either way, it was a horrendous burden to carry. So why was he holding back?

If he had known the smack was cut with something toxic, or if he'd participated in Zoe's death, there was no place on the planet he'd be able to hide from Janek. But that didn't explain Paul's death or the fact that they had both been patients at the Renacido Center. This was about the center. I grabbed my phone and dialed Brynn.

"I forgot to ask earlier, have you gotten any of the information I was looking for on the treatment center?"

"Yeah. Hold on." I could hear paper rustling. "They incorporated in 2005, privately held, your guy, Dr. Wykell, is listed as the principal. The building, however, is in the name of another corporation, Planck Holdings. They purchased the building in the middle of the market crash in '08. No record of a mortgage, so this looks to be a cash purchase."

"Anything odd in the zoning?"

"Looks okay on the surface."

"Maybe," I said. "Chicago's wacky zoning codes aren't so clear. You need a PhD in housing development or an alderman on your payroll to understand that mess. Based on what I've seen, there seems to be at least basic medical treatments being performed at the facility. I'm also not sure these guys are completely forthcoming, perhaps even hiding some of their treatment modalities."

Wykell seemed like an "ask permission later" type of guy. And if there was as much money to be made on a miracle treatment as I suspected, obstacles such as government agencies were nothing but an annoying fly to be swatted away, at least as long as the benefit outweighed the risk. Especially if he thought he could get away with it until it was time to go public.

"Well, if they are concealing medical care, that could be a huge legal mess," Brynn said. "I would imagine the inspection and reporting process for treatment facilities is quite different than for a therapist's office. So how would they get away with that?"

"I don't know. This feels like a drug treatment protocol to me. This might sound like I'm going off the deep end, but what if it's an experimental drug or a unique combo of meds? It's the only thing that I can think of that would lead to enough financial gain to make the risk worthwhile. If they're experimenting with any non-FDA-approved chemical, the question that comes to my mind is, are they hiding something because the regulations are onerous or because they need patients as guinea pigs?"

Stories of quack doctors who'd bilked the vulnerable out of their hard-earned cash were all over the internet. Every year, desperate people forked over millions of dollars for nonexistent miracle cures when the sales pitch was compelling enough. Why not addiction treatment too?

"They could be slipping money to someone to look the other way," Brynn added.

"Yet another possibility," I said, thinking of Alderman Flores. Run-of-the-mill greed was a requirement for the office of alderman. No reason it wouldn't be part of this district as well. "From outward appearances, it's possible none of the neighbors were aware. It's not like there are ambulances pulling in and out. I'm not suggesting they've got a hard-core medical facility set up, but it's certainly conceivable that they're skirting the boundaries of legality with the treatments they're conducting. Let's do some digging to see if we can understand how far they can push the medical angle without needing a whole host of complicated processes and reporting."

"And the prying eyes of inspector types."

"Exactly. There were tons of IV setups in the coach house. I don't know if they're doing anything more advanced. I didn't see a surgical suite or anything."

"I think the insurance angle could also be a good one to explore. Even if they don't accept medical coverage, the business has to have malpractice insurance and property coverage. It could be helpful to know where they're placing their their priorities and how the risk is balanced. I'll add that to the list as well," Brynn said.

"Great idea. Talk to you tomorrow."

From what I could tell, the death over the weekend had not received any news coverage. I assumed the family was arranging an obituary, but a drug-related death printed in a back column of a newspaper wouldn't connect to the center.

A new thought came into my mind. There might be a benefit to making the connection public if raising the heat caused Wykell to react. I ran off the copy in my head, just a simple short piece, appropriately placed, stating the death had occurred while Paul Macanas was a patient at the Renacido Center.

It would force the center to try to explain Paul's death in some way that wouldn't scare off new patients, damage the center's reputation, or bring unwanted attention from regulators. It was a tough ask even for the most experienced of PR reps. Overdoses were explainable, but a death at the center during treatment would require a tightly coordinated campaign, particularly if there were expansion plans. An event like this had the potential to end any shot Dr. Wykell had at a financial windfall, unless he could keep it quiet or spin it as just another example of the ravages of addiction. The important point, for my purposes, was that it would raise the temperature of the pot and make Wykell react. I just had to do it without my byline.

It was late afternoon as I stood on the sidewalk in front of The Rusty Bucket, calling Darna Ocampo for the second time. I stared up at a neon Bud Light sign and weather-beaten door as I left the nurse another message and wondered how long it had been since I'd fit the demographics of this type of watering hole. Probably freshman year of college with a fake ID.

The bar was only two blocks from Wrigley Field, but the street did not yet hint at the crowds that would come over the next few hours. Although the Cubs were scheduled to play this evening in Philadelphia instead of at home, the bars would still be overflowing with fans cheering them on.

As I walked in the door and paused for a moment, letting my eyes adjust to the dim light and hoping my nose would adjust to the stench of a dirty fryer and stale beer. I imagined the scent was embedded in every absorbent surface after years of exposure. Four solo men were settled in with their drinks when I took a seat at the bar. I got the impression a drink at four thirty in the afternoon wasn't an unusual event for these guys, but the raised eyebrows told me seeing someone who looked like me pull up a stool was. One guy in a John Deere T-shirt leaned so far off his chair to check me out, he spilled his beer.

The bartender approached, setting down a coaster and a glass of water. He was about my age with intricate, colorful tattoos covering both forearms. His beard was thick and well maintained, and he sported a T-shirt advertising some brand of tequila that I had never heard of, not that I was any kind of connoisseur.

"What can I get you?" he asked, smiling.

I fumbled for a moment, feeling awkward about ordering my usual. I doubted that their Cabernet would live up to anything I could actually swallow.

"How about a bottle of Corona?" I said, feeling that was a safe choice and more appropriate for the venue.

"You got it." He stepped away and opened the cooler, popped the top on the bottle, inserted a lime slice, and brought it over.

"You're a little early for the game," he said, ESPN playing on the three screens behind the bar.

"I imagine you get quite a crowd in here. I hope you've got some backup help coming in for tonight," I said, lifting the bottle to my mouth.

"The reinforcements will be here within the hour. We always have a lot of prep work to do on game days. Our crowd has simple tastes in booze, but you gotta make sure you're well stocked so the glasses are kept full and the pretzels keep coming."

Mr. John Deere was lumbering toward me, unsteady on his

feet. There was a smile on his face that I assumed he meant as suave but only came across as creepy.

"Henry, go back and sit down," the bartender said. "The lady isn't here to make new friends." JD let out a boozy guffaw but, thankfully, did as he was told. "He's harmless but persistent after tipping back a little liquid courage. Thought I should save you the grief."

I laughed. "I appreciate that. Um, quick question for you. Did a guy named Paul Macanas used to work here?"

He stopped wiping the glass in his hand and looked at me, his eyes curious. "Yes, he did. Left about three months ago, I think."

"Do you know why he left?"

"He said he was going into rehab. It was no secret he had a problem, so I'm not just spreading gossip. He was very public about it. How do you know Paul?"

"Just from the bar," I said, formulating a quick lie. "I don't come in often, but he was always really nice to me. You know how it is when a single woman comes in. Some guys think she's there for more than just a drink, you know?" I tipped my head toward Henry and smiled. "Paul was always considerate that way. Shooed away the assholes that were being obnoxious." Somehow these lies were flowing freely from my mouth. I might not have had the experience I relayed at this particular bar, but it was a universal truth that every woman knew, so I told myself it was only half a lie.

"Yeah, he's a good guy. I hope he gets his act together. I'd sure like him back. Told him he has a job whenever he's ready. Most people aren't so open with their struggles," he said, setting down the glass he'd been cleaning. "Everybody's got shit in their life or knows someone who does. It's no reason to treat people like they're defective."

"That means he felt it was safe to talk here," I said, admiring the openness of the bartender's response. "That's equally important. And something most people don't have, either."

It was surreal to sit here and speak about the man as if I didn't know he was dead. Images of his convulsing body wouldn't leave my mind, but I couldn't be the one to say the words. His former employer would have to learn of his fate from someone else. I wasn't sure if I was being cowardly or calculating, probably both, if I was honest with myself, but it just felt like the news needed to come from someone other than a reporter.

"Fair enough." He nodded pensively, as if the thought hadn't occurred to him before.

"Had he been struggling to get clean for a while?" I asked, taking a swig of the beer. I was trying to sound casual, to figure out how to ask the questions without sounding like a reporter. And the sour stink of old booze was giving me a headache, so I also needed to be efficient if I had any hope of keeping the discomfort from ruining my night.

"Yeah, he's gone twice before. I guess that's normal. Like most people, he said he'd tried a bunch of stuff, but none of it worked for long. He was really excited about this new place. Said they had some out-there philosophies, but he was willing to do just about anything to get clean."

"Sounds expensive. Tough on a bartender's salary."

"Yeah, I asked him about that." He shrugged, clearly finding it odd as well. "And it's not like he has health insurance that would cover it. He said the center had some kind of trade deal and he wouldn't have to pay anything. Sounded wacky to me."

There it was again, another patient who had made some unusual financial accommodations with the center. I understood why the patient would be interested, but what did the center get in return?

"All I could think of was that he was going to become a lab

rat or they'd force him to donate a kidney." The bartender laughed. "What do I know? Maybe they're locking him in a room to perform sex acts. I think he'll do just about anything if it gets him clean."

29

He was going to become a lab rat.

Was the bartender at The Rusty Bucket on to something? I was sitting at a table at Proxi waiting for Cai, furiously Googling drugs used for addiction treatment and trying to remember the medication families Dr. Lecaros had mentioned when I'd spoken to him at the courthouse. Medication-assisted treatment, or MAT, was a common protocol for opioids. Methadone was the most familiar, but there was no real money to be made off a drug with an established history. Buprenorphine. That was it. That was one of the drugs Lecaros had referenced. I scrolled further, learning it was also well established but could be fatal if taken with alcohol or other drugs that slowed breathing. That could explain an accidental death, but I wasn't seeing how a profit motive worked into that theory.

"Can I get you something to drink while you wait?"

A young woman in an industrial-chic apron, retro Levi's, and braids stood at my side. I was on my fourth Tic Tac since forcing down half a beer at "the Bucket" and desperately needed to get rid of the unappealing aftertaste the mints weren't removing.

"You sure can." I took a quick glance at the menu. "Bring me a carafe of Cabernet, the Australian, and an order of the mung bean dumplings to start. We'll figure out the rest after my friend arrives. And we're going to be in the slow group tonight, so no need to rush anything out of the kitchen."

"Got it. Rush the booze, slow the food." She smiled.

Proxi was a wonderful West Loop addition to the Chicago restaurant scene, serving an eclectic but delicious changing array of internationally inspired street food. As bland as they sounded, the dumplings were actually delightfully flavorful, and there was a chance Cai would need to order her own. Despite the international menu, the decor was a modern mix of warm woods, moody colors, encaustic floor tiles, and fabulous unique lighting that I lusted after. I came for the design inspiration as much as for the food.

With the Cabernet poured and beginning to do its job adjusting my taste buds, I struggled to come up with a rational theory on how Wykell could make money off of treatment. The guy didn't run a testing lab. He wasn't working on some new prescription drug to take to market. He didn't play in that world.

But Kendall *had* mentioned mushrooms. Sipping my wine, I was back on Google researching the use and status of psilocybin. Classified as a schedule 1 narcotic, it was considered highly addictive and of no medical use. Despite a long and complicated history, it was illegal to manufacture, distribute, or possess; however, there were a number of existing clinical trials underway exploring the use of psilocybin to possibly treat alcoholism, PTSD, and depression. Could Wykell be conducting his own studies on opioid abuse using patients as guinea pigs?

"Are you drinking that whole carafe yourself?"

Cai was at the table looking as much the radiant, kick-ass attorney as she always did. The jacket to her fitted navy suit was slung over her shoulder, her silk blouse was still perfectly pressed, and the black four-inch Louboutin pumps she favored seem to grace her feet without a pinch. I loved great shoes, but those pointed-toe torture devices were not my idea of fun.

I stood and gave her a hug. "Since you were on a martini kick the last time we went out, I ordered the half bottle. You want a glass, or shall we get the server back?"

"No, this is definitely a martini night."

I flagged over my gal and got Cai taken care of. "So what's driving you to drink now?" I asked, shoving the last dumpling over to Cai.

"Please. You know the drill. Impossible clients who want to litigate every damn point, then don't want to pay the bill. Clients you know are lying through their teeth and then want to use a brother-in-law as their alibi. The list never ends. Some weeks are just more full of shit than others. So is Lane back in town yet?"

"She was supposed to land this afternoon. I haven't heard from her. She'd only get a piece of my mind, anyway. But CPD is done processing the house, so what she does with it from here is her business. I'm out of it."

"Except for the part about why the girl died." She looked at me over the top of her glass, eyebrows raised. "Come on, Nancy Drew. You're neck deep in this. Don't pretend otherwise. So what's the latest on your undercover work? I want the deets."

This was one of the many reasons I adored Cai. She always cut through the BS.

"There's been another death."

"At the house? What?"

"Sorry, I haven't had a chance to catch you up. Here's the short version. The woman that died at Lane's property is a former patient at this rehab center up in Buena Park. Another patient from the facility died over the weekend. Without going into all the details, I think the director might be using off-label drugs or some other protocol outside FDA approval. And the boyfriend may be involved. I was researching psilocybin before you got here, trying to narrow down a theory."

Our server stopped by our table and we added baby octopus, grilled carrots, and yellowtail and grapefruit salad to our order.

"Okay." Cai paused, spearing the last bite of dumpling and contemplating my assertion. "So you're thinking that the off-label drug is having an unintended consequence or an adverse reaction is occurring. Wouldn't the drug show in the tox report?"

"Depends. Janek's niece had no opioids in her system. But you only find what you're looking for, right?"

"What's the ME saying?"

"That it was her heart. An undiagnosed condition. Possibly damage from the heroin."

"I can't say you're making much of a case, but you wouldn't be stuck on this if you didn't have a damn good reason to be, so let's brainstorm. Play out your scenarios, and I'll be your sounding board."

She lifted her martini, then leaned her elbows on the table, waiting.

"Do I need to call you Professor Farrell now?"

She smirked and flipped me a middle finger.

"No sense of humor." I smiled and shook my head at her. "I believe money is at the root of whatever is going on. That the director is trying to package a protocol he can sell. A protocol with claims of dramatic and fast results. Which means it's something not currently recognized or accepted by the traditional addiction treatment programs."

"So a get-sober-quick plan instead of a get-rich-quick plan."

"Yes, and in his implementation, there have been cases of adverse effects. Probably unintended, possibly avoidable, but deadly and certainly not helpful to his sales pitch."

"But Janek's niece didn't die during treatment, did she?"

"Not as far as I know, but we really don't know her timeline,"

I said, remembering Levi's claim that Zoe intended to return to the center. "Maybe the substance damaged her heart, and therefore death wasn't immediate. Or there was an interaction with something else she took. I mentioned a boyfriend. He was her dealer. Maybe his supply was cut with something. Maybe in trying to help, he gave her something that inadvertently killed her. A lot of people play pharmacist when they shouldn't."

"And you started with psilocybin. Makes sense. It fits some of the criteria for an off-label drug. I've heard of its use in treating alcoholism. Any evidence of it causing heart issues or death?"

"No." I shook my head. "Worst case seems to be hallucinations or long-term psychosis. Unless it's combined with other drugs or there's something unique to the victims, it's not high on the list."

"Then maybe you need to start with a drug that has risks for heart issues, and see if the addiction piece works in after. If it's a drug cocktail, that's going to be harder to pinpoint."

"Yeah, I need to consult a pro on the drug front. I'm a little out of my league. I arranged a meeting for tomorrow with Dr. Franklin Lecaros. Do you know the name? He's one of the top experts in addiction in the city, does a lot of expert witness work."

"Only by reputation. Let me know what you think of him. I may have some work for him if he's as good as everyone says." She leaned in. "CEO of an unnamed local institution who has a nose candy problem. Paralyzed a guy on his way home from the strip club. Marriage isn't salvageable, but the guy wants to stay out of jail. Imagine." She shook her head and laughed.

My phone pinged. A text from a number I didn't recognize, but the area code was local.

Cnt stop them crows eating my hnds k.

What? I read the text again.

"What is it?"

"I have no idea. Look."

"Weird. You don't recognize the number?"

"No clue. Probably a misdial." But I was uneasy. I was tempted to text back, but given the distress in the message, I did something uncharacteristic. I phoned. After four rings: "Hey, it's Kendall. You know what to do."

30

I hated being ignored. More accurately, I hated being ignored when someone was trying to avoid answering questions. Yet here I sat in my car, parked across the street from nurse Darna Ocampo's Roscoe Village apartment building. After returning from dinner with Cai last night, I'd placed my third phone call, and surprise, surprise, the woman had ignored me again. So I'd said the hell with it and parked myself on her street at 6:30 this morning. After Paul's death, she was lucky that I was the one stalking her. If they hadn't already, it was only a matter of time before CPD would be asking far more complicated questions. And likely questions that would be asked under the watchful eye of a camera and a recording device.

Brynn had sent me a deeper dive into the nurse's background last night, but I was tired of sitting and getting tired of scrolling my phone out of boredom. I was tempted to get out of the car and stretch my legs, but that would only increase the odds that Darna would see me before I saw her and head out the back door.

I was also deeply concerned by the strange text Kendall had sent. I'd left two phone messages and a text checking on her but had yet to receive a reply. I also knew some rehab centers confiscated electronic devices, so perhaps she'd gotten caught with the contraband. I didn't expect the Renacido Center to be cooperative if I called to inquire about her, but if I didn't hear back from her soon, I'd make that call anyway.

I switched the car radio over to NPR and tried to distract myself with something useful while I waited. As the host droned on with the latest call for fundraising, I saw movement at the front door of the four-story wood-frame building. There she was. I watched for a moment, then grabbed my purse and got out of the car, crossing the street to follow. I didn't know if she was heading toward a car parked further down the block or toward public transportation, so I picked up my pace. If she got into a vehicle before I got to her, I'd be pretty pissed with myself.

A khaki trench coat was belted around her waist, and she carried a plastic grocery bag that seemed to stand in for a tote bag. She was also walking faster than I would've imagined by the looks of her. Her lime green Adidas sneaks were outpacing my wedge-heel espadrilles.

"Excuse me," I called out when I was ten feet behind her. She kept walking as if she hadn't heard me, then brought a hand up to adjust earbuds hidden under her hair.

"Darna Ocampo," I said, calling her name louder this time. She had just reached the crosswalk and turned, removing the earpiece.

"Yes? Who are you?" She looked me up and down, momentarily caught unaware and unable to place me.

"We met at the center over the weekend. My name is Andrea Kellner," I said, handing her a card.

Recognition flooded her face, and she shook her head before tossing the card onto the ground and continuing on her way.

"Paul is dead. You're going to have to talk about it eventually," I said to the back of her head.

"I have nothing to say to you." She stopped as a small Sprinter van barreled into the intersection, giving me a chance to get in front of her. There was anger in her voice, but the flush of red that was just now dotting her cheeks told another story. "If I had wanted to talk, I would've returned your multiple phone calls. Now if you'll excuse me, I need to get to work."

She moved to the right, attempting to step around me, but I matched her.

"You've worked as lead nurse at the Renacido Center for about seven years, ever since Dr. Wykell opened the facility. Prior to that you were at Rush Medical Center. You've never been married, currently provide a home to two cats, both tabbies. Your salary is $65K, and you send some of that to a nursing home in Rockford where your mother is currently receiving care for Alzheimer's."

I rattled off the tidbits of the nurse's life intending them to be a reminder of what she stood to lose. Now I really did owe Brynn.

Darna drew in a rush of air, but she gave no other indication that it would be enough to change her mind. People were always surprised at the level of personal information that was easily found with a few clicks of a mouse—addresses, places of employment, legal history, debt level. In this era of digital information, basic job history was nothing. Brynn could probably find out how much she spent feeding her felines and what brand.

"Have other patients died while you've been associated with the clinic?" Since she'd wasted my time, I went directly for the jugular. By blowing off my first call, she'd frittered away her chance at delicate questioning.

She turned and stared at me, hatred searing her eyes. She swallowed hard, the patches of red now blotching her neck and chest, a sign of discomfort that exceeded her ability to control it.

"How dare you make accusations!" she shot at me, spittle forming at the corner of her mouth.

"That wasn't an accusation. It was a question. The type of question that you will likely get at trial." I knew I was pressing hard, prosecutor mode coming back to me as if I'd never left the law. But it was necessary for her to be scared. Necessary for reality to sink in. A trial wasn't certain, but tough questions were definitely in her future, one way or another.

"Trial? You're just trying to scare me. Now leave me alone." Again she tried to sidestep me but was so unnerved by the confrontation that she couldn't decide on a path.

"Look, you and I were both there when Paul died. I saw you attempt to help him. I saw Dr. Wykell ignore you, saw him push you away. He prevented you from offering medical assistance. Would it have changed the outcome? I don't know. But both of us would be sleeping easier if you had been able to try," I said, my voice softer. "Let's just talk about the center for now. Tell me about the program. What you do and how you do it. Tell me what's unique about your protocol." I paused, giving her time to process. "You're going to want me in your corner."

I was laying on the guilt as thick as I could manage. I was also counting on self-preservation. Her desire to save her own ass would, at some point, have to outweigh her loyalty to her employer. If she knew what I suspected she knew, that calculation would have to enter her mind.

"I can't talk to you." Her eyes were downcast, and she was fiddling with the handle on the grocery bag, as if unsure which hand to hold it in.

"Sooner or later you're not going to have a choice. CPD may not have brought you in yet, but they will. They aren't going to let a young man die without explanation. Particularly after seeing Dr. Wykell practically forbid you to treat him. The medical examiner *is* going to determine cause of death. And

CPD *will* know more than you think they do when they bring you in. They'll know if you lie or if Wykell lies. I hope you have a good attorney."

My pressure campaign seemed to be having the desired effect. Her breathing had gotten heavy, and a bead of sweat appeared on her upper lip. It was hard to tell how she was rationalizing her involvement. The usual explanations generally revolved around fear of losing a job or hey-he-did-it-I-was-just-along-for-the-ride.

I adjusted my tone. "I know that you are just trying to do your job, but if there's something going on—loose standards, inadequate monitoring, something that could have contributed to Paul's death—you need to figure out how to talk about it, because if you don't, you *will have* contributed to his death. At least that's how a prosecutor will present it."

"You don't understand," she burst out, her voice cracking. "When I say I can't talk, I mean *can't*, not I don't want to. I signed a document. A legal document preventing me from saying anything about the center."

"A confidentiality agreement?" It was inherent in HIPAA that patients' medical details were treated with the utmost privacy, but she seemed to be suggesting she couldn't even discuss the center itself.

"Yes, we all have to sign them. And they get renewed every year, if we want to keep our jobs."

"Okay," I said, my mind moving back into lawyer mode. "Documents like this can be nullified in court. I'm sure that Dr. Wykell is being cautious. He has to protect his reputation, particularly in this business, but that doesn't mean it's written in concrete. An attorney can give you an opinion on your risk." Seeing her indecision, I added, "If you don't have one, I know someone who can look over the contract for you. It might help you understand your options."

"No, I don't think you understand. Dr. Wykell is not concerned just with his reputation. This is about the protocol. He doesn't want anyone to discuss the details. There is a fortune on the line. If anyone talks now, it would end his expansion plans. And our careers."

31

Dangerous. Dr. Lecaros had described Wykell as dangerous.

That language wouldn't have been used without an incident or a shared patient. Lecaros would not have used inflammatory language without a very good reason. Attorneys were often preceded by their reputations, and it stood to reason therapists were too, so I had phoned someone I knew would take my call—my own shrink.

"Thanks for seeing me on such short notice, Dr. Takeda."

She was standing in the doorway to her private office when I walked in. It had been a couple of months since I'd felt the need for her guidance, yet her kind smile greeted me as if it had only been last week. She was a tiny, graceful woman, birdlike in stature, whose steel spine wasn't immediately obvious. I loved that about her. There was something I enjoyed about women who were easily dismissed because of their looks, or size, or demeanor, but who, underneath the facade, could take down a country if they had to.

I imagined it said something Freudian about me, but I wasn't sure I cared to know.

"Andrea, I always make time for you if I can. And will you please start calling me Janice. I think we've known each other long enough," she said as we settled in to the club chairs in front of her desk. "So tell me what's going on."

"Actually, I'm not here today about my life. I need some professional input. There's a story I'm working on, well, a potential story, and there are some things about it I don't understand. I was hoping that you could give me a little background or perhaps a referral to someone else who does this kind of work."

"I'm not quite sure what you're asking." She cocked her head slightly and crossed her hands on her lap. "I can't offer a professional opinion on a patient that I have not treated. And if I had treated that individual, as you know, there are confidentiality requirements and expectations between a doctor and a patient."

"No, I wasn't clear. I'm not expecting you to discuss anything related to a specific patient or a diagnosis. And this is completely off the record. I'm looking for background. My questions are more about what would be normal under specific circumstances. And you may not be able to answer directly, but I thought at the very least, you might be able to steer me to someone who could."

My words seemed to satisfy her apprehension, and her brow relaxed.

"Okay, tell me what you want to know, and I'll see if it's something that I can assist with. I'll tell you if anything is out of my range of experience or if I'm uncomfortable with the question, and we can proceed accordingly. Sound good?"

Lavender wafted over from the essential oil diffuser she kept on her bookshelf. I'd forgotten about it, the memory of the calming scent buried in my subconscious. Had that been the intent, or had I simply been too distraught during my visits to identify it? It was immensely pleasant and soothing. Sitting next to the diffuser, an amethyst geode. Perhaps there was something to the crystals and incense I needed to reconsider, but it was a subject for another day.

"Perfect," I said, returning to the subject at hand. "I'm investigating a death. A young woman in her early twenties with a known history of heroin addiction. I've learned that she had been in rehab a number of times yet continued to relapse."

"That certainly is not unusual, particularly with young people who have yet to grapple with the extent of their problems or who do not have family support. It can also be a function of the length of the addiction. If the individual has been addicted for some length of time and has only recently started to deal with their issues, those relapses can be quite a problem."

"As far as you know, is there any gold standard of care when it comes to treatment?"

"We're certainly all familiar with the inpatient residential treatment centers, and for many, that model remains quite effective but that is such an individualized situation. This is an inappropriate analogy, but it's like asking if there's one best method for weight loss. What works for some won't work for others. Different strokes for different folks, if I must continue with the bad euphemisms. But I'm not telling you anything you didn't know already. Is there something specific here that you're looking to gain knowledge of?"

As usual, she cut through the clutter.

"Indulge me for just another minute." I wanted to make sure my base assumptions were on point. "And the tactics used during inpatient treatment are what?"

"I'm not sure I like the word *tactics*." She smiled. "But I understand your point. Treatment has a number of stages. First, one must address the need for detox. Assessment of the physical condition of the individual patient at the point they come into the center. Obviously, talk therapy can be only minimally effective if someone's in liver failure, for example. So the first stage would be evaluating and stabilizing the individual as the drug or drugs of choice work their way out of the body."

"And that would include treating withdrawal symptoms, correct?"

"Absolutely. Those physical symptoms can be quite severe and quite painful. It's an extremely vulnerable time. Ending the pain is a natural instinct for the addict. They know that their substance of choice is the quickest way to end what they're going through, hence the cycle. Drugs and alcohol are self-medication for an underlying issue, after all."

My mind went back to the carriage house, to the images and products I had seen in the storeroom, the numerous hospital beds and IV hookups.

"Are patients typically given any kind of drug treatment to manage withdrawal symptoms?"

"Yes, medication-assisted treatment is still a common protocol for pain management during withdrawal, particularly from opioids, but this really isn't my area of expertise. I would direct you to someone with more current knowledge for those kinds of details. However, we are all familiar with the existence of methadone clinics."

"My understanding is that methadone is used primarily as a transition to sobriety. How is it administered?"

"Typically it's prescribed as a tablet or a concentrate that can be ingested so the individual can manage their pain at home, but there are doctors who prefer to inject. And medication-assisted treatments can continue for quite some time, years even."

"Okay, and after detoxing, what's typically the next step?"

"There are various types of talk therapy—cognitive behavioral therapy, group sessions, individual counseling sessions—and just as many opinions on the situational appropriateness of specific therapies within the psychological community.

"In many ways, the work shares similarities with the type of work you and I have done. An individual has a problem or a repeated behavior set that has been used to address a deficit or to fill a void for something else that is missing. The patient and the therapist work together to discover the root cause and to help the individual learn some healthier behaviors or how to process whatever pain might have challenged their life."

So far there was nothing that Dr. Takeda had said that wasn't common sense, if one stepped back and looked at it logically. What could be so unique about Dr. Wykell's treatment protocol that he stood to make his fortune from it? It sure as hell wasn't talk therapy. My gut was still telling me he was performing experimental drug therapy. It was the only thing I could think of that would yield fast and, more importantly, profitable results.

"Have you heard about any breakthroughs, any new unusual protocols that might be under the radar but showing promise that wouldn't be typical of the Betty Ford–type center?"

"I can't say that I have any great expertise on the subject, so again, you'll need to speak with somebody who is closer to the addiction treatment world than I am. But I have seen papers in professional journals suggesting work with things such as micro-dosing of LSD or psilocybin, better known as mushrooms. But don't take that as gospel. I'm not up-to-date on the cutting-edge treatments, nor do I know what may have moved to clinical trials. The process is slow and cumbersome, but rightly so."

Slow and cumbersome was not going to make Wykell wealthy. I supposed a small clinical trial was possible, but that would mean a lot of red tape and disclosure in a public record database. No, Wykell seemed too anxious. This was a behind-the-scenes operation.

"I can see those wheels turning, Andrea. Do you want to tell me what you're thinking? Is there something specific about this story, this death, that has you puzzled? After all, we are sadly in an era where opioid overdoses are all too common."

"The young woman who died apparently had a brief relationship with a treatment center here in Chicago. I've spoken to the director, and he purports to have a program with a very high success rate—an eighty-five percent success rate. And *cure* is his word choice."

"Those are remarkable numbers, however, I have to admit, I'm skeptical already. The only way to quantify results is through scientific methodology, which isn't done at the treatment-center level. You'd need control groups, ongoing monitoring of blood and urine. Self-reporting doesn't qualify as evidence-based medicine. Personally, I'd be skeptical of anyone who tried to put numbers to their outcomes. We'd all like to, of course, but we're talking about human nature here." She leaned back in her chair, twirling the stem of her reading glasses. "Do you have any insights into how he is achieving that? Or is this a one-off?"

"He's being quite vague about the details of his program. Secretive even, but that's just my gut feeling. It does seem odd to me that there wouldn't be some indication of the treatment protocols if he does indeed have a verifiable level of success."

"May I ask who the therapist is? Not that I can comment, but you've piqued my curiosity."

"His name is Dr. Troy Wykell. He runs a center called the Renacido Center."

I saw Janice flinch ever so slightly at the mention of his name. "Do you know him?" I asked, immediately intrigued.

"No, I don't know him."

"But?"

"But nothing. Somewhere along the way, his name has come up, that's all," she said, shrugging it off. "There are thousands of therapists in Chicago. Nothing more."

"You reacted. Something about this guy made you flinch."

I watched her face intently, but the moment of surprise was gone.

"I had no reaction. I probably just adjusted my posture. Don't read anything into it."

"Okay," I said, not believing her for a minute. But I also knew she would never speak badly of another professional. "Is there some way I can check this guy out? I'm curious about whether there have been any concerns about his dealings with patients. Would the licensing board be the group that heard formal complaints, if there were any?"

She hesitated, seemingly struggling with something. "This woman that died, she was a patient of his?"

"He has admitted to me that he saw her for a brief period of time. In speaking with others, it sounds like it was more than brief."

Janice reached over and pulled a sheet of paper out of a notepad. She jotted something down and handed it to me.

"What is this?"

"This is an attorney that I'm friendly with. He may be willing to speak to you. I understand that he had a run-in with Dr. Wykell, but that's all I can say."

32

"I'm not entirely sure what you want to talk about."

I was walking into attorney Noah Adelman's office, having wrangled a meeting by being mildly evasive when I threw Dr. Janice Takeda's name into the phone conversation I'd had with the man an hour ago. At least I wasn't pretending to be a client this time.

Although grateful that he'd agreed to speak with me, my mind was on Kendall. There had been no response from her, not even an "I'm ok" text after I'd left concerned messages. My most recent call had gone straight to voicemail, so someone had switched the phone off. The call I'd put in to the Renacido Center had been met with "We can't give out that information." I was left to contemplate how to identify and get ahold of her father. Or to storm the gates.

Adelman was a one-man shop. In other words, a legal generalist—divorces, wills, petty disputes over a neighbor's dog, anything that walked in the door and flipped his switch that day or his bank account balance. It wasn't high-paying law, but it kept you sharp.

I followed Adelman into the small office suite he shared with a CPA on the second floor of a dingy South Loop high-rise. There wasn't a window in the place, and the buzzy florescent lighting gave everything a greenish cast, including Adelman's skin. I had no doubt it was the cheapest space they could find within a ten-block radius of the courthouse, and it smelled like wet dog.

He was round and grandfatherly and gruff, but in a sitcom kind of way, and I was having trouble picturing a friendship between him and Janice.

"Sit." He flapped his hand toward a chair as he settled his doughy body behind the desk. "What's this about?"

"I'll get straight to the point," I said, knowing that attorneys like him watched the clock like hawks. Every minute with me was a minute of billing lost to a real client. "I understand that you had a run-in, if that's the right expression, with a Dr. Troy Wykell. He is a psychologist specializing in addiction treatment."

"Yes, I know exactly who he is. But you're an attorney, or at least you used to be, right? So you sure as hell are aware of the confidentiality requirements of our work."

"And I haven't asked you to violate your oath. Talk to me about the public information. There were legal filings. Those filings are public information."

"Then why don't you go find them yourself." He looked at me over the top of his glasses like I was a first-year law student. I could practically see the word *dumbass* forming in a thought bubble above his head.

"I have. You represented the plaintiff." I reached into my bag and pulled out a manila folder. I laid it on his desk and pulled out its contents, pleased with myself for having squeezed in a stop at city hall between my visit with Janice and my appointment here.

"Owen Mosier, Sr. versus Renacido Treatment Center, Inc. September 30th, 2017. Case was dismissed. Fill in the gaps."

"Are you recording this?" He looked at me skeptically.

"Not if you don't want me to."

"Okay, if you have a device hidden somewhere, shut it down now." He paused and chewed a lip, waiting. "I'll give you the basics, but I won't admit to being a source. So my name had better not appear in your next exposé." His tone said he meant it.

"I promise." I smiled and held up a palm. "This is just background. If I get to the point where the story needs a quote, we can renegotiate."

He glared at me and shook his head but didn't throw me out.

"Mr. and Mrs. Mosier came to me after their son, Owen Jr., passed away. Cause of death was basically a heart attack. The kid was only twenty-eight. He'd been a hard-core heroin user for nearly seven years and, like most, had tried nearly everything else you could imagine to kick his habit, including some homemade concoctions. According to the medical examiner, the kid had a defect in one of his heart valves. Probably something he was born with but was undiscovered. After years of hitting the drugs hard, his heart just couldn't handle the strain and gave out one day."

Another heart issue. Adelman loosened his tie and readjusted his rolled-up shirtsleeves. He chewed the corner of his lip mindlessly and picked up a pen, only to put it back down, looking like a guy itching for a cigarette.

"Then why the lawsuit?"

"Mom and Dad were unconvinced. One complication was that they had trouble wrapping their head around the whole concept of an autopsy. Some religious objection. Not that I remember his affiliation. Can't say I can keep all these Christian faiths straight in my head." He shrugged. "But Junior was an adult, and when anybody under thirty drops dead, you know damn well there's going to be an autopsy, whether the parents like it or not. But the autopsy was really the least of it. The parents were suspicious of everything. They knew the kid used drugs, but in their thinking, it was an evil curse. It simply meant they just weren't praying hard enough. Another loony tune expecting prayer to deliver a medical miracle. I'm as religious as the next guy, but these power-of-prayer zealots confuse the shit out of me."

"As in, God would find a way to remove the addiction if they were devoted enough?"

He nodded. "I'm not saying I understand. But they literally believed that the devil had taken over their son's body. They spent hours praying, even took him to some holy water bath where they nearly drowned the kid. It was supposed to scare the devil out of him, but of course, that didn't work either."

"Sounds like throwing a woman suspected of being a witch into the water to see if she'll float."

"Don't laugh. There's a surprising similarity," he said, rubbing a hand over his forehead. "God knows what the kid thought about his parents or their religion. No pun intended. Eventually he sought out more conventional treatment at the Renacido Center. To me, it sounded like he thought it would be less painful than what Mom and Dad were putting him through."

"Was this his only stint in rehab?"

"Is there ever just one?" He raised his brow. "He had been to Bible study, faith-based healing centers, private counseling. His family was made up of hard-core God types. All of it was sanctioned first by the parents. And then sanctioned by their church."

"His church got involved?" I asked, confused by the concept.

"That's how these guys work. Don't expect me to explain it,

but yeah, this church had some kind of religious council that met and tried to come up with an approved treatment plan. They would only agree to individuals or facilities that were willing to honor specific practices and beliefs."

"Like what?" I'd come across people with religious beliefs so strong they dictated associations, but never anyone who filtered their medical treatment past a religious tribunal.

"I haven't the faintest idea. Way too cult-like for my tribe."

"So how did he end up at Renacido? Was it blessed by the church?"

I was struggling to comprehend the idea of needing church approval during a medical crisis. My only religious motto was the classic "Do unto others" philosophy. It wasn't that I didn't believe; it had just never seemed necessary in my life to use an organization as a way to monitor decency in my own behavior. My mind flashed back to the meeting room the afternoon of the open house. The center hadn't struck me as a faith-based organization at the time. There had been no mention of prayer or God in the literature, no crosses or other paraphernalia. If Renacido had a religious affiliation, they hid it well.

"Like I said," Adelman continued. "I don't know exactly how it happened, but the parents were adamant with me that neither they nor their church had sanctioned Owen's participation in treatment at this facility."

"He was going against all of his religious upbringing," I said, thinking out loud. The kid either felt betrayed by the doctrine or was so desperate he'd do anything to shake his vice.

"Or maybe the center told him enough of what he needed to hear to make him think God wouldn't smite him. What do I know about Christianity? Regardless, he signed up. About three weeks into the program, he had his heart event and died. Despite the autopsy reports, the parents came to me wanting to blame the center, and by extension Dr. Wykell, for the death of their son."

"And you believed there was enough there to warrant the suit?"

"At first, not really, but they were so distraught, and so firm in their convictions, that it seemed like they needed to make the effort just to have closure. I was skeptical, so what I agreed to do was to help them get a copy of their son's medical records. I figured we would take this one small hurdle at a time. If we got information that increased any suspicions about his medical care, we could move forward. But if everything looked kosher, perhaps the parents would be appeased. In my mind, it seemed that they just needed to do something in order to accept what had happened to their son. Parental guilt, perhaps. As you know, it's not unusual for the family to need a deeper explanation when the truth is hard to accept. Families need answers, and when those answers are not available, imagination can take over."

"And were you able to get his medical records?"

"That's when things took a turn." He paused and laid his glasses on the desk. "The center, of course, lawyered up. No business wants legal challenges in the public eye. Par for the course, they refused polite requests, so I had to turn up the heat a little and subpoena the records."

"Which meant that you needed to show probable cause."

"Exactly. I had to present the case that we were concerned about the death being suspicious and make the argument that medical records of his treatment would clarify the issue. If everything was on the up-and-up, those medical records would corroborate the medical examiner's findings."

"And did you get the records?"

"The center fought the subpoena, but ultimately they were

ordered to turn them over. They had thirty days to do so, and in the meantime, I scheduled Dr. Wykell for a deposition."

"Did that deposition occur?"

"Sort of. Keep in mind that I was still a bit skeptical of the whole thing, but I figured a few questions directed at the guy who wrote the treatment protocol would accomplish two things. One, it would satisfy my clients if they could hear directly from the doctor who was treating their son. And two, if there was anything that showed up in the medical records later when they were produced, I would have already questioned him enough to know where to look for the bullshit. Well, we all arrived for the deposition, and barely fifteen minutes in, Dr. Wykell decides he doesn't like my line of questioning. He throws a hissy fit and storms out as the parents sat there devastated. So much for empathy. This guy is one obstinate ass. You'd think there'd be a little heartfelt compassion out of a medical professional, but the only thing this guy cared about was himself. Or I should say his bank account."

The little I'd seen of Dr. Wykell's personality told me having a tantrum was not out of character. And there was that profit motive again.

"Did you ever get a copy of the medical records?" I asked.

"This is where it gets interesting. When we were four days away from the court-ordered due date, I got a call from Mr. Mosier telling me they had decided to drop the case." Adelman crossed his arms across his ample chest and raised his brows.

"What reason did he give?"

"I had to pull it out of him, but the bottom line was that they were intimidated. The center's legal team made it clear that they would bury this family financially. Drag it on for years if they needed to. Drive them into bankruptcy. Basically, the Mosiers were outgunned."

"Was there anything else they were afraid of? Do you think Mr. Mosier told you everything?"

"No, I don't. Didn't think I had the whole story at the time, and as time has passed, I'm even more firmly convinced of it. By that point, I believed the Mosiers were right about needing to press forward with a legal inquiry. I was so convinced something stunk to high heaven that I even offered to bill them at half my normal rates, but they still wouldn't bite. Look, the financial hit would scare anyone off, but my gut says it was more than the money."

33

Financial strong-arming. The preferred technique of megacorporations and mobsters. It took arrogance and balls and lots of cash. What gave Wykell the hubris to pull that stunt?

The Mosier family lived in the Irving Park neighborhood, and I was on my way to see if I could knock loose a few more details. Threats of financial ruin would send even the best of us back to our corners. I knew nothing about the financial situation of this family, but typically the reality of a legal grudge match between private citizens and a corporate entity was a tough one to face. I was also realizing that I knew nothing about the financial structure of the Renacido Center. I had made assumptions that this was a single center run by Dr. Wykell. Was it possible there was more money and therefore more legal firepower behind them?

A man who I guessed to be in his early seventies was in the front yard making good use of his edge trimmer when I pulled up. I double-checked the address I had in my notes against the house number, then grabbed my bag and got out of the car.

He didn't notice me at first over the noise of his equipment.

Sweat glistened on his forehead and stained patches on his ratty T-shirt. Bits of grass and other plant material stuck to his forearms and collected on the hem of his baggy Wranglers.

I stepped closer, trying to get into his line of sight, and lifted my hand in a wave. He shut off the Weedwacker, laid it on the ground, then lifted his safety goggles to the top of his head.

"Yes? If you're selling something, just be on your way because I already got everything I need, including the Lord Jesus Christ."

I smiled. "Are you Mr. Mosier?"

He nodded.

"I'd like to talk to you about your son."

His face swung from apprehensive curiosity to get-the-hell-out-of-my-yard in half a second. I handed him my business card.

"And why in the name of Jesus would I want to talk to you? My son has been disparaged enough. The boy is dead. No reporter is going to bring him back. So you can just go on back and find someone else to torment. I don't have anything to say to you or any of your kind."

He reached down and picked up his tool. I could see a woman watching us from inside the house at the front window, her red cardigan glaring through the glass.

"Mr. Mosier, I assure you I have no interest in disparaging you, your son, or your family. When Owen Jr. died, you were concerned about the quality of the medical treatment he had received in the hands of Dr. Wykell at the Renacido Center. I've read the initial court filings." I paused. "There's been another death."

I let the statement sink in for a moment, watching his reaction. His face went ashy, and whatever spark of anger had been in his eyes a moment ago was now a flat, soulless gaze. It was as if I'd stabbed him in the heart all over again. My gut clenched with his pain, and guilt gnawed at me. Reopening his wound for the good of a story was hard to swallow, but if it could expose the truth, wasn't it worth it? Or was that just something I wanted to believe?

"I don't know if there's a connection," I said quietly. "But I'd really like to understand more about your reasons for believing that there was something improper about your son's treatment. Will you talk to me about that?" I asked, my voice full of emotion.

The woman from the window was now walking hurriedly down the front sidewalk. Concern lined her plump face. "Owen, is everything okay?"

He didn't respond.

"Hello, Mrs. Mosier," I said. "My name is Andrea Kellner. I'm a reporter with Link-Media. I came out hoping to speak to you and your husband about Owen Jr."

She shot a steely look at her husband, who simply stared back, seemingly unable to find words.

"We can't talk to you," she said, her voice riddled with irritation. "I don't know what you think you're doing, coming here, trying to dredge up trouble. Owen, come inside."

"Someone else has died, Eileen," he said softly to his wife.

She gasped and covered her mouth, tears welling in her eyes. I could see the debate raging in their minds. The memories and pain of what they had lost now gushing to the surface.

"We'd better go inside," Mr. Mosier said.

I followed the two, now arm in arm, into their living room. It was warm and comforting, a room well lived in. Matching recliners faced the TV, a colorful pieced quilt was draped across the back of the worn sofa, and a stash of magazines was piled on the coffee table, along with a Bible. Two crosses and a Jesus print lined the walls, but not a single family photo graced the room. It struck me as out of character. Perhaps the memories were too painful.

"Please, sit. Can I get you something to drink?" Mrs. Mosier asked, directing me to one of the recliners and showing her Midwestern hospitality.

"No, thank you. Your home is lovely. Did Owen grow up here?" I asked.

"We brought him here right from the hospital when he was born. Top-notch schools are just blocks away," Mr. Mosier said, pride in his voice. "We knew from the beginning we wanted our boy to have a good start."

"I can see that you gave him a tremendous amount of love. It must have been heartbreaking for you to watch Owen's struggles with addiction." The couple exchanged a glance as they sat on the sofa, hand-in-hand. "I understand that he found treatment challenging. Can you tell me about that?"

"Well, we believe in the power of prayer," Mr. Mosier said. "That God, and only God, can give or take away a curse. Junior, well, he didn't always see things that way. He was hurting, and I think he just got desperate. At the end, he was willing to try anything. He had lost faith in God, in himself, and in us." His eyes were hollow, lost in the pain of having disappointed his son and not fully understanding why. He stared at the floor in front of his feet, processing memories that had ripped his family apart.

"We should have tried harder," Mrs. Mosier choked out. Her tears were bubbling up again, and she squeezed her husband's hand.

"I understand that there had been several stints at rehab." I wanted to try to pull back to more neutral territory but also to understand the lead-up. So far the Renacido Center was coming off as the treatment of last resort, but I didn't know if that status meant anything.

"At first, we got him to a good Christian center," Mr. Mosier said. "It was a place our pastor put us in touch with in Missouri.

Outside of St. Louis, and we've got family there. We drove him down. He was there for four weeks." He cleared his throat before continuing. "I think he came back even angrier than when he'd left. Started using again days later."

"He was still living with us then," Mrs. Mosier added, taking a fleeting look at her husband's stricken face.

"I think it was about a year after that when he lost his job. He was a mechanic," Mr. Mosier continued. "Came in to work high one too many times. They just couldn't put up with that anymore. Can't blame his employer. They had tried hard, gave him a lot of leeway to find his way back to God, but eventually our boy had used up his chances. That's when he said he was ready to try rehab again, but not if he had to go back to the church."

"The church treatment center?" I asked.

"Wouldn't go back at all. Not to any church," Mrs. Mosier said. "He said no God would give a man this kind of burden. He didn't want the Christian treatment center. He didn't want to attend services. He didn't want anything to do with our beliefs."

The pain in her face was as fresh as if his rejection of God had happened yesterday. In renouncing his religion, he had renounced his parents.

"He said he wanted to make another try at rehab, but only if he could pick the center," Mr. Mosier said. "Since he didn't have a job, that meant he didn't have health insurance. We were desperate. We would have done anything to help him, so we agreed to pay out-of-pocket. Cost us almost thirty grand. That's a lot of money to us. It took everything we had. But we loved our son, so we figured it out. Sent him out to this fancy place in California that time."

"And was the California center any more successful?" I asked.

"He was clean a little longer." Mr. Mosier shrugged. "As far as we know, it was a couple of months before he was using again. At that point, we just didn't know how to help him anymore. We weren't sure he wanted help, at least not from us. I told him we couldn't have that evil in our home any longer. He moved out. We aren't quite sure who he was living with. Friends, I guess. Sleeping on somebody's couch. Or maybe on the streets."

Mrs. Mosier cried softly as her husband spoke, every word a piece of gravel in the wound. He squeezed her hand tighter and sniffed back his own tears.

"He didn't involve us when he made the decision to go to that Renacido place," he said. "Owen just stopped by the house unexpectedly the day before to let us know. We hadn't seen him in over four months by then."

"He seemed at peace," Mrs. Mosier added. "As if he felt really good about this decision. He said this center was different, that they had some special treatment. Some experimental procedures that showed promise. But we don't know if that was just his hopes and dreams talking or if he was trying to convince us."

"And did you speak to him while he was at the center?"

I knew I was getting into delicate territory and had to be careful about how I phrased my questions. Parental guilt found a way to rear its ugly head, regardless of the reality of the circumstances, but the last thing I wanted to do was sound accusatory.

"Only once," Mrs. Mosier said. "He called us about three weeks later. I put him on speaker phone so we could both hear his voice. He said he felt really good. That the treatment was working. He could feel something was different this time."

"But he just wasn't himself," her husband jumped in. "He sounded a little spacey, maybe 'slow' is a better word, and kind of wheezy. Like he was having a hard time breathing or couldn't catch his breath. I asked him about it. And he said there was some medication he'd been given as part of his treatment that made him feel a little 'floaty.' That was his word. Said it slowed everything down. But it only lasted a day or two, so he wasn't worried."

"You don't think this was an ongoing medication, then?" I asked.

"No, I think it was something that he took once a week. He said they monitored him. Hooked him up to an IV while the drug was being administered," Mr. Mosier answered.

The image of the rooms in the carriage house came back to my mind. The drug could have been something administered intravenously, or the IV could have been part of a backup protection. It could even have been straight saline just to get a line into his arm as a safety measure. However, that ruled out methadone.

"Did he tell you what the drug was?"

"No, his speech was getting pretty slurred by that point in the conversation. It was something that started with an *I* but I couldn't make it out. It sounded more like it was a cocktail of drugs."

"A week later he was dead." Mrs. Mosier was trembling now, her eyes locked on me.

"And you filed suit a month later. Correct?" I asked.

Again the couple exchanged a glance. "At the time it seemed like the right thing to do," he said. "They wouldn't tell us anything at the center. Like what drugs he'd been given. They said he was an adult and we weren't entitled to his records. That the information was confidential."

"The way he sounded on the phone and the fact that he died just days later, well, we got scared," Mrs. Mosier said. "Our boy was dead, and they wouldn't tell us anything. When we couldn't get any information from them, that's when we decided we needed a lawyer."

"I know this is difficult, but can you tell me why you dropped the lawsuit?"

The couple looked at each other, the unspoken language of a long-term marriage. Mrs. Mosier nodded to her husband.

"This attorney paid us a visit. A guy named Reda," he said. "Out of the blue. No phone call. Just knocked on our door one night. Said he was the attorney for the center. He told us flat out that if we continued with legal action, he personally guaranteed he would bankrupt us. Said there was a lot of money behind them, that they had a big announcement coming, and our choices were to benefit when that happened or lose everything we had." He lowered his head. "This lawyer also said they would accuse Owen of all kinds of depravities—engaging with other men and such—and that they'd do it publicly if we went to court."

Humiliation and financial ruin. Scum lawyering at its worst.

"That's a disgusting legal approach. You used the word 'benefit.' Did you interpret his comments as basically offering you a bribe to stay quiet? A cut of the center's future financial windfall?" I asked, my mind jumping to ramifications. "I'm not passing judgment, I'm just wanting to clarify," I added quickly, realizing my tone might be misinterpreted.

"We didn't take any bribe," Mr. Mosier shot back, anger in his voice. "Good Christian folks don't make money off other people's sorrow. And I sure as hell wasn't going to make money off my dead son. I told him never to contact us again. That's when we dropped the suit. I didn't want their blood money, but they would have crushed us financially and denigrated our son in the process. So we let it go and moved on. And I don't have a minute of regret."

34

As painful as it was for them, the Mosiers had made the right decision. But could justice be delivered another way?

I'd sent a third text to Kendall after leaving their home and had Brynn working behind the scenes to dig deeper into the business structure of Renacido and the attorney who'd used intimidation tactics against the Mosiers. At the very least, the Illinois Bar Association needed to hear about it, but I was more interested in why Renacido had felt compelled to go to those lengths.

I was standing outside a Gold Coast rehab center prepping for a loosely arranged meeting with Dr. Lecaros. He'd promised me a fifteen-minute block of time, provided I didn't mind waiting around for him during a break between appointments. Annoying, but if he was willing to talk to me without the consult bill, I'd sit quietly and bow to his schedule. The psychologist had described Wykell as dangerous, and he certainly seemed it to me, but that didn't mean we were working off the same definition. Given Lecaros's area of expertise, I was speculating that there was either a patient or a practice at the heart of their rift.

The red brick building I'd been directed to was elegant and discreet. Its Georgian architecture and rich green shutters blended seamlessly into the neighborhood. To anyone walking past, the purpose of the business establishment would have been unknown; the small brass plaque near the door was the only mark identifying it as one of the most highly regarded treatment centers in the Midwest—and then only if you happened to be familiar with the name. I'd walked past the facility myself many times and not given it a second thought.

Two young men stood outside, taking time out for a smoke near the iron fence as I approached. I nodded hello, then stepped toward the heavy green door. Immediately inside was a reception area, more parlor-like in feel than the clinical atmosphere I had expected. Traditional furniture, wingback chairs, even a small area fashioned into a library. Like the Renacido Center, this facility made an attempt at disguising its purpose. However, given the cameras and manned reception desk, it didn't seem likely patients were wandering aimlessly out of this facility without supervision, certainly not those in physical distress.

If you had $30K to drop on treatment, I imagined the homey atmosphere took the sting out of the reality of being consigned to the facility.

I approached the woman at the desk and asked for Dr. Lecaros.

"Please have a seat. I'm sure he will be out shortly," she said after putting in a call.

I settled into a chair and killed time by Googling Dr. Wykell, looking for any connection I could find to business associates, past or present. The intimidation tactics used on the Mosiers screamed big money or big risk. There was a lot to lose, or a lot to gain, if the tactic of choice was to hire a thug.

Zoe had died of a heart complication, as had Owen Mosier.

If Paul's life had ended for the same reason, it would be impossible for CPD not to explore the connections. It was unlikely that the ME had completed their work yet but I sent Michael a text asking anyway, before moving back to the internet to explore drugs with risks of heart-related side effects.

Dr. Lecaros poked his head out of the doorway and motioned me over. I tucked my phone into my bag and scurried after him as he moved down the hall.

He led me to a small room outfitted with a desk, a couple of upholstered chairs, and bookcases stacked to capacity. He settled into one of the chairs, and I did the same.

"You'll forgive me for the limited time. My schedule is such that I have to squeeze in meetings where I can, even if it means using facilities other than my own." He flapped his hand at the room, which clearly didn't meet his standards. "If I recall correctly, and I believe I do, you were interested in cutting-edge opioid treatment modalities," he said.

"Before we get to that, you said something the other day that I'd like to follow up on. It was about Dr. Wykell. You cautioned me to stay away. Why was that?"

"You clearly mistook my intent. I simply meant that there are psychologists far more knowledgeable in this area. After all, why consult with the second string?"

"Then you're familiar with his work. I got the impression that perhaps there was a conflict there. Was I mistaken?"

I had to be careful of how I approached the conversation, as I had yet to correct Dr. Lecaros's assumption that I was still an attorney shopping for a hired gun. If I had to fess up to being a reporter, I'd have about two seconds to get out of the room.

"It's nothing other than philosophical differences. So, you have questions on the newest treatments."

As I suspected, Dr. Lecaros had recognized his moment of indiscretion and was dialing it back.

"Could we start with an overview of some of the practices in your world," I said. "As a leader in the field, how would you define the gold standard of addiction treatment?"

May as well start with the suck-up. Admiration, real or not, was going to be the fastest way to get Lecaros to talk. If he disagreed with the current standard of care, he'd let me know just to show how smart he was.

"Flattery will get you everywhere." He laughed while I resisted an eye roll. "Although your question is like asking me to describe the gold standard in building a house. There is no one way. I happen to have strong opinions, opinions based on my years of work in the field, I might add, but the gold standard is more accurately thought of as a positive end result."

"Fair enough. I can only imagine the patience and the compassion required to make addiction treatment your life's work," I said, continuing the unpleasant ego stroking. "Perhaps I need to rephrase the question. Would it be accurate to say that various methods of talk therapy are the primary methodology?"

"Yes, although talk therapy is an immensely generic term. We do utilize practices such as cognitive behavioral therapy, biofeedback therapy, and a whole host of other modalities that would fall into that category, but then there are also treatments such as EMDR, which access other mechanisms in the brain. Often it's a combination of protocols that have been individualized for the needs of the patient."

I had two primary lines of questioning in my mind, and I had to be careful how I layered them if I was going to keep Lecaros engaged. There was the concern about what might be going on financially that would heighten the risk of a PR black eye impacting the Renacido Center, and then there was the issue of experimental treatments. They weren't mutually exclusive, but I had to be deliberate in my questioning so that I didn't appear to be going after Wykell directly. Like in the law, it was out of bounds for one doc to publicly disparage another, and Lecaros was certainly aware that he had already toed up to that line, even if he hadn't given me any context.

"Would it be accurate to say that treatment at a facility such as this is one of the more expensive options?"

"Individualized treatment is never cheap. Although I only consult here, this is a facility that believes strongly in a period of inpatient care, followed by outpatient therapy, and then ongoing support for as long as necessary. A lifetime, perhaps, for some. Each leg of the treatment is interconnected with the others. It's quite labor intensive."

"Excuse me, I wasn't intending to sound critical of the cost. I just wanted to establish the fact that if a patient came to you, whether through this facility or through direct contact, and did not have insurance coverage, there would be some kind of expectation of an out-of-pocket payment plan."

"Yes, of course. Although these days, my work directly with patients is limited. I'm primarily a consultant serving the therapist community and the legal community. This process is a costly endeavor, and the money spent is an investment in life. So many lives are ruined by addiction, it's difficult to think about it as a simple ROI equation."

He snuck a peek at his watch, reminding me that my time with him was not unlimited.

"Have you ever run across a center, a private center, that treats patients for free?" I asked.

"Completely free? I'm certainly familiar with a few charity organizations that provide treatment to individuals, but those facilities would either have been funded by some type of endowment or they are a need-based sliding scale with supplemental funds coming from the community or a government source."

"But not a for-profit facility?"

"I don't see how that would work. Staff *does* expect to be paid, utilities are not cheap, and then there is the pesky problem of taxes." He gave me a weak but condescending smile.

"How about more of a barter system?" I said, throwing out an unformed thought, brainstorming just to see where it got me.

"It's a preposterous idea. Why in the world would you ask?"

"Just curious," I said, quickly changing the subject. I'd irritated the man. Time for a little stroking. "Given your prominence in this field, I assume you are up on the cutting edge of treatment protocols, protocols that might be considered experimental or are in early stages of evaluation. Would that be accurate?"

"I do my best to keep up. As I'm sure you know, we have a significant problem in our country right now, particularly in the area of opioids, and we in the field are all anxious to make an impact. Not only for individual lives but for the greater good of society. That is the heart of why we do the work we do."

"And what would some of the newer, more experimental drug treatments be? And by that I mean medication-assisted treatments."

He sat up straighter in his chair. I'd finally found something that interested him.

"One of the things becoming more common now is NAD therapy, nicotinamide adenine dinucleotide. It's a coenzyme of niacin that helps our bodies produce energy. Drug and alcohol abuse depletes the body's production, and this can contribute to a co-occurring disorder. But I view the treatment more as an adjunct support versus a stand-alone treatment."

"And how is NAD administered?"

"Typically through an IV. As I said, it is a co-treatment, not a stand-alone. It assists with flushing drugs out of the user's system and helps curb cravings. It also reduces the pain of withdrawals, which puts the patient into a place where they are more able to work with the other therapies."

Although the IV part seemed to fit the bill, I wasn't sure a naturally occurring enzyme did, unless the usage was brand or dosage dependent or used in combination with other drugs.

"Are there any potential risks or toxicities to NAD?"

"It's a fairly recent addition to the arsenal, and although I can't imagine any obvious problems—after all, it is a naturally occurring enzyme—in reality, we don't yet have long studies to clarify."

"What about medications or combinations of medications that perhaps have not yet reached acceptance?"

"Are you talking about off-label use?"

"Is that an issue?"

"Of course, but not at any facility that wants to keep its license. There are treatment centers outside of the US utilizing hallucinogenics, LSD, psilocybin, and ibogaine. But none of that is currently legal in the US. I'm not up-to-date on the current clinical trials, but there are people who leave the country. Have you heard the term 'medical tourist'?"

"Yes, I have, but only in the context of cost savings for things like cosmetic or dental surgeries. You're talking about going overseas for addiction treatment not approved in the States." My mind was running ahead with this thought. "If a US-based facility wanted to utilize some of these products, these medications you just mentioned, even though they're not legal currently, how would they go about doing that?"

"By smuggling it in and not telling anyone what they were doing."

35

Umm, body odor, beer, and cheap perfume. Why hadn't I anticipated the foul cocktail that assaulted my nose?

It had easily been a decade since I'd walked into a club, and the reasons why were on full display—the lights, the unyielding beat of the bass, the stench of stale alcohol, the stickiness of the floor, the crush of bodies around me. I shuddered, feeling like I'd just landed in a foreign country and was decades older than everyone around me.

Immediately after my conversation with Dr. Lecaros, I'd phoned Michael but had yet to hear back from him. Lecaros had mentioned a drug called ibogaine being used for addiction treatment outside of the US. Had that been the drug Owen Mosier mentioned? The coincidence was too strong not to investigate. There was enough information online about the substance to be concerned, particularly about the heart-related deaths associated with the chemical.

Ibogaine was a naturally occurring psychoactive alkaloid that came from the bark of the iboga plant. Although used in a number of countries for opioid treatment, the science wasn't settled on its safety, its contraindications, or its effectiveness, so I'd need the full participation of the ME to move forward. From my light research, it wasn't clear if or how long the substance could be detected postmortem. In situations where death had been reported, all seemed to include either poorly screened recipients, drug interactions, or existing but unrevealed medical issues. But again, that was territory for the ME.

What also wasn't clear was how Wykell could make money off its use. Plant-based products, at least in their natural form, weren't profitable from a drug standpoint. There was no ability to patent them without chemical modification. And then there was the small issue of the FDA. To make this pay off, Wykell was either going to have to hide the ingredient under another mantle and try to work around the legality or promote the entire process as a package deal, perhaps coming up with a brand name for the process versus the drug. He flat-out couldn't publicly disclose the ingredient, but if it was layered with enough steps, he could probably get away with selling the success of the protocol. Provided pesky things like dead bodies didn't get in the way.

With my progress on the ME front hampered for the moment, I was making another run at Levi to see if ibogaine rang any bells for him. And if I could settle my nerves on his involvement.

Levi worked somewhere behind the scenes setting up equipment and organizing the tools necessary for the show. And if it was anything like most bands, that meant he was a jack-of-all-trades—fetching drinks, adjusting mics, anything and everything to make sure that the show went on flawlessly.

I squeezed through a throng of people at the bar holding their bottles and plastic cups close, and I felt the unwanted gazes of men on my body. A hand grazed my ass as I passed, and reflexively I turned around to tell the asshole what I thought of his cowardly move, but in the crush I couldn't tell which idiot had done it. Just another reminder of why I hated the environment.

Snaking my way through to a spot between the stage and the bar, I found a step where I could get about twelve inches above the heads of the crowd. I wedged myself onto the narrow berm hoping to get a decent viewpoint of the stage and, more importantly, any comings and goings.

There was a smoky haze near the stage where the lights lit the group of musicians currently performing. Lost in their own revelation, they stomped and swayed to the beat as the crowd echoed their movements. From my vantage point, I could make out a few individuals huddled just beyond the stage near the edge of a black curtain, attending to equipment. Levi wasn't with them, but it was as likely a place as any to watch for him.

Already the beat of the heavy metal band was drilling into my brain in a way that I didn't want. It thumped in with its repeating bass, causing a throb in the back of my skull that threatened to work its way around to my temples. I fished in my bag for a bottle of water and some Advil, knowing this was only the beginning of the discomfort.

I should have corralled Cai, or maybe Brynn, to come with me.

After about fifteen minutes, I caught sight of Levi. He was adjusting a speaker that seemed to have lost its juice on the left side of the stage. Luckily, right in my line of sight. I watched him do his work, debating whether to approach immediately or wait for them to finish the set. After fiddling with the equipment, he made my decision easy and moved toward me, likely on a mission to make a pit stop for drinks. What fun, I'd get to wade back through grabby-hands territory.

"Levi," I shouted, following him to the right side of the long bar. Initially he didn't hear me over the roar, so I reached out and put my hand on his shoulder. He looked at me, confusion in his face for a moment.

"What are you doing here? This doesn't seem like your crowd."

"It's not. I need to talk to you." His hair was a sweaty just-got-out-of-bed mess. And his light gray T-shirt was stained at the neck and the pits. I didn't even want to think about how bad the guy would smell by the end of the night.

"Yeah, well, I'm working, and in case you haven't noticed, this is hardly the place for conversation," he shouted back at me. "I need to get drinks for the guys. Sorry you wasted your time." He continued moving forward, lifting three fingers to the bartender, while I stuck on his heels. The volume was a little lower now, and the bartender had already started to pour.

"What kind of drugs was Zoe using?" I said, loud enough to make sure he could hear.

"You already know the answer to that. Your cop friend, he's got it all figured out, right? Knows what she did. Knows it was my fault. Blah, blah, blah. You come all the way down here to ask something you already know? Please, give me a fuckin' break. I said I got work to do."

The bartender handed him a bottle of beer and three plastic cups full of ice, lime, and something clear. Levi tipped the bottle back, finishing a third of it in one fell swoop.

"I'm not talking about those drugs," I said. "I'm talking about the truth. You were around her, you know what she was really using. And you know, at least I think you know, what she was being given at the treatment center."

"I told you already. No point in repeating myself. Nothing else to say, so get off my case." He chugged the balance of the brew like a man stranded in the desert. "You enjoy the music. The next set is really killer."

"You're going to want to talk to me, Levi. A new toxicology

report is being ordered," I said, playing the odds that I could get Michael and Janek to take the next step. "They're going deep. So this, whatever it was she was taking, it's going to come out. Why don't we make this easy and you can tell me what they gave her at the center."

"Why do you think I know that? They don't tell the patients what they're on, and I wasn't there when they shot her up."

"Interesting choice of words, 'shot her up.' You knew enough to walk into the treatment center and accuse Dr. Wykell. I heard you say, 'What did you give her?' So don't stand here and tell me that you don't know that they're using a pharmacological product in some fashion. You wouldn't have said that to him. You would not have made those accusations if you thought nothing other than talk therapy was going on. So why don't we cut the bull and you can tell me what you meant by that."

"I gotta go," he said, but his tone had gone from arrogant to nervous, and he looked over at the stage for an escape route.

"Did you think it was an adverse reaction?" I said, trying to give him an out, a way to soften the blow of the truth if it would get him talking. "Maybe something that she was taking before she went into the center, coupled with something they gave her? Surely you have some suspicions? Don't you think it's time you spoke up? Or do you want to wait for CPD to make sure you talk? You've got a chance to fess up, to explain what you know." I softened my tone. "If you know something and you're holding back, CPD is not going to be all that happy with you when those tox results come back. You seem like a smart guy. Don't you think that it's time to be honest?"

He motioned to the bartender for another beer.

"I don't know what they gave her," he said, his voice cracking. "I know they gave her something. But I, I can't answer what it is. Look, I'm really messed up over this. All I ever wanted to do was the right thing by her. And instead she's dead."

"What are you getting at? What does that mean, *you* wanted to do the right thing?" I asked, aware that he was swinging the question back to his own behavior. I could see the fear and hurt in his eyes, as if he wasn't sure whether to collapse in grief or to sprint off.

"We were both messed up, but we knew we needed to get off the shit. We were trying. We were trying really hard. But those withdrawals, they kill you. And before you know it, you gotta use again just to feel human. You need something to end the pain. So we tag teamed. I went first, broke through the sweats and the fever and the vomiting and all that shit while she nursed me through it. It was the worst thing I'd ever experienced.

"I didn't want her to go through that," Levi said. "So when I'd detoxed enough and it was her turn, I wanted to help her out. This guy I know, he had some stuff that helps take the edge off. Helps you ease down. So I gave her some."

"What was it?"

"Kratom. It's not illegal. Doesn't really get you high. It just knocks you down a bit off the edge. She was nervous, wanted to go cold turkey, but it was bad. It was so bad." Tears ran down his cheeks as he looked at me, pleading. "I just couldn't stand it, so I took some, told her we'd do it together."

"And what happened after that?"

"I don't know exactly. It was the last time I saw her. We were at that house on Pierce. I fell asleep, and she was gone when I woke up. That was the night before she went into the treatment center. All I've been able to think about is what if that was it? What if the shit I gave her, the kratom, what if it killed her? How the hell can I live with myself? I've been sick about it every day since. I can't stand to even look at myself in the mirror. And that's what I think about every night. Did I kill her?"

36

I saw Michael immediately.

Between work, my jaunt to the club to speak to Levi, and the late hour last night, we hadn't yet spoken about my ibogaine theory, and as far as I was concerned, it couldn't wait another minute, so I'd invited myself to the party, otherwise known as breakfast.

Michael was parked on a bench in the back of the coffee shop, a cup lifted to his mouth, while Janek sat across from him in the booth. Unless something earth-shattering had happened or the chief was calling for an all-hands-on-deck early morning meeting, this very booth was where the men could be found from 7:00 to 7:45 a.m. Their regular waitress set up a reserved sign, lest some unknowing fool had the audacity to try to home in on the seat.

"Good morning, gentlemen. What's on the greasy spoon menu today?"

I looked down at their plates, feeling my stomach curl with the heaping servings of bacon, eggs, biscuits, and gravy. All likely cooked with enough lard to bring a cardiologist to his knees. Just the thought of the heavy food was more than my system could handle. I asked the waitress for a glass of water and passed on the heartburn.

"I'm tempted to lecture you on the dangers of an unhealthy diet," I said, "but we've been down this path before. I will let you clog your arteries in peace."

"Sweetheart, you're making a good choice." Michael slid closer to the window to let me sit down, a smile on his face.

Public displays of affection were still an iffy subject, even when no one else from CPD was in sight, so I settled for a squeeze of his hand under the table.

"Good morning, Karl. How are you? How's your sister?"

"I'm fine," he said, his tone telling me he wasn't even in the same universe as fine. "Theresa, she's balled up on the floor or balled up in bed. Can't seem to find a way to stop the tears. It's so senseless. She's hurt, angry. All I want to do is take down that little fuck that did this to her."

He stabbed a piece of egg dripping with runny yolk, along with a shovel of hash browns, and chewed like it was a spoonful of gravel. He wore his pain like a shield, but underneath it all, I had seen firsthand his warm heart. I looked at Michael, who drew in a breath and stared at his coffee mug.

"I think you need to ask for a deeper dive on the toxicology tests," I said to the men, my eyes shifting from Michael to Janek.

"What are you talking about?" Michael asked.

"I've been talking to a few people. People who've had encounters with the center. And I think we've got to take a harder look at them. We have to look at their medication-assisted treatment protocols. At lot of these drugs don't show up on the tox screen unless you're looking for them."

The men looked at each other and then at me. "We?" Janek said, rolling his eyes. "Can you just get to the point? You're always coming at us with these conspiracy theories, and my breakfast is getting cold."

"Well, don't let me stop you from your grits," I said, a bit more harshly than I should have. I had the urge to remind him of how often my so-called conspiracy theories had panned out, but today wasn't the day. "Let's just review, in addition to Zoe, we also have Paul Macanas. Both were connected to the center. And there was a third."

Finally, I had the men's attention.

"Okay, I'm listening," Michael said. He looked at me with his cop eyes—probing, intense, waiting for a flaw or inconsistency—while Janek contemplated his java.

"The third death was a year ago. A young man named Owen Mosier, Jr., also a patient at the center. He died about three weeks into his treatment at Renacido. I spoke to his parents yesterday. According to them, they'd spoken to their son a few days before his death and described him as slurring his words. He also seemed to be having trouble catching his breath. Their religious beliefs disagreed with an autopsy, but given the man's young age, the medical examiner performed one anyway and determined that the young man died because of a heart defect. He speculated that, similar to Zoe's condition, the drug use amplified a heart issue."

"And?" Janek chimed in, getting impatient.

"That's three dead patients in just over a year. Young people who, other than their drug use, seemed to be in reasonable health. At the time of Zoe's death, she had no heroin in her system, correct?"

Janek nodded.

"So how does that translate into a toxicology concern?" Michael asked.

"Owen Mosier's parents believe that their son was receiving experimental treatments. They claim Owen chose this specific center because of those experimental treatments, against the family's wishes, by the way, although they didn't know what that treatment entailed. They believe it may have been some kind of drug cocktail. He referenced an IV protocol, but because his speech was impaired, it wasn't terribly clear to them what he was saying or what he was taking. When they attempted to get his medical records from the center, they were met with nothing but obstacles, strong legal obstacles, from the treatment center."

"Okay, that's odd," Michael said. "If the center is not cooperating after the death of a patient, one has to ask what they have to hide."

"Exactly," I said, watching Janek. "The center contends that this young man was an adult and therefore the parents really had no right to see those records without authorization, which had not been provided before his death. Seeing nothing on the surface, the medical examiner ran the standard tox panel, nothing more."

"Did the family get lawyers involved?" Michael asked.

"They started. They hired counsel and began a wrongful death lawsuit."

"And what happened with that?" Janek asked. "As if we don't already know."

"Not much. You're right, Karl, without more to go on, it wouldn't seem to be much of a case. However, I spoke to the attorney who represented the Mosiers. A subpoena had been issued for the medical records and a deposition with Dr. Wykell was scheduled, but Wykell walked out of the questioning almost as soon as he arrived."

"And the medical records?" Michael asked.

"Before the records were produced, the family was paid a visit by the center's attorney. Completely out of line, of course. The guy is not going to win any awards for ethics, but he played a bet and essentially threatened to destroy them, and their son's reputation, if they continued with the lawsuit."

The men were looking at each other, their partner telepathy at work.

"The Mosiers are people of modest means and didn't know quite what they were up against, but they knew enough to be scared and they backed down. Paying for their son's previous attempts at rehab had drained them financially, and they just didn't have the resources to carry on with the case. Not when they were up against legal slime like that."

Michael nodded. "Okay, we've got some similarities here. What are you thinking on the tox results?"

"I spoke to a forensic psychologist and I asked him about experimental treatments. He gave me some drug protocols that, although not approved for use in this country, are being used in Mexico and other places where the legal requirements are less restrictive. He said individuals fly down, spend chunks of time in these offshore treatment centers. Sometimes making multiple trips. I think it's worth looking into."

"And you think that these kids all finagled a trip to Mexico or someplace?" Janek asked.

"Probably not. I'm thinking that the center has a connection and may be illegally importing drugs that aren't approved here. Whether that's individual drugs or some kind of drug cocktail. One particular drug that's come up is called ibogaine." I paused, looking at Janek. "Its side effects correlate with heart-related symptoms, specifically bradycardia, a slowing of the heart. I think that's the first place the ME should go. Apparently, LSD is also being used off-label, but a regular screen would pick that up if they were expecting to see opioids. I assume the report hasn't come back on Paul yet?"

Michael shook his head, then added, "We can also shake down some of the center's employees, hopefully get them on the record with off-label product claims."

I opened my mouth intending to tell the men about my

financial suspicions, but thought better of it. I was already pushing my luck on additional toxicology, but it wasn't something I could accomplish on my own—I needed their help. The financial piece I could manage.

"That might be difficult," I said instead, my mind on Darna, aware that I needed to take another pass at her, this time with reinforcements. "They're secretive. Employees sign NDAs that specifically spell out the treatment protocol as off-limits."

Janek grunted. Cops hated dealing with NDAs because it also meant they had to deal with lawyers.

"That's why it makes sense to have another go at toxicology," I said. "Find out if some of these substances might have been in Zoe's system or in Paul's. It's probably been too long to test Owen without having the body exhumed, unless the lab still has samples." I looked at Janek. "I know this is a big ask, but I think this will play out faster if Theresa asked the ME for the additional tox screen. Would she do that?"

"I'm not sure. But I think I can convince her. Thanks, Andrea," Janek said, looking a little less tight now that he had a task.

"Okay, I'm gonna run." I turned to Michael. "Give me a call later." I leaned over and gave him a kiss, smiling. "Sorry, couldn't help myself." I winked and left the coffee shop.

37

"Grab your coffee and a notepad. We've got some work to do. Actually, bring your laptop, too," I said, flagging Brynn down the minute I saw her after I returned to the office.

I flipped open my laptop and sank into the chair, a legal pad within reach. It was only 8:15. Plenty of time to get a head start on a financial investigation into the Renacido Center before I met Nurse Ocampo at her apartment. I'd corralled Cai into offering an opinion on the NDA, and we were scheduled to meet at 10:30.

"Okay, boss, what do you need? Oh, before I forget, I met that Darius guy yesterday at the check-cashing place. The guy is freaking out. Says he's willing to talk, but only if we can guarantee he won't be prosecuted."

"He said that?"

"Sure did. Obviously that's beyond my pay grade, but I said I'd see what I could do. Translation, I'd throw it back in your lap."

"Nicely done." I laughed. "Keep in contact with him. Let him know it's being worked on, but be evasive. Just smooth it over enough to keep him calm. I'll reach out to my legal contacts and see if that's an option. They'll want some tidbit proving what he knows before committing, however."

I sent a brief text to my former boss, State's Attorney Denton Tierney. I'd need the big guns on this.

"Set Darius aside for now. I want to dive into the financial situation of the Renacido Center. We know a little bit about their legal structure, but we need a deep dive into their finances. I want names of anyone who might be associated with the company that aren't listed on the website. I want to know who's on their board. I want to know any properties they own. I want to know any loans they have outstanding with anyone. Basically, I want to know how they're making their money and who stands to benefit from their success or their failure."

Brynn was jotting down notes on her laptop. "Is this about that death a year ago? The one with the legal action?"

I nodded. "In looking through the filings, I saw that the attorney handling the case had specifically subpoenaed records about the company ownership and asked for names of any unidentified individuals. Common practice. You ask for things sometimes just to see what might float to the surface. He was setting the foundation to go after them for a financial payout and wanted to make sure there was no money buried. Normal lawyer work.

"Most rehab centers are small businesses, unless they've been gobbled up by a larger entity. And I've been assuming the same about Renacido, but now I'm wondering whether there might be other money behind this. This phrase keeps coming up, 'future rewards,' as if there's some kind of financial payout coming at some point down the road or a plan for expansion in the future. And then there's the secrecy. Dr. Wykell is withholding protocol details, putting a lot of conditions on his staff, and it's got me suspicious. What if there *is* something and

Wykell has come up with a breakthrough in treating addiction?"

"He'd be a gazillionaire overnight," Brynn said, eyes glued to her screen, fingers already working their magic on the keyboard.

"Exactly, provided it was something that he, and he alone, could control. It would have to be proprietary," I said, thinking out loud. "The guy isn't running a drug company. He's not developing a new magic pill."

"Are you sure about that?"

I considered it for a moment. "Well, that would require him to be working with someone else, a drug company or a lab somewhere. One of the possibilities is use of an off-label drug called ibogaine. It's illegal in the US but taken in capsule form in some other countries."

"But there are private labs that would do the work."

"There are, but at some point, in order to move down that path, there's an awful lot of government red tape to go through."

"Would that require some kind of drug trial? Wouldn't the FDA be involved?"

"If you think about vitamins, for instance, there are things being done, like high doses of vitamin C delivered intravenously that the FDA really doesn't control. What they do control are any claims made."

"You mean they can't claim the infusion would make you twenty years younger or cure your cancer. That would be false advertising."

"Exactly. However, there are doctors who've seen results in their own patients and feel they've cured quite a number of diseases using these methods, whether it's intense nutritional therapy or compounds used in conjunction with conventional treatment. They wouldn't make promises and would never make claims in advertising, but they would be able to discuss the options with patients in person."

"Sounds like a way to skirt the law," Brynn said.

"Maybe, in the wrong hands. It's always about money, right? Maybe they intend to hide the inclusion of the ibogaine. Remember the energy drink story? Caffeine, taurine, there were all kinds of suspect ingredients and quantities. Lots of supplements have unidentified compounds in them, purposefully or not. Maybe Wykell intends to create a brand name or use marketing language that doesn't identify the substance. Ibogaine is plant based."

"So, more like a trade secret. A Big Mac special sauce kind of thing."

"Nobody releases the formula for making Kentucky Fried Chicken. It's kept under lock and key. Couldn't addiction treatment be handled the same way?"

"I guess, but you'd know more about the legal process than I would."

"If we start with the premise that the center is working on some kind of unique protocol and wants to make money off of it, then the whole picture changes."

"You mean these deaths might be an overdose of one of the ingredients, or some sign that they don't have the formula worked out. They are the clinical trial."

"That's why I want to know who stands to profit. Desperation can lead to all kinds of cover-ups."

"You've asked for some unusual favors along the way, but this is a new one. I'd prefer a little foreplay, but are you at least going to buy me dinner after?"

Cai had just jumped out of a cab in front of Darna Ocampo's apartment, where I waited.

"I'll buy you whatever you want," I said, laughing.

"How's this going to go down?" Cai asked, lifting her Dior sunglasses to her head.

"As I said on the phone, Darna is conflicted. She's signed an NDA with her employer that says she won't speak about any of their treatment protocols. However, I believe that there is some indication of medical malpractice. She's nervous enough to understand that she's at risk, but she is equally concerned about her employer's wrath. So what I need you to do is to take a look at the contract and give her whatever legal advice you would give any client who walked into your office. Should she do the right thing for the greater good or protect her own ass?"

"Sometimes they are one and the same," Cai said.

"Let's go see if she's home." We walked up to the building, and I rang the buzzer for apartment four, waiting a moment before hearing the electronic click of the door. We walked in and proceeded to the second floor. Darna's door was already open when we got there, and she peered at us around the frame, looking cautiously from me to Cai.

"Come on in," she said. We followed her into a cozy but extremely small living room, where we were offered seats on a floral couch.

"Darna, this is Cai Farrell. She's an attorney, a friend that I trust completely, and she specializes in contract law."

Darna looked at Cai expectantly, nervously clenching her hands in her lap.

"Ms. Ocampo," Cai said. "This is an informal conversation. I am here simply to look at the contract. Based on the details, I can get a sense of your risks and perhaps offer up an opinion on your options. Is that okay with you?"

Darna nodded.

"Do you happen to have a copy of the contract?"

"Yes." She picked up a manila folder from the coffee table and handed it to Cai. Pulling open the contents, Cai leaned forward, her elbows on her knees as she read. Darna distracted herself by petting one of the tabbies now rubbing his head against her leg.

"You're correct," Cai said, looking directly at Darna. "This contract prohibits you from speaking in any form about patients, doctors, the facilities, or the protocols of the center. And you are right to be cautious, as there are some significant legal and financial consequences for breaking the terms. So, the issue becomes, what is the level of risk. And by that I mean, are the behaviors, let's just call them that, of the center so egregious that they negate the intent of this document."

"What does that mean?"

"Well, as one example, you can't be compelled to cover up a crime using the NDA to gag you. Whether you are clear of risk is not something *I* can answer for you. I'm not privy to the center's culpability. So what you need to decide is whether or not what you've seen at the center constitutes danger or risk to the life and well-being of the patients under your care. If there are behaviors that the ownership or management of the company knowingly forced employees to engage in that in turn compromised patient health, then the likely outcome of any legal jeopardy you are in today is extremely different." Cai paused. "I'm afraid I must also state that your own behavior may be called into question in the event of an incident. And the NDA would not protect you."

"So what you're saying is I'm protected only if I become a whistleblower." Darna's voice had gone flat. She stared back at Cai with the eyes of someone who had everything to lose. It was an agonizing dilemma and, sadly, a tactic I'd seen many times in the past—the wealthy and well-connected running legal roughshod over anyone in their path. She stood and moved over to the window, the cat still at her feet. Cai and I waited, giving her a moment to process.

"Can you help me?" Darna said. "Can you represent me or find someone who will? I'll tell you everything I know after I have a lawyer."

"I'll speak to a colleague of mine," Cai said.

"With Paul dying over the weekend, I can't pretend anymore," Darna continued, her voice cracking. "This treatment works, I know it does, but we clearly don't have all of the information. We're missing something. Maybe there's a problem with the quality of the ingredients or the dose is wrong. But I can't be part of this if others might die and I could have prevented it."

"I'll get your contact information from Andrea and we'll be in touch later today," Cai said. "In the meantime, could you give me the name and phone number of the individual who runs things at Quantum Holdings?"

"Wait. Quantum Holdings?" I said as Cai and Darna stared at me.

"That is the company name listed on the NDA," Cai said. "Is something wrong?"

"Quantum Holdings was also the owner of the house Lane bought." I turned to Darna, who clearly wasn't following the connection. "The same house that Zoe Symanski died in."

38

"What happened in there? I'm completely confused."

Cai and I were standing on the sidewalk outside of Darna Ocampo's building, and she was looking to me to explain why the connection between Renacido, Quantum, and Wykell had set off my alarm buttons, but I was already mentally speeding through the implications.

"Sorry, I gotta run. I'll fill you in later, promise. Please, just get Darna locked down with counsel as soon as you can," I said, already in the street. "You called an Uber, right?"

Cai lifted her hands in a what-just-happened gesture. "Go. I love standing on the street corner by myself. If I get mugged, I'll blame you. Forever."

"Our next dinner is on me. An expensive one." I smiled and blew her a kiss as I got in my car.

QUANTUM HOLDINGS *WAS* the Renacido Center. Or was the parent company, or a holding company, and that connected them to Zoe's death. Her presence in that home was not coincidence.

I flew into the Link-Media office, nearly knocking Brynn's laptop out of her hands as we collided at the elevator.

"You might want to go hide out at the coffee shop for a little while," she said. "Borkowski's in a snit about me running out by Midway yesterday to see Darius. Just to give you a heads-up, he's not happy with you. Or with me. Apparently, he'd rather I work on something meaty, like calling the Anti-Cruelty Society and PAWS about the next pet adoption week. We might want to show him a rough draft of where this story is going to get him off our asses for a bit."

"What's he gonna do? Fire me?" I retorted, continuing toward my office. Borkowski would thank me after the fact, even if he didn't know it yet. "You coming? Or would you prefer dog duty?"

Brynn let out a snort and was fast on my heels.

"Do you remember the name of the company that was listed as having purchased the building that houses the Renacido Center?" I asked, not giving her a moment to adjust. Flipping open my laptop, I logged in to LexisNexis.

"Umm, starts with a *P*. Oh, I think it was Planck Holdings." She dropped into the chair, rested her elbows on her knees, and stared at me expectantly. "You wanna fill me in? Might make it easier for me to help."

"Let me check something." I opened a second browser window and typed in *Planck Holdings*, scrolling the search results before letting out a laugh.

"Planck. Max Planck. The father of quantum theory. Someone has a sense of humor, as well as a fascination with advanced science."

"Okay, now I'm completely lost."

"Quantum Holdings is the company that owned the building

where Zoe Symanski died. The same company that owns two other properties nearby, now in default. Turns out Quantum Holdings is the company controlling the NDAs that employees of the Renacido Center are locked in to, and Planck Holdings owns the center. Well, the building, anyway, so this is all one big connected mess. And I'd bet Wykell's name is on every one of the articles of organizations for these LLCs and that the same mailing service address is in use as well."

Brynn sat back in the chair and chewed the corner of her lip. "Okay. So, things must not be going too well financially if three of the properties in their portfolio ended up in foreclosure," she said.

"Or they needed cash. Or they changed tactics and needed to scratch the plans they had for Pierce Street," I said, turning my attention back to the computer.

"Why not just sell the properties if they needed cash?"

"Exactly. That would have been the logical next step. Generally speaking, going the foreclosure route means they tried to sell and couldn't find a buyer before the bank was at the door changing the locks. But that doesn't make sense to me. Humboldt Park is one of the hottest investments in the city. They should have been able to sell these in heartbeat."

"So why the foreclosure, then?"

"I don't know. But there are two reasons companies are set up using all this layering—different names, different organizational structure—to obscure the owner's identity or to isolate risk. And they aren't mutually exclusive."

"So Quantum Holdings could appear to be broke, while Planck has all the assets. Do you think another rehab center was planned for those properties?"

"It's as good a guess as any. So the question is, what fell apart? If they decided to give up the real estate, that means they'd scrapped the plan or run into an obstacle." Walking away from the real estate was confusing me. It seemed a pointless financial move, and at its core, this was about money.

"Maybe the reason they bolted isn't relevant," Brynn said. "Wykell seemed to believe he was on the verge of a financial breakthrough, even without the properties, so maybe the additional treatment centers weren't essential, or not essential right now. Or maybe it's as simple as a permit problem. After all, the city of Chicago can be a strange bedfellow."

"That could be it. That could be why they walked away," I said to Brynn, a new thought coming to the forefront. "Maybe it's not a permit problem but a partner problem. Someone behind the scenes exerting pressure. Or maybe they had a falling out, and walking away from the mortgage payments was damage control or someone's idea of a hissy fit? Continue with the financial piece," I said to Brynn. "Look for an investment or a loan history associated with any of these entities. I'm going to work on people. Wykell wasn't in this alone."

My fingers were flying, clicking on links, sorting data, trying to find a connection from Renacido, Planck, or Quantum to another individual. I was convinced Wykell wasn't alone in this venture, but no new names were surfacing, so I went to the second tier, plugging in Darna Ocampo, Francesca, the administrator, Levi, and even Zoe, while Brynn worked across the desk. The room was silent aside from the click of our respective keyboards.

Five pages in a small news article caught my attention, and I clicked through. "Three years ago, Levi Vinson was picked up coming back into the US after a trip to Mexico," I said to Brynn. "He had a stash of heroin in a pocket of his backpack, which one of the TSA dogs alerted on. And here's the kicker. The attorney that defended Levi is a guy named Stephan Reda."

"That's a familiar name. Wasn't he associated with that property your sister bought?"

"He was the contact the bank named when I asked about the foreclosure history. He's also the attorney who threatened to bankrupt the Mosiers if they tried to prosecute Renacido."

"I think we just found our drug mule," I added. "I'd bet money that Levi Vinson's passport is full of ink."

A text from Cai popped up. *Darna's locked down. Can you get over here?*

―――

DARNA OCAMPO SAT HUDDLED on the side of a conference table with a thirtyish man in a suit when I entered the room. Her body seemed to have shrunk in the hours since I'd last seen her. Her skin, lacking makeup, seemed even more pasty and transparent than normal. She looked up, nodding silently.

Cai introduced me to her associate, then directed me to a seat across the table before leaving the room.

"Ms. Ocampo has provided me with an overview of the situation at the Renacido Center as she knows it, as well as her personal role in their activities," the attorney said. "We understand that the situation is developing and that no charges have been filed. However, Ms. Ocampo has agreed to answer some of your questions in a desire to help prevent any future injury to patients. We ask that you refrain from publication of anything you learn from this conversation until such time as we can determine if there is a role for law enforcement."

"No, I'm not agreeing, I'm *insisting*," Darna interrupted, shooting a stern look at her attorney. He nodded.

"Agreed," I said. "For the sake of efficiency, could we focus on the treatment protocol today and come back to other issues at another time?"

Darna nodded. If I could get Darna on record confirming my

suspicions about ibogaine, I could get the center shut down, buying time to unearth money and people.

"Do you agree to be recorded during this conversation?"

Darna looked at the attorney, who gave his consent, so I hit my recording app.

"The Renacido Center bills itself as having developed a groundbreaking treatment protocol for opioid addiction. You've been an integral part of administering that treatment. Are you familiar with the components involved?" I asked.

"Yes, the program involves several stages—medical evaluation, detox, a series of medication-assisted treatments, and cognitive behavior treatments that then integrate the prior steps for long-lasting results," she replied.

"And what stages have you been involved in personally?"

"I'm involved at all stages. Others, Dr. Wykell primarily, handle the cognitive behavior work, but I'm monitoring patients throughout their time at the center."

"Are medications used during detox?"

"To some extent. We give IV fluids, and we provide nutritional support in most cases. Certain drugs drain the body of nutrients, causing imbalances that can interfere with healing. For example, depression is often a problem that contributes to addiction and presents during recovery. We can treat that with Omega-3s and B12. Supplements alone won't solve the problem, but getting the nutrient levels back up helps everything else work. If pain management is a problem," she continued, "we can use medications such as methadone."

"Talk to me about 'medication-assisted treatment.' That is the phrase you used."

Darna looked down at the table for a moment, then at her attorney. If she was having second thoughts, they were raging in her now.

"Weeks two and three are the core of the program. Each

Monday, patients who are in that stage are installed in a room in the carriage house, hooked up to a saline IV, and then given a dose of what Dr. Wykell calls Renewal 1. A dose of Renewal 2 is given the following week."

"And what is in that?"

"I don't know."

I looked at her and crossed my arms over my chest. "Ms. Ocampo, I thought you were here to cooperate. Are you really going to sit here and tell me you are administering drugs and you don't know what they are?"

"I don't know officially. Wykell brings it in from a lab somewhere else. They're capsules. Containers are already labeled." She looked at the attorney again. "About a year ago I overheard Dr. Wykell on the phone. Two words stood out to me, ibogaine and MDMA."

"What's MDMA?"

"The street name is Molly. What I believe, but can't prove, is that one dose is ibogaine, the other is MDMA, and that the combined effects of using both drugs are what give results. And by the way, I do believe the treatment works. I've seen it work, even if the drugs aren't legal yet. I'm not someone just standing by passing out evil. We're helping people who can't get help any other way." Tears were pooling in her eyes, and her voice was choked with emotion.

"So how do you explain the death of Paul Macanas? Paul was under your care when he died, likely on one of these drugs at the time."

I could see the attorney tense. I was stepping into culpability territory.

"After I heard Dr. Wykell mention ibogaine, I did some research. I wasn't familiar with it. Ibogaine has caused death in some cases, but there was always an underlying medical problem—other drugs in the system, heart issues—so I made sure that my screening process was more detailed. I didn't tell Dr. Wykell. I just did what I thought was right. The only answer I have is that Paul must not have been honest on his health questionnaire."

Zoe and Owen were also on my mind, but there would be time to explore those situations after I'd gotten Wykell behind bars.

"I assume you have access to the two Renewal products. Would you be willing to provide samples to CPD for testing? We'll need to confirm the presence of the illegal ingredients."

"Of course. Do you need me to get them secretly?"

"Let me speak with my contact at CPD before I answer that. Do nothing for now. It's better that Dr. Wykell isn't suspicious."

A text pinged my phone.

Cn u get me out? K.

39

The phone rang endlessly, bouncing menacingly through the speaker system in my car as I drove north on Lake Shore Drive, but Kendall wasn't picking up. Images of Paul's convulsing body and Zoe's decaying one wouldn't leave my mind. This couldn't be Kendall's fate, not if I could help it, anyway.

I pulled off the drive at Irving Park and phoned Michael, shouting a message into his voicemail about where I was going and why, then dialed 911 as I screeched onto Marine Drive, nearly causing an accident as I made the turn. Panic sweat was rolling down my back as I barreled into the driveway of the Renacido Center. I sprinted toward the carriage house, not even bothering to close the car door.

The doorknob refused to budge. I pounded and kicked and screamed Kendall's name, hoping she could hear me, wanting her to know I was here. That she wasn't alone. My phone still rang into nothingness, so with a glance around, I picked up the largest rock I could find and smashed it repeatedly against the doorknob until the old metal was dented and hanging by a screw. I pushed in the door and charged up the stairs.

The space was dark other than a glow from the back where exterior light entered. I could hear Kendall's phone now, but softly, as if buried in her purse. It was the faint rhythm of a popular Taylor Swift song, downloaded as a ringtone and completely incongruous with the tough-girl image she projected. Treatment rooms lined the hall, and she could be in any one of them. Knowing minutes could make the difference, I tried to locate the source of the sound. It was distant, and I couldn't tell if the ring was coming from behind a closed door or the large treatment room in the back where Paul had died.

Suddenly angry male voices bounced at me from down the hall, and I paused.

"What kind of mess have you gotten me into?" one screamed. "Your impatience has ruined everything I've worked for."

Dr. Wykell? I crept forward as silently as I could, peering into treatment rooms as I moved.

"Everything *you've* worked for? You're nothing," the second man bellowed. "Nothing but a talking head, paid to hawk what I've told you to hawk. You haven't the intellect or the skill to have done any of this on your own. You have no vision. You have no plan. You apparently can't even keep a phone away from a kid. How would you have executed any of this without me? I'm the brains behind this. You're merely the front man. All I've heard from you is fear and caution, when the greatest advancement in addiction treatment is at your feet and you don't even see it. You need to stop being an obstacle. We are on the brink of greatness, but you can't even do the one job you've been hired to do. So get behind me or get out of my way."

"But the deaths? Clearly, we've missed something in—"

"I've missed nothing. Scientific journals will speak of me forever in reverence for bringing this treatment to the world, while you'll be nothing but an asterisk. No one will remember the name Troy Wykell if you don't start doing your job. This is just the price to be paid for research. The death of a few is nothing if it pays for the lives of many. Sacrifices are occasionally required for the greater good."

"Not when sacrifices involve unwitting children," I roared at the men.

I stared, eyes blazing, hatred pouring out of me without restraint at Dr. Troy Wykell and the man who it was now clear was his partner, Dr. Franklin Lecaros.

Kendall lay nearly comatose on a hospital bed five feet behind the men, hooked up to an IV. Hearing my voice, she lifted a hand, only to let it fall back to her side, the effort too great.

Wykell froze, all color leaving his face. He looked to Lecaros, who stared back at me, but neither said a word.

"You men need to step aside now," I said. "I'm taking Kendall out of here, and you will both face the consequences of your greed."

My phone was still in my hand, on an endless call to Kendall's, and tapped to end the incessant ring. While Wykell cowered, Lecaros clenched his jaw in rage, anger coursing in his veins and turning his face beet red. Kendall moaned softly from her bed, and I rushed to her side.

It wasn't clear if she was capable of walking, but I needed to get her out of this room and away from these men any way I could.

"Kendall, it's Andrea. Can you hear me?" She mumbled something unintelligible and swung her head from side to side. "I'm going to try to help you sit up."

"You're not going anywhere," Lecaros said, his voice a low growl.

I watched the men out of the corner of my eye as I assessed Kendall's condition and the risk. I had nothing I could use to protect myself. Lecaros had accepted death as an acceptable consequence of perfecting his treatment. How far would he go to prevent exposure?

I couldn't manage Kendall and the IV stand she was tethered to, so I shoved my phone in my pocket, grabbed gauze from the nearby tray, and pulled off the tape stabilizing the line in her arm. Then I pinched my fingers around the end of the cannula.

"Do you really think I'd let fools like you destroy my greatest accomplishment?" Lecaros said to me, his voice dripping with hate.

I shot Wykell a pleading look and held tight to Kendall's arm. I needed an ally, or I needed help buying some time until my CPD reinforcements arrived. The one thing I had in my favor right now was that the men weren't aware I'd made the 911 call.

"Let her go," Wykell said, his voice wavering. "This doesn't have to slow us down. The kid will go back home, and this will just be another failed attempt at sobriety. Nothing has changed."

"And what about her?" Lecaros nodded at me. "You're still missing the full picture, Wykell. What's her story going to be? Who is she going to talk to?"

Lecaros pushed past his partner and stood two feet from me, his eyes dark and menacing. "Did you think you were being cute pretending you were still an attorney needing help with a case?" he said to me. "How dumb do you think I am? I looked you up the minute you mentioned Wykell."

My heart pounded in my chest as Wykell stared at Lecaros. Confusion was on his face as he mumbled weak objections, but he seemed unable or unwilling to stand up to the man. I looked over at Kendall. Her eyes fluttered and she swatted feebly at the equipment still piercing her vein, and I had little confidence she'd even be able to stand unsupported. I was on my own.

Shooting my eyes around the space, I took stock of my surroundings, looking for anything I could use as a weapon if I needed one but saw only the IV stand. Where was that patrol car?

"Do you know who we have here, Wykell?" Lecaros said, turning to the therapist. "A journalist. A journalist who is also a former prosecutor. Do you want to tell me again how this isn't a problem, you dumb fuck? She'll spin this into a hole so deep, neither one of us will ever get out of it. I'm not about to let either of you destroy me or my work!"

Lecaros rushed at me and I gripped the needle in Kendall's arm tighter and pulled, but it wasn't enough. If I could extract the IV, I could at least flail at him with the stand. It wasn't much, but it was the best I had.

Lecaros got to me before I had dislodged the metal tip of the cannula, grabbing my shoulder and then reaching for the IV tubing. He yanked the rubber hard, wrapping it around my throat as I struggled to pull the needle from Kendall's vein.

I clawed at the ligature as Lecaros encircled my neck with it a second time and pulled, cutting off my air supply. Kendall's blood gushed as the cannula was ripped from her arm, and she fell to the floor, choking and gasping for air. I could hear Wykell yelling at his partner to stop, but Lecaros wrenched the tubing even tighter. Lightheaded now, I tore at the plastic as best I could with one hand and reached back, desperate to dig my fingers into Lecaros with the other. His eyes. His neck. Anything I could make contact with.

"Freeze! Or I'll blow your fucking head off!" A commanding voice shouted the order as the room grew dark and I felt my body sink.

Michael. It was Michael.

40

"She's going to be okay. She's going to be okay."

Kendall's father crouched by the side of her hospital bed, clutching her hand, his body shaking with tears of relief. Repeating the words as if saying them out loud, over and over, would make the physician's promise come true faster. The doctor smiled, then gave the nurse additional instructions before leaving the room.

Surrounded by the hospital monitors, Kendall looked tiny and young and vulnerable. I wondered if her father was flashing on images of her as a young girl, a girl ignorant of drugs and addiction and angst. I saw that innocence in her face as she lay there, her body flushing itself of the drugs she'd been given, and felt hope. Hope for her future and hope for her relationship with her father.

Michael stood protectively by my side as we'd received the update on her prognosis, but he was strangely quiet. I could see the worry in his eyes when he looked at me.

"Well, Kellner, you did it again. Another bad guy off the streets," Karl Janek said, joining us at the end of Kendall's bed. "How's the neck?" he asked, lifting my hair to inspect the injury.

"Just bruised," I said. "I'm lucky that plastic was the first thing Lecaros could get his hands on."

"Yep, that stretch probably saved your ass," Janek said, and Michael tensed.

"You've got Lecaros and Wykell locked up by now, I assume," I said. "What sob story are they giving you?"

"Please, Wykell is singing like a little girl. Guess the idea of being confined to a treatment room for ten to twenty ain't sounding so good to him right now. The odd thing is, through it all, both of these assholes are spouting off their greatest hits as if it were some contest to see which of them is the most self-involved."

"Unfortunately for them, malignant narcissism is not a legal defense," I said. "And I wonder which expert witness Lecaros will want to testify at *his* trial."

Janek laughed. "And even better, I personally got to haul in that little fuck Levi on smuggling charges. He's been bringing in their ibogaine from Mexico for almost two years. Turns out Levi was deep in debt to his own dealer and shuffling his mule money to pay it off before they whacked him." Janek shook his head, a smug smile on his face. "The thing that really burns me is that this piece of dog shit knew Zoe was in that damn basement months ago. He now says he found her dead on the floor back in January. He was so freaked out that it would look bad for him, that instead of calling someone, he put Zoe in that chair thinking that whoever found her would think she died of natural causes. What a moron."

"The warped logic of drug users is never easy to follow," I said.

"We arrested two crazy-ass shrinks, a slimeball attorney, and a lowlife drug pusher. That's a damn good day. You sure you don't want a job on the force, Kellner? Cut out the middle man, so to speak?"

"I'm good." I looked at Janek and laughed. It was the closest thing to a compliment I'd ever gotten from him. Janek winked and left the room.

Once Janek was gone, Michael pulled me into his arms and held me as if he were afraid my legs would go out from under me again. We stood quietly, letting the adrenaline leave our bodies, watching Kendall, knowing that while her path forward with addiction was uncertain, she at least had a chance. And so did we.

DID YOU ENJOY THE BOOK?

Thank you so much for reading TELL ME A LIE. I'm truly honored that you've spent your time with me.

Reviews are the most powerful tool in an authors' arsenal for getting attention to our books to other readers. If you've enjoyed the story, I would be very grateful if you could spend a moment leaving an honest review.

You can leave your review by visiting your retailer of choice or Goodreads.

NEXT IN THE SERIES

GET INFORMATION ON THE NEXT ANDREA KELLNER STORY

Also by Dana Killion
    Fatal Choices - a free prequel short story
    Lies in High Places - Andrea Kellner Book 1
    The Last Lie - Andrea Kellner Book 2
    Lies of Men - Andrea Kellner Book 3

I love to hear from my readers. Did you have a favorite scene? Have an idea for who I should kill off next? Jot me a note. I occasionally send newsletters with details on the next release, special offers, and other bits of news about the series.

Sign up for my Mailing List at www.danakillion.com

ACKNOWLEDGMENTS

Writing a novel involves months, sometimes years, of plotting, planning, and fretting over every word, and this book was no different. It also involves the support and dedication of wonderful friends and loyal fans. Thank you all!

My heartfelt thanks to the readers who have stuck with me through this wonderful journey. Your encouragement and kind words are priceless.

To my wonderful editor Kate Schomaker, thank you for your enthusiasm, for tightening my prose, and for your patience with my refusal to learn the proper placement of commas. Glad to find a kindred spirit who drinks red wine on all occasions.

To my boys, Alex and Zach, I hope you live dreams of your own. And finally, to my husband Theo, thank you for continually reminding me of your love and that making the tough choice was worth it. xoxo

ABOUT THE AUTHOR

Dana Killion grew up in a small town in northern Wisconsin, reading Nancy Drew and dreaming of living surrounded by tall buildings. A career in the apparel industry satisfied her city living urge and Nancy Drew evolved into Cornwell, Fairstein, and Evanovich.

One day, frustrated that her favorite authors weren't writing fast enough, an insane thought crossed her mind. "Maybe I could write a novel?"

Silly, naïve, downright ludicrous. But she did it. She plotted and planned and got 80,000 words on the page. That manuscript lives permanently in the back of a closet. But the writing bug had bitten.

Tell Me a Lie is her fourth novel. Dana lives in Chicago and St Petersburg, Florida with her husband and her kitty, Isabel, happily avoiding temperatures below fifty.

Copyright © 2020 by Dana Killion

Published by Obscura Press

ISBN-13: 978-0-9991874-8-7

All rights reserved.

No part of this book may be reproduced in any form or by any electronic or mechanical means, including information storage and retrieval systems, without written permission from the author, except for the use of brief quotations in a book review.

DanaKillion.com

Made in the USA
Coppell, TX
14 December 2020